NAIVETE

TRACY BROEMMER

Naivete

by

Tracy Broemmer

Contemporary Romance

Published by Tracy Broemmer

Edited by Lexie Broemmer

Cover by Nora of Covers by Sophie

All Rights Reserved

For Lex

For years, you've bounced ideas around with me, proofread & edited countless stories, all the while pouring your heart & soul into your education and your career.

Thank you for the fantastic work you do & the time and heart you give me for my work. I am so very proud of you, and I love that you let me use your class syllabus for Booker Gannon in {A Naughty Lesson} Naivete.

One day soon, I will dedicate a book to

Dr. Broemmer, PhD.

FILM, CULTURE, AND LITERATURE

Dr. Booker Gannon, PhD.

English 2660
bookergannon@killdareu.edu

(555) 555-6666

MWF, 8:00-8:50 a.m

Lecture Hall P301

P305 — Office

Hours: F 1-3 p.m. or by appointment

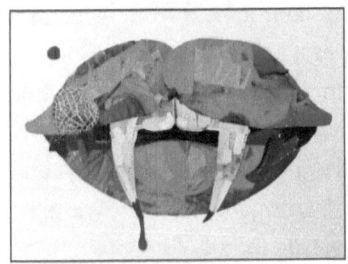

Course Description:

Throughout this course, we will explore texts ranging from the 19th Century to the present day. Our class texts will include novels, novellas, and films, all of which center on one very popular creature of the night: the vampire. Although one may think the word vampire synonymous with eroticism or horror, we will dive deep into the meaning behind this mythical monster in order to better understand its historical, cultural, and political contexts— and how these contexts change—over the course of time.

Guiding our course will be the following questions:

· What or who is the vampire?

· How do gender, sexuality, race, and class play into the mythos of the vampire? Or, in other words, what role does identity play in constructing the vampire?

· Are Gothicism and horror relevant today, especially in conversation with the vampire?

· Who consumes vampire media, and how are such consumers perceived in our larger culture?

The goal of this course and your assignments, including three short papers, a short presentation, one major paper, and a creative final project, is to help you hone your analytical, argumentative, and writing skills. While I want this course to challenge you intellectually and to make you reflect on social goings-on, I also want it to be fun and genuinely interesting for all of us.

*Disclaimer: Please note that you will encounter texts with sensitive and distressing topics in this class. You will also encounter graphic descriptions of gore in at least one book, *The Southern Book Club Guide's to Slaying Vampires*.

The English Department's Expectations for 2000-level Coursework:

·	Read texts or view films by authors from a variety of periods and nationalities.

·	Read closely and critically, learning to interpret literature, film, and modes of rhetorical argument in ways that are both intellectually rigorous and personally significant.

·	Discuss their own written reflections on literature, film and rhetorical argument in group settings, enriching their ability to express clearly their points and insights.

Students who complete this course will be able to:

·	Generate engaged and responsive close readings of texts

·	Describe and analyze the various ways in which texts reflect and help shape wider cultural conditions

·	Construct clear spoken and written arguments that demonstrate an awareness of purpose and audience

I.	Required Texts:

Writing Handbook:

- *Writing About Movies* (5th Edition), Karen Gocsik, Dave Monohan, and Richard Barsam

Novels/Novellas:

- *The Vampyre*, John William Polidori

- *Carmilla*, Joseph Sheridan Le Fanu

- *Dracula*, Bram Stoker

- *The Southern Book Club Guide's to Slaying Vampires*, Grady Hendrix

- *Twilight*, Stephenie Meyer

Films:

- *Carmilla*, dir. by Emily Harris

- *Nosferatu*, dir. by F.W. Murnau

- *Blacula*, dir. by William Crain

- *Fright Night*, dir. by Tom Holland

- *Twilight*, dir. by Catherine Hardwicke

Some course readings will be available online via Canvas as PDF files. Such readings will likely consist of excerpts of theoretical texts or relevant peer-reviewed articles. Please print these out and bring them to class; alternatively, bring your laptop to class and make sure you have them available. We will look closely at passages from all the course texts, and you should always have the text(s) of the day with you for discussion.

II.   Assignments and Grading:

·   Class Participation (attendance, discussion, reading quizzes, etc.): 15%

·   Short Papers: 20%

·   Cultural Artifact Presentation: 10%

·   Major Paper: 25%

·   Final Project: 30%

III.   Course Policies Deadlines:

Assignments are due when they are due. Generally speaking, for each day an assignment is late, it will receive a 10-point penalty. With that being said, I know life can get overwhelming sometimes and that sometimes you might have an extenuating circumstance. If you are struggling to meet a deadline for some reason, please talk to me. Please remember, though, that at the end of the day, it is up to me to determine if you have a legitimate reason for missing deadlines.

Attendance and Tardiness:

Regular attendance is expected and is fundamental to your success in this class. We will be working constantly with your writing, so your presence is important. If you need to miss class, please let me know ahead of time. Please also arrive on time. (Again, I understand that sometimes there are circumstances in which you have to be absent or late. Although I am the judge regarding unexcused absences, please let me know if you are struggling to make it to class for some reason.)

Maintain a respectful learning environment:

I expect common courtesy in the classroom, so any disruptive or disrespectful behavior (e.g., talking while I'm talking, using inappropriate language in the classroom, intimidating classmates, etc.) may result in your dismissal from the day's class. If I dismiss you, you will not be present, which means you will be *absent*; I will count you thus. *Your actions are your choices: if you choose to treat a classmate or me with disrespect, you choose to risk dismissal and the resulting loss of points.* In return for your cooperation, you may expect the same respect from me.

IV.   Readings

Please note that the following schedule is a **tentative reading and assignment schedule**. Throughout the semester, we may have to adjust assignment dates and readings based upon our discussions and your progress. I reserve the right to make these changes and will be sure to announce any changes in class and post announcements on our Blackboard site.

·(Another) Course Content Disclaimer: In this course, students may be required to read texts or view materials that they may consider offensive. The ideas expressed in any given text do not necessarily reflect the views of the instructor, the English Department, or Killdare University. Course materials are selected for their artistic, historical, and/or cultural relevance, or as an example of stylistic technique. They are meant to be examined in the context of intellectual inquiry of the sort encountered at the university level.

Concerns?

If you feel you may not be able to meet these requirements or have any questions, please come to see me **at the beginning of the semester** to discuss your concerns. Make sure to speak with me *as your concerns arise*, not during the final weeks of class. I will not help you if you wait until the end of the semester.

<u>Reading and Assignment Schedule</u>

W 1/18   Course Introduction

F 1/20   Botting, "Introduction: Gothic Excess and Transgression," pp. 1-20 (on Canvas)

M 1/23   Polidori, *The Vampyre*

W 1/25   Cohen, "Monster Culture (Seven Theses)," pp. 44-54

F 1/27   Adaptation work

Introduce Cultural Artifact Presentations

M 1/30   Le Fanu, *Carmilla*, Prologue—Chapter VI W 2/1 *Carmilla*, Chapters VII—XIV

F 2/3   *Carmilla*, Chapters XV—XVI

Creed, from *The Monstrous Feminine*, pp. TBA

M 2/6   *Carmilla*, dir. by Emily Harris

Gocsik, et. al., "The Challenges of Writing About Movies," pp. 1-12 Gocsik, et. al., Gocsik, et. al., "Looking at Movies," pp. 19-34

W 2/8   Gocsik, et. al., "Formal Analysis," pp. 35-54

Reflection paper due by midnight 2/9

F 2/10   No Class—Wellness Day

M 2/13   Stoker, *Dracula*, Chapters I—X W 2/15 *Dracula*, Chapters XI—XIV

F 2/17   *Dracula*, Chapters XV—XVIII M 2/20 *Dracula*, Chapters XIX—XXIII W 2/22   *Dracula*. Chapters XXIV—XXV

F 2/24   *Dracula*, Chapters XXVI—XXVII M 2/27 *Nosferatu*, dir. by F.W. Murnau

W 3/1   Roberts, "Demons Within and Without: F.W. Murnau's *Nosferatu*"

F 3/3   Gocsik, et. al., "Cultural Analysis," pp. 55-100

Formal analysis paper due by midnight 3/4

M 3/6   No Class—Spring Break

W 3/8   No Class—Spring Break

F 3/10   No Class—Spring Break M 3/13   *Blacula*, dir. William Crain

W 3/15   Hefner, "Rethinking *Blacula*: Ideological Critique at the Intersection of Genres" pp. 62-74

F 3/17   Halbertsam, "Parasites and Perverts: An Introduction to Gothic Monstrosity," pp. 76- 88

Cultural analysis paper due by midnight 3/19

M 3/20   Hendrix, *The Southern Book Club's Guide to Slaying Vampires*, Author's Note to Chapter 7, pp. 7—80

W 3/22   *Book Club*, Chapters 8—13, pp. 81—144

F 3/24   *Book Club*, Chapters 14—19, pp. 145—200

M 3/27   *Book Club*, Chapters 20—28, pp. 201—281

W 3/29   *Book Club*, Chapters 29—35, pp. 282—343

F 3/31   *Book Club*, Chapters 36—42, pp. 344—404 M 4/3   *Fright Night*, dir. by Tom Holland

W 4/5   Peer Review for major paper

F 4/7   No Class—Easter Break

Major paper due by midnight 4/8

M 4/10   No Class—Easter Break

W 4/12   Meyer, *Twilight*, Preface— Chapter 5, pp. 1—109

F 4/14 *Twilight*, Chapters 6—8, pp. 110—178

M 4/17   *Twilight*, Chapters 9—12, pp. 179—259 W 4/19 *Twilight*, Chapters 13—16, pp. 260—347

F 4/21   *Twilight*, Chapters 17—20, pp. 348—422

M 4/24   *Twilight*, Chapters 21—Epilogue, pp. 423—498

W 4/26 *Twilight*, dir. by Catherine Hardwicke

F 4/28   Dungan, "Vegetarian vampires of the Anthro-
pocene: Re-reading the animal blood diet in Stephanie
Meyer's *Twilight Saga*," pp. 42-62

M 5/1   Work Day

W 5/3   Presentations of Final Project F 5/5 Presentations of Final Project

M 5/8   Presentations of Final Project

Exams: 5/10 to 5/16

Final Project Due Wednesday, May 10

BOOKER

In.

Out.

In.

Out.

"Need anything?"

Booker Gannon stared at the fingers of his right hand as he drew them in to make a tight fist and relaxed them out again. He shook his head in response to the bartender without looking at him. Left fingers curled around a rocks glass, he continued to squeeze and relax his fist, almost in time with the slow, dark groove of the jazz music playing in the dimly lit bar.

Useless.

He'd used his fists a few times when he was younger, when he was in high school. Pounded the fucking brains out of a kid when he was fifteen. The fucker had looked at Booker's sister one too many times.

The high of that fight, the ass-kicking he had delivered, had pumped him up as surely as steroids. Booker had walked into his junior year of high school with a reputation as a badass for the first time in all his academic years. Thank Christ he had started pumping iron the summer between freshman and sophomore year. Like a snake shedding its skin, Booker had gladly shaken off the nerdy, bookworm label and accepted the mantle of bad boy.

Still smart—educated, well-read, *and* street smart. But cold and cruel.

His fists hadn't been good for a damned thing *last* year, last April. True, he'd pummeled the hell out of the wall in the mudroom. Beaten both fists against the wall over and over until he cracked a hole in the drywall. Until his knuckles were bruised and bleeding.

Until Ashley was screaming and crying.

Begging him to stop.

The relief of that beating lasted all of five seconds. Seeing the damage he had done to their house had been like a punch in his gut. And recognizing the fear on Ashley's face had driven him to his knees.

He wouldn't have hurt her.

Eyes still on his right hand, Booker lifted the glass and sipped the biting rye whiskey.

Could have been worse.

He didn't have the energy, the wherewithal, to snort at the thought. Sure, things could have been worse. At least he was here now, right? *Working*, again.

But he hated it here.

Not *here*. Not *Sidecar*. The dim lighting and vintage furnishings here, the dark, brooding instrumental jazz, and the liquor—can't forget the liquor. Nope, Sidecar was currently his favorite place here.

Here. In *Killdare Springs*.

He hated the fucking town. The university. Every student he laid eyes on every day on campus, especially the ones he had to look at every day in his classrooms or during office hours. He wasn't sure that would ever get better.

And that thought only lit the rage inside him all over again.

The semester would begin tomorrow.

There was a time when Booker was excited about starting a new semester. Meeting a new group of students. Learning their likes and dislikes, their strengths and weaknesses. Building mentor and mentee relationships with them. Watching them learn, watching their enthusiasm for learning.

Right now, all he had left of that excitement was memories. A hope that he would find his way back to that kind of compassion for students.

He still loved literature and the avenue it provided to teach a whole slew of concepts. And he looked forward to his own journey through the literature of his choosing and a deeper learning for himself on that same slew of concepts. Thank

God he was able to choose the texts and films for his classes. The gothic theme of his class certainly matched his dark mood.

Booker lifted his finger and nodded at the bartender. He watched the hipster-looking guy splash another pour of rye in the glass and nodded his thanks when their eyes met. Tuesdays were quiet here; he would know. He was here most Tuesdays, most days that ended in y. The bartenders —there were four of them—didn't know his name. Both because they weren't chatty, and because Booker would tell them to fuck off if they were. He was pretty sure he had a resting fuck-off face. He got it when he traded in his happily-married, hoping-for-a-family, I-like-my job-face.

The bartender glanced at the big, heavy oak door across the room as it opened. Booker looked his fill at the guy, at his gangster hat, the gold earring in his left earlobe, and dragged his eyes away. Never bothered him, and never refused to serve him. He swung his own gaze over to the door to see two women come in. Dressed in the same sort of getup—skinny jeans and blazers over tank tops—they leaned together and laughed as they made their way to the bar.

Booker held his breath, only letting it out when they chose stools around the corner, nearly as far from him as they could get.

One was blond, the other a brunette.

Booker hadn't been with a woman since Ashley left.

A hundred and sixty-one days since the divorce was final. A hundred and ninety-nine days since the last time he and Ashley tried to have sex.

Not that he was counting.

The women at the bar could have been supermodels. But Ashley Spencer Gannon was beautiful. And sexy as fuck.

At the moment, he hated women more than he hated anything else in his world.

Then again, his world had shrunk considerably in the last two hundred and seventy-three days, so maybe that wasn't saying much.

The bartender flirted with the women at the bar. Talked them up as he mixed vermouth and gin in a glass, stirred them, and then strained the drinks into chilled martini glasses. From this distance, Booker couldn't guess how old the women were.

Maybe they were here hoping to score a hot night.

Maybe they were lovers, and they were here for a drink before going home to climb into bed together and make their own hot night. They were attractive women, but even that thought didn't do much for his dick.

He had Sofie and Reese to thank for that.

Another sip of the rye burned down his throat. His phone lay on the bar, screen down, untouched since he had walked in here. Probably hours ago. The fuck if he knew. But with the semester starting tomorrow, he should probably get his ass off the barstool and back to his house.

The rental house on Sylvia Rise wasn't bad. In fact, it was his second favorite place in Killdare Springs, second only because Sidecar had a hell of a bar, and at home, he had only two bottles of liquor, both damned near empty.

Downing the whiskey in one more swallow, Booker shifted to pull his wallet from his pocket. He tossed his credit card down as the blond woman slipped off her stool and rounded the bar. She walked directly at him, close enough that he noticed her eyes were the color of a stormy sea and her thick eyebrows were much darker than her dirty-blond hair.

She stared at him boldly as she passed, distaste written all over her face.

Maybe she *was* a lesbian. A *man-hating* lesbian. Booker turned his head and watched her hips sway as she walked to the restroom. Shame. She had a nice ass. Once upon a time, he might have taken that visual home with him. Thought about sinking his teeth into her ass cheeks while he drove his fingers into her and made her beg.

"Thanks."

Booker jerked his attention back to the bartender as the guy put his credit card and a copy of the bill in front of him. He nodded, scribbled a generous tip and his name on the paper, and tossed the pen down.

While he doubted it would happen here in Killdare Springs, he hoped someday he wanted to fuck someone again. Mid-thirties and zero sex drive was enough to make a guy depressed.

2

LENNOX

Lennox Clarke laid her hand over the top of her glass and shook her head at Banks Drummond. The bartender drew back to study her face.

"Water?" he offered her instead. Before she could answer, he moved to fill a tall glass with ice water for her.

"Thanks." She nodded as she took it from him and turned to look at Collins Drummond—landlord and somehow, though eleven years her senior, her best friend. Collins had quoted her a ridiculously cheap monthly rent, helped her move into the upscale but still cozy duplex a few days later, and insinuated herself into Lennox's life seamlessly. So much so that Lennox was now close to her younger brother, Banks, too. Banks, only four years older than Lennox, had made it clear he was interested in dating her, but Lennox had argued that she wanted to be friends. "I need to get home."

Collins glanced at her phone with a nod.

"What time's your first class?"

"Eight."

Collins lifted her glass and finished the last of her drink. Two martinis to Lennox's one. Neither of them drank much, at least not on a random Tuesday in January.

"Leaving already?" Banks took the martini glasses as the girls pushed them toward him.

"Classes start tomorrow," Lennox reminded Banks.

"Mm." Banks nodded. "Whatcha got? Science stuff?"

"Bio," she answered as she slipped off the stool. "And a lab. Comm. U.S. History."

"That could be fun."

Of course, Banks would think a U.S. History course would be fun. That would be because he didn't have a precocious five-year-old, soon to be six-year-old, at home, always wired, always talkative, keeping him up late at night, making it hard to concentrate on reading and homework.

"And a lit class," she added.

"Oh?" Banks tipped his head.

Collins snorted. "Exactly."

"You have *him*?"

Rumors had traveled Killdare Springs at the speed of light when the university hired Booker Gannon as a visiting professor. Lennox had left her taste for rumors and gossip behind in high school; she didn't have time to give a damn what people thought or said about anything. Not with

Eloise at home. Being a single mother usurped her entire life.

She wouldn't change a thing.

However, Lennox was intelligent, and despite getting pregnant when she was eighteen, she was well-educated. Enough to know that most rumors started in some basis of fact. She wasn't *afraid* of Booker Gannon. After what she'd been through the past six years, Lennox wasn't sure she could be afraid of the *boogeyman*.

But she wasn't looking forward to the class for a number of reasons, not the least of which was Booker Gannon. She had done well enough in her rhetoric classes as a freshman, and she was an avid reader. But neither of those things made her think this lit class with Dr. Gannon would be fun or easy.

"I liked my lit classes," Banks mumbled, eyes on the glasses as he rinsed them and set them on the bar mat. "But I didn't have him, obviously."

"I gotta hit the ladies' room," Collins announced with a quick peek at Lennox. "Be right back."

Lennox nodded.

"That was him," Lennox told Banks.

"What?" Banks jerked his gaze around the dimly lit bar and finally looked back at her. "Who was him?"

"That guy over on that side of the bar. Black sweater. Longish dark hair. That's Booker Gannon."

"You're kidding. Right?"

"Nope. I see him all the time on campus."

"That guy's here every night."

"Well, from what I gather he doesn't have any friends or family. So." She shrugged.

"Oh, I've heard things about him." Banks nodded. "Just didn't realize that was him. He's quiet. Never says much."

Lennox met Banks' eyes and shrugged. "I heard his syllabus is, like, fifteen pages long."

Banks flinched.

"He's hot, though," Collins said as she rejoined them at the bar.

"Who?" Lennox looked at her quickly.

"That Gannon guy. Isn't that who you're talking about?"

"Mmm." Lennox shuddered. "Whatever. See ya, Banks."

"Don't be a stranger." He nodded as he stepped around the bar to give each of them a quick hug.

"You don't think so?" Collins asked Lennox as the two of them left the bar together. Damp, frigid air touched Lennox's skin—the tank top left too much skin bare. She shivered as they hurried across the parking lot to Collins' car.

"I don't know." She shook her head as she settled into the passenger seat. "I mean, maybe? But he just seems so full of himself."

"How many times have you reminded me not to listen to gossip?" Collins dropped the car in reverse and whipped it out of the parking space in two seconds. Lennox had long since learned not to gasp or comment when riding anywhere with her friend. It would only make her more reckless.

"That's not gossip," Lennox mumbled. "I've seen him around campus a lot. It's his vibe."

"He reminds you of Monty."

Lennox considered denying it. But there was no point. Flopped comfortably in her seat, head turned toward the passenger window, she shrugged. "Maybe. A little."

"They're not the same."

They weren't. Monty McArthur and Booker Gannon were not in the same ballpark. And yet, Collins' comment was close enough to being true that it needled Lennox under her skin. No desire to talk about either man—not even with Collins and they normally talked about everything— Lennox closed her eyes and opted for a change of subject.

"I hope Mom has Eloise down when we get home."

"Me, too, for your sake." Collins nodded as she floored the accelerator, and the sporty Lexus flew west on Main Street. Assuming her friend was now driving at least fifty, Lennox squeezed her eyes closed. In another life, Collins Drummond would come back as a driver in the Brickyard or Daytona. "She cornered me Sunday afternoon about horse collars."

"Excuse me?" Lennox rolled her head on the seat and blinked her eyes open.

"Football."

"Oh." Lennox straightened with a laugh.

"Except, Lex, she was explaining to me what a horse collar is."

"My dad." Lennox shrugged. "They watch football together."

Actually, Eloise and Lennox's dad and brother were big into football. Baseball. Basketball. Eloise, petite and fragile look-ing, adored her grandpa and uncle, and therefore, she shared all their interests. However, she loved her grandma, too, so that same little girl who carried a football through the house, tucked under arm, hell bent to get from one room to another to "score" also loved baking and dressing for tea parties.

"Oh, I know." Collins nodded now. "I have never seen a kid who talks so much."

Lennox laughed softly.

"So." Collins finally eased off the gas and let the car cruise around forty for a bit. She glanced at Lennox. "Did he recognize you? Did he see you tonight?"

"He saw me," Lennox answered easily. "But I've never had occasion to introduce myself. So, no, he doesn't know who I am."

"Do you think he really did it?"

The quiet, serious tone made her stomach clench. It was one thing to ignore gossip, to refuse to spread rumors. Another to be stupid about something that could be a threat.

"I don't know." She shrugged. "I just have to get through this semester."

"Lex, if he tries anything..."

Lennox groaned and shook her head. She didn't want to talk about it. She didn't want to think about it.

"You'll tell me." Collins slowed to a stop at a red light and looked at her pointedly. "Right? You *will* tell me."

"He's not gonna do anything." Lennox knew the words were just as much to assure herself as to assure Collins. "Even if he *is* that guy, it doesn't mean I would be his target."

"Right. Because you're not blond with a beautiful smile and stormy eyes—"

Lennox couldn't help the rumble of laughter. "I'm not stupid, Collins. I can handle myself."

"I know you can," Collins said quietly. "Just reminding you that you don't have to do it all alone."

3

Lennox

The syllabus was *twelve* pages long. Lennox had looked at it last week. Some of the verbiage was simply the university's mission statement, statement on course work and assessment in the English department, and the department's statement on social justice.

But several pages did pertain to Dr. Gannon's reading assignments, the books and films they would be discussing in class, and his grading system.

Lennox had purchased the books listed and assumed that he would either provide copies of the articles he assigned or give them links when he was ready to discuss each of them.

She arrived for class fifteen minutes early. Even after dropping Eloise off at her mom's, Lennox had too much time on her hands, but not enough to go back home. Killdare Springs was a mid-sized city with a small town feel. Traffic was nothing compared to Chicago or St. Louis, and yet, Capsey Road—where she lived—was a good ten minutes from campus and not much less than that from where her parents lived.

P301 was the small lecture hall to the left of the stairwell on the third floor of Palmer Hall, the humanities building. The first to arrive, Lennox ducked inside the room and claimed the aisle seat in the fourth row of chairs. The hall seated fifty. If she had to guess, she would assume there would be fifteen students or less in this class. The fourth row was bound to be the last row of students, and yet, not choosing the very last row made it appear less calculated.

She pulled her laptop from her backpack and put it on the white table in front of her. Her parents and her brother had given it to her when she turned twenty-two and announced she wanted to go to college. Though getting pregnant with Eloise had been a wrench in her plans and had certainly been a shock to her parents, Lennox was grateful they had recovered quickly and been there to help her with her daughter when she needed it and support her dreams of nursing school. Her brother didn't have to do either, but he did. Four years her senior, Jaxon had been her buddy when she was little, the bane of her existence when she was a tween, and her protector since she had turned eighteen and he, twenty-two.

Next, she slipped her phone from her bag and tapped the screen to wake it. Not interested in checking social media at the moment, she opened her Kindle app and read a few lines of the last book she had downloaded. Wasn't long before she remembered why she was only four chapters into it. She didn't love it. Rather than torture herself, she watched her classmates file into the room, some in small groups, some alone. She wasn't that much older than most of the students around her. But she felt ancient compared with some of these kids—the hulking athletes with their huge muscles and chunky earphones and the girls with their tiny crop tops and baggy jeans.

Surrounded by small conversations and quiet laughter, the anticipation and anxiety over a new semester starting, Lennox considered the rumors about Booker Gannon.

The fifteen-page syllabus was inaccurate, though not far off.

Everyone on campus grumbled about how arrogant the man was. Judging from what she had seen of him, Lennox tended to agree. He had taught this same class last semester, which was most likely the root of the rumor that he was a vampire. That one still made her snicker; she had a good old-fashioned belly laugh when she first heard that one.

While she read vampire books, and she and Eloise hung a goofy-looking cartoonish cardboard vampire every Halloween in the living room window, Lennox didn't believe in anything paranormal, especially not real blood-sucking immortal beings.

She *had seen* Booker Gannon. Often. And yes, *those* whispers were right on the money. Even if she hadn't wanted to agree with Collins last night, the guy was every woman's fantasy with his thick, dark hair, vivid green eyes, and thick lashes and brows. Even Lennox caught herself staring at him now and then when she saw him on campus. Hard to resist a look at the five o'clock shadow on his lean face. The cut of the suits he wore. The cruel mouth that she had never seen smile.

But because she had seen him, Lennox couldn't believe he might be one of those human beings who truly thought he was a vampire. He might be a beautiful, well-dressed, cold-hearted son-of-a-bitch, but she doubted he had billions of dollars of old money stashed in offshore accounts or hidden away in a creepy, damp cellar somewhere. She couldn't picture him walking around with a vial of blood hanging from a cord around his neck. He didn't avoid sunlight, although he *was* mysterious, and he wasn't often seen around campus or most of Killdare Springs in general. While she could picture him sipping red wine, the idea that he sat around in some dungeon in the dark drinking human blood from a chalice was ridiculous.

Next someone would start whispering about him having some coed chained up in his basement for sexual torture and enjoyment. That's how rumors worked. Lennox assumed there was some truth to the rumor of why he had left his last school. But she also knew how rumors gained girth and malice as they spread.

The door opened, and the low buzz of conversation in the lecture hall went silent. Lennox slipped her phone in her backpack, eased the bag down to the floor, and trained her eyes on her professor. His suit today was navy. When he reached the front of the room and turned, she clocked the crisp white shirt and the silver and navy tie. With a different teacher, she might wonder if he was a Dallas Cowboys fan. But this guy didn't seem the kind who would enjoy football. Or any sport.

Or life, really.

Booker Gannon was easily the most striking, gorgeous man she had ever seen. But he looked like he had a stick wedged permanently up his butt. She didn't need a nursing degree to tell her that would be painfully uncomfortable and could create the sour look on the guy's face.

He *did* remind her of Monty. But he was even more of what she found intimidating about Monty McArthur.

"English 2660." His voice was a mix of silk and gravel. Lennox snorted to herself at the thought. *Here we go. Already falling prey to the bullshit romanticism of the vampire lore.* His voice was gruff, but he was so pretty, Lennox wanted to smooth that description over. When the guy in front and to the right of her glanced back at her, she covered her mouth with her fingertips and cleared her throat.

"Film, culture, and literature," the man at the front of the room continued. "I'm Dr. Gannon. If you're in the wrong room, go now."

Lennox cringed when a girl three rows in front of her gathered her books and climbed to her feet. She expected Dr. Gannon to make a smartass comment as the girl hurried to the door, but he simply waited patiently for her to step out before addressing the class again.

"What's a vampire?"

Lennox watched as several heads dipped and fingers flipped through books. She wondered what they were looking at. It wasn't like they had vampire *textbooks*. They had literature *about* vampires. There was a difference.

"Yeah." Dr. Gannon pointed at a guy in the front row, one of the Neanderthal-looking rugby players with the huge earphones, although they were now down around his neck.

"Someone who drinks blood."

Lennox eased back in her chair when Gannon nodded his head back and forth and then pointed at the girl next to the rugby guy.

"A paranormal being that uses sharp teeth to bite and suck blood."

Again, Gannon did the little nod and swept his gaze over the room. Lennox didn't raise her hand, but she didn't look away when their eyes locked. The silence between them vibrated as she waited for him to say something.

Did he recognize her from last night?

"What do you think?" He leaned his elbows on the podium in front of him and tipped his chin at her. Now she wished she would have looked away. She wasn't one to shy away from attention, but she didn't love it, either. Reasonably intelligent, Lennox was reserved until she was comfortable in a setting, with the people around her.

"Someone who preys on others," she answered boldly.

In that context, that vampire rumor she had heard about Booker Gannon *could* be true.

"Interesting," he mumbled with a nod. Eyes still locked with hers, he asked, "What fictional character comes to mind when you hear the word vampire?"

Edward from Twilight.

She wouldn't say it. Nobody in the room would even know who the hell she was talking about. Lennox herself had been a little too young to get caught up in the *Twilight* craze. But she'd had plenty of time to read the books and watch the movies when Eloise was a baby. She loved her daughter to the moon and back, but Eloise Clarke had not been a good sleeper. Lennox had gone through a lot of TV Land, Netflix, and other streaming services, not to mention half the Killdare Springs public library while she was up with her baby.

Then again, *Twilight* was on their required text list.

Did he want her to say Dracula? Or was that too obvious?

Does it matter, Lex?

"Dracula."

He nodded, though there was no smile. No flicker of pride or celebration anywhere on his face.

"Who else?"

Was he still talking to her? Did she know other vampires?

A hand went up closer to the front of the classroom. Gannon nodded to acknowledge the guy, but he lifted a hand to hold his answer off and kept his eyes on Lennox.

"The count on Sesame Street."

That cruel, hard mouth split into a grin. That vibration between them a moment ago pinged her again, like the electric shock of touching a live wire.

"What's his name?"

Lennox forgot there were students all around her, staring at her, as she conversed with Booker Gannon.

"Count von Count."

The grin faded, but he nodded. Finally, he turned his attention to the guy who had a hand up.

"Count Chocula."

"Yep."

Gannon stepped away from the podium and shrugged out of his suit jacket. Lennox watched him hang it on the back of his chair and then unbutton his shirtsleeves to roll them. She assumed this was all part of a show for him. But was it his way of establishing power as the professor? Reminding them all that his word was gospel in his class?

Or was he baring his forearms so the young girls in his class would drool over him?

Again, the definition she had tossed out came to her.

Someone who preys on others.

As a visiting professor, he was mysterious. As a *good-looking male* visiting professor, he was intriguing. Lennox watched him turn his back to them and pick up a marker.

Was there any truth to the stories of him sleeping with his students? Did it matter?

It did.

To her.

Hard to respect anyone in a power position who preyed on others.

4

BOOKER

"Let's talk a little more about—" Booker glanced at the blond-haired girl in the second to last row again, waiting for her to share her name.

"Lennox," she supplied it simply, no fan fair, no flirty smiles or giggles. Booker much preferred simple, no fan fair, and no flirting. The woman just earned a point in his book.

"About what Lennox said," he continued with a nod. "Someone who preys on others. Like whom?"

He was tempted to press her again, to make her say more. But he made himself move on, calling on a tall black-haired guy.

"Serial killers?"

Booker shrugged and nodded. "Sure." He sighed and tucked his hands in his pockets. "Most people think the word, the creature, *vampire* is about eroticism and horror. And it can be. But we're going to dig a little deeper in this class."

"What do you mean?"

Booker snapped his gaze to a girl with spiked blue hair in the front row. She bit her lip when he stared at her, like she thought he might chastise her for speaking out of turn, as if this was elementary school and not a sophomore level college lit class.

"Good question." He nodded. She stared back at him silently. "We're going to dig deeper and look at the meaning of the mythical monster. We want to understand the historical, cultural, and political contexts of the creature, and we're going to look at how those contexts have changed through the years."

"You're talking about racism and sexism."

Surprised she spoke again, Booker turned his attention back to the woman named Lennox.

"Yes, I am." He nodded. "We're going to look at the mythical vampire in terms of racism. Sexism. Class. Gender. Sexuality."

He waited for a few quiet snickers to subside, ignoring them, both because it irritated him and because he wasn't oblivious. Booker knew his female students—even a few of his male students—talked about him inappropriately. He had heard some of the crazy rumors that got started about him before he had even set foot on Killdare University's campus. He was here to teach, and he had no intention of adding fuel to the fire of gossip.

Nor did he plan to share his truth.

"The goal of this class is to hone your analytical, argumentative, and writing skills. Yes, I want to challenge you intellectually, and yes, I want all of you to walk out of this class in May with a broader understanding, a broader social point of view, than where you are today."

He waited for someone to argue, for someone to challenge him and tell him he had no right to change their way of thinking. For some reason, he found himself looking at Lennox again. Though she didn't speak, the look on her face was certainly bold and challenging.

"I'm not asking you to think like I do." He shrugged. "All I ask is that you *think*. For yourself. You'll have three short papers, a major paper, a major presentation, and a creative final project to do, in addition to your course reading. Class participation will count toward your grade. Which means what?"

Blank faces stared back at him.

"You have to be in class to participate," he announced. "That simple. If you can't make it to class, maybe you don't need the credit."

Anger flashed over a few faces. Sure, there were excused absences, but Booker didn't make it a habit of discussing them. To him, it sounded like a subliminal message to go ahead and skip class. He preferred to deal with each student, each absence, each grade, individually and arbitrarily. If the dean wanted to ride his ass about it, Booker would handle it. Not like he hadn't already had his ass ridden harder than a Derby horse.

"Your reading schedule is tentative," he went on, scanning the room as he spoke. Several of his students were staring right back at him, Lennox included. A few of them were picking at their fingernails which he thought was gross.

And a few of them were looking at books. Not to read, but to avoid eye contact with him.

Booker had been a student once; he knew the drill.

"There might be times I'll change the schedule," he told them. "Some of your reading will be graphic." He shrugged. "I'm not into trigger warnings. If you believe you'll have a problem with it, drop my class and find something with unicorns and sunflowers."

A quiet murmur went around the room. This was probably where the rumor that he was a dick had started. Booker preferred to think of himself as demanding and maybe unforgiving. But if his stance on these things made him a dick, he was okay with that.

"If at any time in the semester, you feel you can't meet the class requirements, come to me immediately. Do not wait until the final weeks of class."

He wasn't unreasonable. He was tough. And he had high expectations. But he also understood not everyone was cut out for academic life. And not everyone would be able to tolerate the gore and the distressing topics they would cover.

"For Friday." He moved back to the podium and leaned. "Read the introduction to the Gothic on your syllabus and be ready to discuss it. And by discuss it, I mean discuss. Discourse. Talk to each other. Talk to me. Ask questions. Answer questions."

He looked around, seeing a few nods and even more students avoiding his gaze.

"Class dismissed." He backed away from the podium and leaned over the chair at the desk to pull his laptop from his backpack. In front of him, his English 2660 students filed out of the room, some of them engaged in conversation, and some quiet.

He found himself watching Lennox move gracefully down the side steps of the lecture hall. Dressed in faded denim, Ugg boots, and a sweatshirt under a dark blue puffer coat, she looked like a college student from his school days. Easy and comfortable. Not trying to turn any heads or impress anyone. She wore a touch of makeup, but no jewelry that he could see. Her dark blond hair fell in short messy waves around her face.

She was pretty in a completely different way than all the other girls he'd had in classes since he started teaching. Pretty like she didn't care. Like she had more important things to worry about. Booker made himself look away. Didn't matter what sort of pretty the woman was. She was his student; therefore, she was off-limits.

He opened his laptop and tapped his password in when prompted. Sensing he wasn't alone, Booker looked up from the laptop, surprised to find her standing in front of the desk.

Lennox.

A little disappointed, he barely bit back his sarcasm. He wouldn't have guessed this one to choose unicorns and sunflowers over vampires.

"What?"

She narrowed her eyes at him, her stare calm and cool. A shudder ripped through him, though he refused to show any emotion.

This was the woman he had seen at Sidecar, the one who had looked at him with such distaste. Had she known last night who he was?

Yes. Only one reason a woman would look at him like that. Lennox knew exactly who he was, and she had apparently heard the rumors. *All of them.*

5

LENNOX

"On Fridays, I have a nine o'clock class at south campus."

Gannon simply stared at her. Up close like this, his green eyes nearly made her shiver. He appeared younger than she assumed, too.

"And?" He shrugged.

"Not sure how long it's gonna take me to get to south campus."

"If you're a sophomore, you've been in Killdare Springs—"

"I grew up in Killdare Springs," she interrupted him. "And I've *driven* all over Killdare Springs. But I don't know what traffic will be like at eight fifty in the mornings, and I don't know what Dr. Rutledge's policy on tardies is."

"But somehow his policy on tardies trumps my policy on attendance?"

Lennox caught herself before she rolled her eyes. While she didn't plan to cower in front of him—she wasn't afraid of Booker Gannon, English professor or actual vampire—she wouldn't be outright rude, either.

"It's one day a week," she said simply, "maybe five minutes one day a week."

Gannon, hands in his pockets again, studied her silently for a moment.

"What's your major?"

"Nursing."

Hence the reason she was more concerned about Matthew Rutledge's tardy policy than anything in Gannon's class. Again, not something she would say to him, but there it was. Her bio classes mattered more to her than lit. She could cruise through lit and walk away with a decent grade, as long as Gannon wasn't an ass about how he graded.

"My sister's a cardiac nurse," he told her. "She worked hard in school."

Lennox had no doubt.

"So did I," he continued. "For my English major."

"Are you suggesting I don't plan to work hard? Just because I might need to leave class a few minutes early on Fridays to get to my next class on time?"

"I'm not." He shook his head. "I'm having a conversation with you."

At a loss for anything else to say, Lennox nodded and took a step back from his desk.

"Have you read *Dracula?*"

"No." It didn't bother her to admit it.

"Are you a reader?"

"Yes."

"You've read *Twilight?*"

She laughed softly. "I have."

"And your opinion?"

"On the book? The series? Movies?"

Gannon simply shrugged. Lennox sighed and tipped her head.

"It's not really something I can just say good or bad."

"No?"

"There were things in the books I liked. Things I didn't."

"And the movies?"

"Didn't care for them."

"Not a Robert Pattinson fan? Or was it Taylor Lautner you didn't care for?"

"Neither. Just didn't love the movies."

"How would you change them?"

Lennox opened her mouth to answer him.

"Booker?"

Gannon jerked his gaze from her to the doorway where a

man dressed in khakis and a white button-down now stood.

"Hey." Gannon offered the guy a smile. Lennox wondered about that. This one looked real. Was he one of those *man's man* kind of guys? Or just ridiculously serious in a class-room environment? "How ya doin', Chuck?"

With their conversation clearly over, Lennox turned to leave.

"See you Friday, Lennox."

Surprised that Gannon had said anything to her, she simply nodded at him and slipped by Professor Whisman standing in the doorway. Their conversation followed her down the hall, but she wasn't interested in Shakespeare, so she tuned them out.

She considered the rumors as she bumped the bar on the stairwell door with her hip and stepped through when it opened. Compared the rumors to the man she had finally met in person.

He did seem like he might be a dick. He might grade hard, and that might be because he expected a lot, but also, it might be because he was a power-hungry dick. He was every bit as good-looking, as sexy, as the rumors hinted at, but Lennox hadn't felt any flirty vibes from him aimed at anyone in the room.

Too soon to tell, she decided as she hurried down the stairs. And really, other than how he graded, she didn't care. If he was banging female students in his office, that was his problem. Surely one he would lose his job over again if anyone proved it was happening. Lennox had no plans to get herself in a situation where she had to blow him for a passing grade.

And if she did find herself in that position, she would go to the dean. She didn't have time for that kind of crap.

Outside, she huddled deeper into her coat as she hurried across campus to her car. Nothing worth stealing inside it —if someone needed Eloise's car seat so badly they would steal it, Lennox could afford to buy her a new one—she pulled the driver's door open, threw her backpack over to the passenger side, and settled into her cold, leather seat. Shivering, she started the engine and turned the blower down, so the cold air wouldn't freeze her face off.

She glanced at the clock on the dashboard. Just after nine. There was no way in hell she would be able to leave Gannon's class, get out to her car, drive to south campus, and get to her bio classroom on time. *Now*, she rolled her eyes.

6

BOOKER

His sister, the cardiac nurse, had worked her ass off in school, just as he had said to Lennox. But so had he. There had been times he and Randi had clashed about school and intellect. Their parents had chalked it up to sibling rivalry. Maybe that was the case, but Booker got sick of people kissing Randi's ass because she worked so hard. Nursing, sciences, were a different sort of intelligence, different studies, but it didn't mean humanities was a slack major that didn't deserve respect.

They had grown out of it. In fact, he probably talked to Randi more than anyone these days. Booker hadn't dumped all the shit about Ashley, the shit Sofie and Reese had pulled, at Randi's feet. But she knew more about it than their parents did. Randi worried about him, though, and that drove him crazy. He didn't want or need his big sister sticking her nose into his business, telling him to get out more, to quit talking to students altogether, to make an account on a dating app, or even just to keep his chin up.

He had told her as much last month when he went home for Christmas. Randi had been out with friends—she had done her damnedest to drag him out with them, to set him up with one of the girls. Booker flat out refused to go; rather, he stayed at his parents', guzzling first a six-pack of some hazy IPA and then hitting the bottle of Jack Daniels he found shoved to the back of his parents' liquor cabinet. Instead of going to her apartment when her night out broke up, Randi had come back to their parents' house.

Tipsy enough to start in on him. Rattling about him being a good guy, how Ashley should have stood by him, and all Randi wanted was for her little brother to be happy. Flat out drunk, and still ridiculously angry at women—three in particular—Booker had told Randi to back off. If he remembered correctly, he had sneered at her. Told her he didn't need a cardiac nurse to fix his broken heart. And he might have told her his friends Jack and Jim were all he needed.

He didn't particularly want to remember. But if he were honest with himself, he had to admit he said that thing about a nurse and added that ugly sneer to it because he was being childish, and it was a good dig at how everyone had always treated Randi like she was a rocket scientist and Booker—well, as if Booker just liked to read, and it was a waste of time.

And what made that even worse? Booker liked to read horror books. Thrillers. He liked the abject. The uncanny.

Randi could have gone on the attack. Could have told him to go fuck himself. But she hadn't. She'd stomped up the basement steps, spent the night in her teenage bedroom, and joined them for breakfast the next morning. She had been her usual bubbly, fun self with their parents, but she hadn't said a word to him.

Booker deserved it. That night wasn't one of his finer moments. He hadn't had any fine moments in a long time. Definitely not since before last April. He hadn't attempted an apology yet. Nearly three weeks had passed, and he hadn't talked to his sister at all.

Ironic then, that he would be thinking about her now. Eyes trained on his light brown oxford dress shoes as he walked the campus path to Crave, he considered texting her. Like him, Randi was stubborn, and she could wait him out. She wouldn't contact him; she would remind him he had told her to butt out.

Loud indie rock greeted him when he pulled the door of Crave open. He shouldn't be here. But the campus coffeehouse was open to all professors and students; it was open to the public. On the corner of campus, just off Lincoln Avenue, it was a convenient stop for Killdare Springs businesspeople. The drive-thru no doubt added to that convenience.

Booker had only dropped in a time or two last semester, both times just after seven, when most college students were either dragging their hungover asses back to their dorms or already in their dorms sleeping it off. He wasn't sure what had possessed him to head this way when he left Palmer Hall this afternoon, but here he was in line for a cup of ridiculously overpriced coffee. Surrounded by kids.

He glanced around the cozy coffeehouse and noted a few professors seated here and there. That made him feel somewhat better. The song switched to something even more raucous and earsplitting. Booker lifted his hand and cupped it around the back of his neck. Maybe the headache had driven him here for caffeine. If that was the case, the joke was on him, because this hideous crap kids called music was like a fucking shovel pounding the back of his head in.

"Dr. Gannon." The girl behind the counter offered him a smile. He tipped his head and studied her, recognizing the spiky-blue hair. She had been in his Film, Culture, and Literature class this morning. "Kara. I'm in your eight-a.m. class."

He nodded. "Hi, Kara." Clearing his throat, he looked up at the chalkboard menu on the wall behind her. "Can I just get a large dark roast?"

"You bet." She tapped the iPad at her station, announced his total, and turned away to fill his order in one smooth motion. Backpack over his left shoulder, Booker pulled his wallet from his hip pocket, plucked his credit card from it, and tapped the card reader. He dropped a buck in the tip jar, tucked his card away, and nodded his thank you to Kara when she handed the oversized red mug to him.

He caught himself before he could growl at her. He wanted the coffee to go, but he hadn't specified that.

"There's some people from class over there." She tossed her hand toward the north side of the small place. Tables— two-tops and four-tops—and couches and loveseats clustered around small decorative tables. A fireplace. And a sea of college students.

"Thanks." He took the mug from her and considered asking her to pour it into a to-go cup.

"Josh is kinda holding court." The girl rolled her eyes. "Guy thinks he knows everything."

Intrigued by her tone as much as her words—Booker had no idea who the hell Josh was—he changed his mind, nodded at her again, and wandered over to the seating area. Four students from his eight-a.m. class were gathered on two loveseats arranged around a low-slung rough-hewn coffee table.

Two guys. Two girls.

Wondering which one was Josh, he took a sip of his coffee, flinching when the hot liquid hit his tongue.

"I'm just sayin'." The tall guy in the Killdare University hoodie shrugged so dramatically, Booker thought he might be better suited to the theater department. He also knew without a doubt this must be Josh.

"I gotta go."

Booker jerked his gaze away from the hoodie heart throb and watched the blonde reach for her backpack.

Lennox.

"It's just sensationalism. It sells."

Booker saw a laptop screen opened to the article he had assigned on the Gothic.

"Go home." The other girl sounded annoyed. She snatched an empty mug from the table and stood. "Oh. Dr. Gannon. Hi."

This girl hadn't said a word in class today. Her annoyance with Josh faded in the face of her discomfort with Booker.

The other three looked up in unison. Josh appeared like he wanted to chat, most likely to kiss ass for his grade or to walk away later and squeeze some lighter fluid on the bonfire that was Booker's life.

Booker had no desire to sit around and bullshit with the hoodie guy.

The other kid, the one sitting next to Josh, stood and offered Booker a neutral smile.

"Trying to make sense of the reading," he explained.

"Mm." Booker nodded noncommittally.

"Okay. I'm out. Gotta get to work." The other girl grabbed her bag, called a general goodbye, and gave Booker one last nervous glance.

Josh stood up. Booker saw the way the kid was sizing him up, ready to be smug over the fact that he was taller, bigger. When they stood eye to eye, Josh cleared his throat.

"Gotta work out," he announced. Booker simply stepped aside to let the kid leave.

The remaining guy shot Lennox a look, and they shared a laugh.

"See ya Friday," the guy mumbled to Lennox as he slapped the lid of the laptop closed and picked it up. "See ya, Dr. Gannon."

"See ya," Booker repeated. He watched the kid walk away, laptop tucked to his side. Lennox was watching him when he looked back at her. "Something I said?"

She snorted softly and raised her eyebrows.

7

Lennox

"Actually," she sighed, "thanks for the rescue."

Dr. Gannon looked over his shoulder and then back at her.

"He's been rambling for the past forty..." Lennox glanced at her phone. "Three minutes. That's enough of the Josh Stone show for me for one day."

Dr. Gannon appeared surprised at the laugh that escaped him.

"I assume he was talking about the Botting reading?"

"Trying to," she agreed. She grabbed her notebook and pen from the table and dropped them in her bag. "Sorry. I really do need to go."

"Work?"

"Hmm?" She watched him step around the loveseat across from her and sit down.

"Heading off to work?"

"No." She cleared her throat, suddenly tongue-tied. He was still in the suit, but he had loosened the tie. Not enough that she could see anything, but still, the look was relaxed, easy. He didn't look like the arrogant jerk he had earlier today standing at the front of the lecture hall. "Off tonight."

"I didn't specify I needed my coffee to go," he mumbled with a sigh.

"She'll give you a to-go cup."

He nodded.

"How did you find the reading?"

Poised and ready to escape, Lennox deflated and fell back to rest on the loveseat. "Parts of it were over my head."

"But in general?"

"Okay." She shrugged. "Interesting, I guess."

"And I gather Josh Stone says the Gothic is sensational."

"Yeah." She nodded. "But I think he was using that as his argument for anything goes."

"In Gothic literature?"

"Life."

"Mm." Dr. Gannon sipped his coffee and put his mug down.

"I had rhetoric with him last year." She squeezed her eyes closed. "Let's just say there's not much character growth there."

Gannon laughed softly.

"So, tell me now."

"Tell you what now?"

"Your thoughts on *Twilight*."

Lennox glanced at her phone again and sat forward. She needed to pick Eloise up from her parents' house and get her home. Fix something for dinner. Get Eloise through whatever homework her kindergarten teacher had sent home with her. And then read her own assignments.

"Creepy." She shrugged.

"You think vampires are creepy."

"No." Lennox sighed and let go of her bag. "Well. I mean, *Salem's Lot*? Creepy vampire, yes. *Twilight*, not so much."

"Then why say the books are creepy?"

"The idea that some hundred-and-some-year-old being was sneaking in to watch the girl sleep? That's creepy."

"He was protecting her."

"He was probably fantasizing about having her for lunch," she corrected him. "And no, I haven't read the one that's in his POV. I liked the first book. By the time I got to book four, I was..." She shrugged. "I liked them okay. Let's leave it at that."

"What're you reading right now?"

Lennox swallowed hard and reminded herself they were in a public place. No matter if the rumors were true or not, Dr. Gannon couldn't do anything to her here. And no one could say she was being flirtatious with him.

Jesus. Just what she needed.

"Um." *Grow up, Lennox. He's not flirting with you.* "Book three of a series by Ellen Michelle." Lennox didn't elaborate. She doubted a college professor was familiar with the *Blood Rite* fantasy series.

"First series or the spinoff?"

Stunned by his question, she simply stared at him for a moment. Around them, a laid-back rap song played, and conversations piqued and swelled. Lennox squirmed under Dr. Gannon's intense gaze.

"First." Her answer was little more than a whisper.

Without comment, he picked his mug up and took another drink.

"You've read them?"

"Both." He nodded. "Wrote an article about them, actually."

"You wrote an article about Ellen Michelle's books."

"You don't believe me?"

"I...Sure, but why?"

"I studied Raiah. In contrast to Eve."

"Eve," she repeated. "Of the Bible? That Eve?"

"Mm." He nodded.

"I'm not sure I follow that comparison."

Raiah, after all, was a demon. If Eve of Genesis had been labeled a demon, Lennox had missed that part.

"Mother of creation."

"So, Raiah as *mother of demons*."

Dr. Gannon nodded. "As well as Eve tempting Adam."

Lennox rolled her eyes. "That again, huh?"

"Explain."

"Adam could have said no. *Sorry, Eve, but no. Nope. Not interested*."

Dr. Gannon's smirk needled her.

"And what about Raiah? No mortal man could resist her."

"Yeah, well, maybe mortal men are weak, Dr. Gannon." Lennox shrugged.

"Maybe."

Lennox sat still under his stare, but her stomach was clenched in fight or flight mode.

"Are you religious?" he asked. Taken aback by the question, Lennox held her breath for a second. She broke the intense eye contact and let her gaze roam over his face. His thin lips were pale in contrast to the dark five o'clock shadow on his angular face.

Monty was blond. Blue eyed. Athletic.

And rich. And arrogant.

And cruel when push had come to shove.

"I gotta go." She grabbed her bag and stood.

"And where do you have to rush off to?" Still seated, he

tipped his chin up to watch her as she stepped away from what now felt like a very personal, cozy sitting area.

"I have to pick up my daughter."

The second the words were out of her mouth, she tasted regret. It wasn't like Booker Gannon was some depraved psychopath who was going to follow her home and kidnap Eloise, but *still*. The idea that he now knew she had a child bothered her. It felt like a violation, even though she had been the one to say the words.

LENNOX

She could feel Eloise watching her from the doorway. Lennox finished the sentence she was reading before looking up at her daughter. Getting pregnant at eighteen had been a surprise, but Lennox never referred to her daughter as a mistake or even an accident.

"What're you doing up?" She put her laptop aside on the sofa and eyed Eloise. Her light-bulb-bright blond hair was matted and smooshed to her head on one side; the other stood on end with static electricity. Her purple nightgown was getting too small, but it was Eloise's favorite, and whenever Lennox tried to get rid of it, the girl had a fit.

"Can't sleep, Mommy."

Lennox doubted that. Bedhead like that didn't happen from not sleeping.

"C'mere."

As if she was just waiting for the invitation, Eloise scampered across the living room and threw herself on Lennox's lap. Lennox wrapped her arms around her and pressed her cheek to the top of her head. She breathed in the sweet little girl smell of baby shampoo and soap and lotion. Eloise would be six soon; and Lennox knew that she would blink, and her daughter would be ten and then thirteen and then sixteen and—

"What're you reading?"

"Stuff for school."

"Want me to help you with your homework?" Eloise tipped her head back and looked up at Lennox with big, dark eyes.

"Would you?"

Eloise grinned, revealing the loose tooth Lennox had been wanting to pull.

"Let me get that tooth—"

"No, Mommy!" Eloise squealed. "Let's do your homework."

Lennox glanced at the time stamp in the upper corner of her laptop screen. It was nearly ten. Eloise should be in bed. But Lennox liked the extra snuggle time with her, so she would give her a few minutes.

"Okay. I'm reading about the Gothic."

"What's that?"

"Mmm." Lennox rested her head on the sofa as Eloise turned in her lap to sit face to face. "It's spooky stuff."

"You study spooky stuff in school?"

Her frown, her obvious confusion, tickled Lennox. She supposed even that much was hard for a five-year-old to understand. There was no way she was going to get into the details of the article she was reading—a discussion of the Gothic, how it was thought of as the promotion of vice, violence, and sexual desire. She could imagine Eloise heading into school tomorrow armed with *those* words and proposing a discussion of *The Monk* by Matthew Gregory Lewis, published in 1796 and considered sacrilegious and obscene.

"Yeah." Lennox nodded. "I will be this semester."

"What's *smester* mean?" Eloise lifted her hands and touched the heart charm on the necklace Lennox wore every day. She was fascinated with it now; gold and bling always caught her little girl's eye. Lennox often wondered if there would be a day when Eloise was fascinated with it, wondering if it had been a gift to her mother from her father, rather than just because it was gold and shiny.

It hadn't.

Lennox's parents had given it to her when she turned sixteen.

"It's a certain amount of time for college classes," Lennox explained. "This is for my English class."

"Gofic is English stuff?"

Lennox laughed softly. "Well, the class is a literature class, so we'll be reading a lot of stuff."

"Spooky stuff?" Eloise repeated as she tipped her head.

"Mm-hmm."

"Like ghosts?"

"Yes." Lennox nodded. As far as she had read on the syllabus, there were no readings about *ghosts*, per se. But she had no desire to tell Eloise they were studying vampires. Eloise liked the Count on *Sesame Street* and Dracula in *Hotel Transylvania*, but Lennox suspected talking about any other vampires might put ideas in her head. Scary ideas that would lead to bad dreams.

Eloise giggled. "I know one!"

"Yeah? What ghost do you know?"

"Casper!"

"Good job." Lennox nodded.

"What's your teacher's name?"

"Doctor Gannon."

"Why is a doctor your teacher?"

Lennox laughed again and circled her fingers around Eloise's skinny wrists. "I think we need to get you back in bed."

Eloise shook her head. "Ghosts might get me."

Lennox kissed Eloise's hands and then wrapped her arms around her daughter as she climbed up from the couch. "The only ghost you know is Casper," she reminded Eloise. "He would probably be fun to hang out with. Don't you think?"

"I love you, Mommy." Eloise rested her head on Lennox's shoulder as she carried her into her bedroom.

"Love you, too, El." Lennox stood at her bedside, and Eloise put her feet down. Lennox watched, wishing she had the energy her daughter did, as the little girl jumped and flopped down on her bed. She scrambled to pull her covers up and then beamed up at Lennox with big eyes.

"Can we get ice cream this weekend?"

"Maybe." Lennox leaned over to kiss Eloise on the forehead. "Goodnight."

"Maybe means yes!" Eloise hollered after her as she left the room.

She was right; nine times out of ten, when Lennox told Eloise maybe, it was a yes.

Before going back out to hit the books again, Lennox ducked into her bedroom and changed from her jeans and sweatshirt to pajamas. She could take her laptop to her room and read in bed for a while, but it would make her sleepy. Something told her she would need to be on her A-game this semester with Booker Gannon, so she needed to be alert while she was reading.

He had completely unnerved her earlier this afternoon with that question. It made no sense. Why asking her if she was religious bothered her, she had no idea, but she had gathered her stuff and hurried away from him, a little out of breath and definitely unsettled. If he was power-hungry, her rushing out of Crave like that had probably fed the monster.

Curled up in the corner of the couch again, Lennox pulled her computer back to her lap. But she couldn't concentrate. After

staring at the article on her screen for another few moments—
she had read it once, and now she was reading it a second time,
highlighting lines that piqued her curiosity and making notes
in case Gannon called on her Friday—Lennox minimized the
shared article he had sent them and opened her web browser.

A wave of awareness, almost like heat, flowed from her
wrists to her fingers, as she settled her fingertips on the
keyboard. Should she—? Not like anyone would know. And
it wasn't like there was anything wrong with just looking
him up.

Curious about the article he had written about the Ellen
Michelle series, Lennox typed Booker Gannon, PhD into the
search bar. That heat, that jolt of electricity in her fingers,
now rolled through her chest, pushing her oxygen up and
out. Breathless, fingers still on the keys, Lennox eyed the
list of hits with Dr. Gannon's name. Most of them were
about scholarly articles he had written or panels and
conferences he had participated in.

Slowly, as if worried someone would catch her, she scrolled
down the list. Her mouth went dry when she saw the article
from last spring. She could click on it. Read the *real news*
and put the questions in her head to bed. Then again, she
hadn't given *it, him*, enough thought to have questions, and
besides, sometimes the news stories *weren't* the whole
story.

But it would be closer to the truth than anything she heard
on campus.

The text message tone on her phone beeped. The sound in
the otherwise quiet living room made her jump. Belly flut-

tering with nerves now, she leaned forward and snatched the phone from the sofa cushion in front of her.

How was class today?

Lennox flopped back on the arm of the couch and let out a long sigh. Collins texted often. Even if she was right on the other side of the main wall in the house, the two of them texted if they were too busy to visit through the day. Her friend wasn't texting right now just because Lennox was about to snoop into something that was none of her business, even though her timing was impeccable.

Sitting up again, she fired an innocent text back.

Good. Looks like a lot of reading.

Well, you expected that. It is lit, after all.

Lennox chuckled and scrolled back to the top of the page. She almost clicked out of the browser, but she hesitated. She was curious about the article Dr. Gannon had written regarding Ellen Michelle's *Blood Rite* series.

Plans Friday?

Lennox held her phone in one hand and tapped the fingers of her other on the edge of her laptop. The *Blood Rite* series was very sensual—none of the *smut words* used in sex scenes, and yet, the scenes in those books were steamy enough, Lennox wouldn't want Eloise to get her hands on the books until she was twenty. Twenty-seven.

Ever.

She scrolled down again until the cursor hovered over the article she was interested in.

Gannon, Booker. "Ellen Michelle's Rajah Cojocaru as mother and lover in the *Blood Rite* series." *American Literature Studies* V. 4, pp. 27-42.

Her text tone made her jump again.

Lex? You there?

Lennox held her breath as she clicked on the link, eyes on her phone as she responded to Collins.

Yeah. Nothing Friday. What's up?

Movie night? With Eloise?

Rather than answer Collins, she skimmed the first paragraph of the article.

Ellen Michelle's titular character in Book 1 of the Blood Rite *series,* Raiah Awakens, *is symbolic of motherhood as well as man's lustful desire to possess, both mentally and sexually, all women. As a demon, Raiah feels no more maternal bond to the creatures she bears than to those she turns into vampires. However—*

Her phone rang in her hand. Lennox jumped again, dropping the phone to her lap. It bounced off the laptop, hitting the space bar, and falling between her thighs.

"Movie night's good," she answered as a greeting. Eyes still on Dr. Gannon's words, her hand hovered over the keyboard, as if she were afraid Collins could see what she was doing.

"What the hell are you doing?"

Breathless with—what? Fear? Maybe. A little. But anticipation, too. She wanted to read the rest of what Dr. Gannon said about the books, about the sensuality, the exchange of blood and sex, the killings—Lennox saved the article and snapped the laptop closed.

"Studying." She cleared her throat, hoping nothing in her tone gave away the way her heart was racing.

There was nothing wrong with being curious about an academic paper your professor wrote. Nothing wrong with being curious about the story behind his leaving his last college, either. Not if it meant keeping herself safe.

Never mind that he was such a pretty man.

After all, Lennox had met a wolf in sheep's clothing before. *That* family of vampires had tried their damnedest to suck her dry.

BOOKER

Booker wasn't a joiner. He had never been one to jump on a bandwagon and follow the crowd. When he and Ashley were married, he would have scoffed at the idea of joining a gym for exercise. Rather, the two of them had invested in a small workout room in the basement of their Americana brick ranch-style home. They'd had free weights, which he used more often than she did. And they'd had a spin bike, which she used more often than him. Both had used the treadmill, but Booker preferred to run outside, weather permitting.

At least the gym he had joined here in Killdare Springs had insane hours so he could knock out the workout first thing in the morning. His house on Sylvia Rise was a gorgeous old Victorian style home, but the basement was nothing more than a stone cellar. The interior of the two-story home was elegant and dark, the perfect complement to Booker's life now. And yet, there was nowhere he could put a treadmill or free weights with a bench.

Didn't matter. He'd left it all behind in the divorce. Ashley had sold it before the ink was dry on the papers.

At Killdare Fitness, he went in at five and worked himself as hard as he could before limping out and going back home to shower and get ready for the rest of his day. He kept to himself, started every morning with a cardio warm-up and made the rounds on the weight machines. The place offered organized classes; Booker was somewhat interested in the boxing ring in the back room. He could pummel out a hell of a lot of his residual rage in a ring. But he would also have to sign up to spar. And by definition, sparring with someone in a boxing ring required him to interact with someone.

To avoid stopping into Crave today, Booker carried his own coffee mug up the stairs to the third floor. While the other day had been interesting—bumping into Lennox and the three other students from the film and lit class—he didn't plan to make that a habit. No doubt there was someone just watching, waiting with bated breath for him to fuck up. Not to mention the way Lennox had hightailed it out of the coffeehouse the other day when he asked if she was religious. He had only been curious about her reading habits and if she was sensitive to anything in particular. Rushing out of there the way she had painted a picture of a sensitive, skittish girl that didn't mesh with who she was in his classroom.

Then again, this was day two, so what the hell did he know?

The lecture hall was empty when he pulled the door open and stepped inside. Booker bumped the light switch and headed to the desk. He took a drink before depositing his mug on the ancient metal piece that looked as if they'd salvaged it up from the seventies. He swung his backpack down off his arm and let the bag plop in the chair behind the desk.

Once upon a time, he had loved this. The empty lecture hall, the slow, steady filling of said lecture hall. Students conversing while they waited for class to start. Booker used to perch on the edge of the desk and take it all in—the conversations about weekend parties to reading assignments to progress on papers and projects. More often than not, a couple of the guys and girls would approach him and ask him to clarify something from a previous lecture or the reading from the night before. Booker would explain whatever was needed; he loved delving into those conversations. Once the point was clear, talk always steered to casual things. The athletes liked to share with him about their home runs or their three-point shots. The partiers liked to brag about how many kegs they went through at the farm over the weekend. The sorority girls quizzed him on what he thought they should do for community fundraisers.

Butt on the edge of the desk now, Booker stared silently at the empty seats in front of him. He wanted to think he would get back to that, to enjoying his job. To enjoying not just class discussions with his students, but general talk, too. He wanted to think he could look at Kara, the blue-haired girl, who looked nothing like Sofie and *not* think of Sofie.

He wanted to want someone to come home to after a day at school. While the thought was okay, pressing any further into that fantasy just made him think of Ashley.

The door opened and pulled Booker from his thoughts. He turned his head and watched Lennox come inside and dash up the steps to the same seat she'd had Wednesday. He tried not to notice the way her skinny jeans molded her slender thighs and her nice little ass. When that didn't work, he told himself he was only noticing because she dressed so differently from most of the coeds on campus.

She slipped her coat off, revealing a button-up navy blouse. Buttoned not to the very top, but enough that she would give no one a show if she leaned over. A hint of gold gleamed at the top of the blouse; he had noticed the necklace at Crave. No wedding rings. No rings of any sort.

But she had a daughter.

Lennox tossed her coat on the chair next to her and unzipped her bag. As she dug around inside it, she happened to glance up and catch him watching her. Her movements slowed for just a moment. Booker would swear her cheeks flushed, but she ducked her head toward the bag and fished out her laptop and a pen.

It wasn't doing anyone any good for him to sit here and stare at her. He had things to do for class, too. Dumb of him to get caught up in the used-to-be fun in teaching. With a small sigh, he slipped off the edge and rounded the desk. He'd worn dark wash denim today. A button-down and a green sweater over it. Fridays felt different, but the only concession he made to Fridays now was dressing down a bit.

He would still work all day. And he would still go home alone. Find something to eat. And end up at Sidecar, sipping on something strong enough to numb the sharp edges the last year had carved into his skin and bones.

The rest of the class filed in a few at a time as Booker set his laptop up and readied his PowerPoint presentation. With the first slide—an introduction to the Gothic—on his screen and the big screen at the front of the room, he grabbed his coffee and stood at the podium, watching everyone quietly settle in. Kara met his eyes and flashed him a quick smile. Nothing over the top. Freckles dotted her face, and her chapped lips framed a crooked tooth. Sofie, at eighteen, had never come to class without a full face of makeup on. Including fake eyelashes.

They couldn't be more different. Not one of the girls, the young women in this class, looked like Sofie or Reese. And yet, Booker feared he would see those two faces in every woman he met from now until he was dead.

10

LENNOX

Lennox kept her laptop closed, and she resisted the urge to slide her hand over it as if to protect it when Dr. Gannon glanced at her just before class started. She hadn't read any more of his article last night; when she got off the phone with Collins, she had made herself reread the article on the Gothic so she would be prepared for discussion today.

She didn't feel all that prepared.

For one thing, she had Dr. Gannon's article bookmarked on her computer. The thought of him moseying by her open laptop and seeing the name of his article pinned in her search bar made her belly flip flop. Dumb for all sorts of reasons, the first of which—it was a college lit class. She highly doubted Dr. Gannon would move up and down the steps of the lecture hall to conduct class. On Wednesday, he hadn't wondered far from the desk or podium. Second, who cared if he saw that she had his article saved? She was an avid reader. She loved the *Blood Rite* series, and she was intellectually interested in his thoughts on the series. Never mind that she was genuinely curious about his thoughts on the sex scenes.

"Gothic." Dr. Gannon's voice in the silent room chased a shiver up her spine. Lennox glanced at her coat and considered slipping it back on. "In one word."

She wasn't cold, though.

Stupid, maybe. She was being stupid. It was okay to admit that she was a little bit excited about this class. That Dr. Gannon was interesting. That didn't have to mean a damned thing. It *couldn't* mean a damned thing.

Dr. Gannon swung his gaze from her to Josh. Reminded of the conversation at the coffeehouse the other day, Lennox had to bite the inside of her cheek to keep from smiling. Her friends—the girls she had met in her classes last year, last semester—thought Josh Stone was hot. Lennox could agree with that until the guy opened his mouth. Then she only wanted to punch him in the face.

"Josh?"

Lennox waited for him to spout off about sensationalism, but Josh seemed to be thinking before speaking. First time for everything, she guessed.

"It's a—"

"One word," Dr. Gannon interrupted him.

Josh tipped his head back and sighed. "Fearmongering."

Dr. Gannon, elbows resting on the podium, raised his eyebrows and gave Josh a curt nod.

"Not bad." He cleared his throat. "Kara?"

"I was going to say fear," she answered.

Lennox had talked to Kara a bit at the coffeehouse the other day, but she had never seen the blue-haired girl before. While she had been ready to answer, certain Dr. Gannon would nail her immediately, Lennox wouldn't raise her hand. Not now. Not when it almost felt like he was going out of his way to not call on her as he looked around the room. Most people reiterated Josh's idea of fear.

"Lennox?"

She sat perfectly still for a moment when Dr. Gannon finally did call on her. Their eyes locked. Lennox finally roused herself out of the stupor—be it awe or fear-inspired —and took a deep breath.

"Haunting."

"Isn't that the same as fear?"

"But the Gothic is about supernatural things. And about the fear of the past. Which is...a haunting." She slowed as she finished her answer, aware of Josh watching her. Dr. Gannon simply stared at her a moment longer and finally tapped the keyboard of his laptop.

The introduction slide vanished and the second one appeared with verbiage similar to what all of them had said.

"What do you think about Botting's claim that supernatural events aren't really part of the Gothic after the 18th century?"

"I disagree," Josh called.

"Why?" A rumble of laughter went around the room when Dr. Gannon batted the question back at him. "Has anyone read *The Monk*? Matthew Gregory Lewis?"

Lennox shook her head when Dr. Gannon looked at her. She'd heard of it, but she had never read it.

"I ask because gothic literature was considered low culture or popular culture. So, useless in terms of societal value in the 18th and 19th centuries. *The Monk* was especially disparaged because it was considered obscene."

Why was he still looking at her?

Lennox wanted to look away, but she wouldn't give him the satisfaction. Not to mention, what would her fellow students say if she did? If she caved and broke the eye contact first? Would they think Dr. Gannon was bullying her? She wasn't about to let that rumor get started.

Then again, what if by challenging him, by refusing to look away, she appeared to be coming onto him, trying to impress him? She didn't need any rumors like that going around, either.

She held her breath for a moment, feeling a bit of sweat on her lower back.

First of all, she had a little girl. An intelligent, precocious little girl. Lennox wanted Eloise to be proud of her mom as she grew up, not embarrassed by her. And second, her little girl had a father, and he had a family.

One that had no use for Lennox.

"Is that like how some people still consider the horror genre to be...less than?" Josh asked Dr. Gannon.

"Yeah, but a lot of people think any *genre fiction* is lowbrow." Kara twisted in her seat to look up at Josh.

"Like romance." He tipped his head.

"Yeah, but also horror. And science fiction."

"Some people only read *proper* literature."

Lennox swung her gaze to the guy two rows down directly in front of her. Rupe had been with them at the coffeehouse Wednesday.

"All true," Dr. Gannon agreed with a simple nod. He slipped around to stand in front of the podium and reached for a coffee mug on the desk. "But let's get back to the Gothic."

He took a drink and tapped his keyboard again.

The new slide was a picture of a giant, old church.

"Other than a genre of literature," he spoke as he looked up at the picture, "what does the word gothic make you think of?"

"Architecture."

Her stomach buzzed like she had swallowed a bee when Dr. Gannon glanced at her.

"Yes." He nodded. "Dark and grotesque. Right?"

"I like it," Kara mumbled.

"Sure, but that's the style, right? Dark? Intricate?" Dr. Gannon leaned an elbow on the podium and took a moment to study all of them. "This picture is a church, as you can see. What other gothic sorts of buildings can you think of?"

No one answered. Lennox glanced at Josh, wondering if he was being stubborn. When she saw him looking at his phone, she arched her eyebrows and looked away.

"Lennox?"

She tipped her chin up to look at Dr. Gannon.

"If you've read the *Blood Rite* series. If you've read Jennifer L. Armentrout's books. If you ever dragged out the dime store paperbacks from under your grandma's bed, you know—"

"Castles," she interrupted him.

"Thank you." He nodded and turned back to the screen. "Castles."

Josh put his phone down, drawing Lennox's attention again.

"Kara, tell me something you read in high school lit class that would be considered gothic literature."

"*Frankenstein.*"

"Yes." He nodded. "Many consider it to be the first gothic text. But the roots of Gothic literature go much further back. They can be traced back to the Middle Ages. I'm not going to read all my notes to you. You're adults. I'll share the PowerPoint. It's your responsibility to look at it. What happens in the 18th century? Tell me before I go to the next slide."

"The gothic genre is linked to romanticism."

Gannon nodded at Rupe. "Yep. What's that mean? More love and sex in books?"

"Romanticism was a literary movement. Like, William Wordsworth is in that period."

"Good. Let's talk about *excess*. You read it. What's it mean?" Dr. Gannon was still looking at Rupe. When he didn't answer, Dr. Gannon raised his eyebrows. "*Did you* read it?"

"A lack of rationalization," Rupe finally answered.

"Yes." Dr. Gannon looked around the room again and nodded at a guy in the front row.

"It's a lack of rationalization because of excess of feeling."

Lennox watched Dr. Gannon back up and tap his keyboard again to move to the next slide about *transgression*. She'd had a professor last semester who spoon fed the class every word of each of his slides, rather than trusting that as college students they knew how to read. She had hated that class—the lectures were boring and flat, and she hated writing essays.

She had assumed she would hate this class, just because she hadn't enjoyed either of her rhetoric and composition classes. And, if she were being honest, she had dreaded having to deal with Booker Gannon.

Now, she was surprised to find herself almost enjoying the lecture.

"Lennox."

She tipped her head in askance when Dr. Gannon called her name.

"Do you see the connection between Romanticism and Gothicism?"

She huffed out a quick breath and thought back on what she had read for class and today's discussion.

"I think they're both...reactionary to everyday life. Reality. But Gothic is gloomy and...dark. And Romanticism is..." She hesitated again, struggling to express her thoughts.

"The Gothic is about the limits of what we, what humans do. Like the gloomy side of that. And Romanticism is more about faith. In order. They have some things in common, but they're sort of opposites."

Lennox kind of agreed with Rupe, but she also felt like she needed to read more and think about it longer to have a good answer. She glanced at the clock and realized she needed to get moving so she wouldn't be late for her biology class across town.

11

BOOKER

Booker sipped his pour of bourbon, eyes on his phone. He rarely looked at it when he was here. Another nice thing about Sidecar. Being here was like stepping backwards, or maybe just sideways, in time. Nothing mattered here. No ghosts lingered in the shadowy corners of the bar. No one was peeking around a corner watching him nurse his liquor, waiting for him to lose control. No vapid, flirty coeds. No puffed-up male students kissing his ass, trying to impress him.

Sidecar was his escape.

Or had been. Randi had texted him on his way in earlier. He hadn't answered her, but he had read his sister's text several times already.

I know you're not speaking to me, but Mom said you haven't checked in with her since Christmas, either.

Everything about it pissed him off. He tossed the phone down on the bar again and tipped his chin to his chest. He had a headache the size of Rhode Island, and while it was a small state, it made for a hell of an afternoon, pounding in his head.

It was a good day. Discussion in both of his classes had gone well. The freshmen rhetoric and comp class had surprised him. He hadn't expected much of anything from them, even if it was the second semester, and the majority of the students had been in either his or Ms. Bingham's class first semester.

Lennox had left early, just as she had announced on Wednesday she would do. A few of the remaining students had watched her slip out the door, but no one had commented. Made him wonder how well they knew her. Particularly Rupe and Josh, since she had been with them at Crave the first day after class.

But she had contributed in class, and though she hadn't made any awe-inspiring definitive statements, it was clear to Booker that she had read the assignment and had spent time thinking about it.

He enjoyed Fridays, weekends, but on the other hand, he had a whole window of time with nothing specific to do. While he was completely at home in Sidecar, they didn't open until five in the evening, which still left a lot of open hours for him to fill.

Ashley was dating again, and that knowledge had been enough for him to delete his social media accounts. They had been sitting dormant and private since sometime early last spring, sometime in April. For some stupid reason,

Booker had scrolled Instagram before he got up this morning and seen the picture his ex-wife had posted. She and some guy name Billy watching Thursday night football over beers and nachos.

It wouldn't last. Ashley was not a basic beer and nacho kind of girl. And her knowledge of football extended no further than knowing there was a team called the Chicago Bears.

Even knowing that her new romance wouldn't last, seeing the picture had put Booker in a bad mood first thing this morning. Might be the cause of the headache now, but he had to admit that his class discussions today had almost been fun.

He picked his phone up and looked at Randi's text again. The mature thing to do would be to step outside and call her. Because text messages could be read with the wrong tone. And also because he would be sending a message with that *wrong* tone, *intentionally*. His first instinct had been to jump down Randi's throat and remind her they weren't speaking.

"Banks."

The familiar voice caught his attention, even though he had no idea what or who *Banks* was. Dropping his phone to the bar again, he looked up as Lennox, the girl from his class, approached the bar with a smile. The bartender, glass and rag in hand, turned to look at her and flashed her a big smile.

They leaned toward each other over the bar, though they weren't close enough to indicate anything sexy or personal being said. Most likely so they could hear each other over the music. The bartender was nodding and then Lennox backed away from him. She took a step toward the door, but something made her stop and look toward him.

Their eyes locked.

Did she frequent this place like he did? How had he not noticed her before? Well, he wasn't noticing women these days. Period. Or he hadn't been.

Not until seeing the dirty blonde with the dark eyebrows in here earlier this week. Now he was bumping into her everywhere and having a hard time getting her off his mind.

Which was unacceptable.

Lennox hesitated for a moment, maybe wondering if she was supposed to come over and speak to him. Wondering if he would dock her grade for snubbing him in a bar outside of class. Interestingly enough, he kind of wanted to. Hell, he kind of wanted to dock her for the hesitation, even if she did eventually wave or walk over to say hello. He had wanted to dock her for walking out of his class early today, but he decided against it.

On the other hand, Booker didn't want her near him. Especially not in a dimly lit speakeasy with sexy, bluesy, jazz playing. He held the eye contact as he picked up his rocks glass for a sip. The trouble with this girl was the resting fuck-off face didn't seem to scare her.

From this far away, he couldn't see the darker flecks of blue in her stormy eyes. But he let his eyes roam over her face, her shoulders, noted the gold hoop earrings and her plump pink lips. Didn't seem to have a lot of makeup on, but again he was too far away to tell.

And it didn't matter, in the big scheme of things.

But damned if that look on her face, the way her lips were slightly parted didn't intrigue the fuck out of him. He should look away or frown or something to break the staring contest, and yet, he wouldn't. Damned if he would show discomfort under her intense stare.

The bartender stepped between them, and like someone walking in front of a movie screen, the interruption was enough to make Booker look away. A little bit angry with the guy and a little bit relieved, Booker stared at his phone again. But he didn't pick it up.

He breathed a sigh of relief when he caught Lennox leaving from the corner of his eye. Maybe he needed to broach the subject with her. Booker had no desire to see her every damned time he was here, but he wasn't going to give up his one escape, either.

12

LENNOX

Eloise played a mean air guitar. Lennox loved her kid's imagination. She supposed she had to chalk at least part of that up to Monty, but she would take credit for it, too. For a few months, she and Monty had lived it up and had a blast. They had gone to a concert together—Shinedown—and loved it. Monty had played the air guitar and the air drums and sang the whole way home from Cedar Rapids.

"That was fantastic, El," Lennox told Eloise. The little blonde beamed up at her as she pushed her hair off her face.

"For my next song..."

Collins' snort from the bistro table behind Lennox drew her attention. She glanced at her friend over her shoulder. Collins was watching Eloise, clearly amused by her antics. Lennox rinsed the last plate and set it in the dishwasher. Banks had been here earlier; he'd brought a pizza over to share and suggested Eloise do a kitchen concert. Lennox thought it was convenient that he had to meet a friend as soon as the pizza was gone, and Eloise decided to sing louder.

"Sing with me!" Eloise hollered as she broke into a song by The Black Keys. Lennox sang along as she dried her hands on the dish towel, folded it over the oven door handle, and closed the dishwasher. She glanced at her daughter, knees bent, strumming an invisible guitar, face twisted in a dramatic mask as she sang.

The doorbell rang. Since there was no real music playing, the sound was a loud, unwelcome surprise. Lennox sighed. She rolled her head on her neck as she made her way to the front door. It wouldn't be her parents. She and Eloise would see them tomorrow for lunch. Jaxon would be there, too, most likely, but he didn't make a habit of showing up at her house unannounced, anyway.

Still smiling about Eloise singing away in the kitchen, Lennox pulled the door open and froze when she saw Eve McArthur on her front porch.

"Eve." She cleared her throat wishing she could send Eloise a telepathic message to stop singing. Thankful Banks was already gone—Eve had looked down her nose at him more than once when she'd dropped in and found him here—Lennox reminded herself to breathe.

"May I come in?"

"Of course." Lennox nodded and stepped aside to allow the woman room to enter.

"I'll get right to the point."

As she spoke, she surveyed the living room, as if looking for joints or pills or empty liquor bottles. The woman had been looking for reasons to take Eloise away from Lennox since the moment Lennox had announced that she was pregnant. The fact that she never found anything questionable to call her on sometimes seemed to infuriate her.

Tonight, her eyes caught on Lennox's laptop and the stack of papers by it on her second-hand coffee table. A beat-up paperback copy of *Dracula* lay on the table, too. They weren't reading it yet, but Lennox had found it earlier today when she and Eloise were at the library. She had it on her Kindle, but she'd grabbed the print copy at the library's second-hand store for fifty cents. Lennox liked marking up books she read, tabbing important pages, important quotes.

"*Dracula.*" Eve frowned.

Lennox pressed her lips together to hold her sigh, her exasperation, inside. Eve, dressed in winter white slacks and blouse topped with a deep, crimson-colored wool coat, stood with her hands folded primly at her waist. The color of her coat made Lennox think of blood. But then again, it seemed like Eve McArthur was always after blood when she was around Lennox.

If Monty was the good-looking, compelling boy vampire who seduced naïve girls, Eve was the evil, sinister all-knowing mother or queen of vampires who didn't bother with seduction and went straight for blood and death.

Lennox should jot that down and share it with Dr. Gannon.

Flustered at the thought of Dr. Gannon now, a deep blush

rushed her cheeks. Just in time for Eve to turn back to her and see it.

"It's for an English class," she mumbled.

"And does Eloise look at your books?" Eve tipped her head. "We both know she reads well above her age."

"No." Lennox shook her head and folded her arms over her chest. "No. Of course I don't let Eloise read my books."

"Then why is it out?"

"I just got it—" Lennox stopped talking and took a deep breath. "We just had dinner, Eve. Eloise is in the kitchen."

Eve stared at her with a pinched face, a deep groove between her eyebrows. "There's a mother-daughter luncheon next Saturday at the museum. I'd like to take Eloise."

"My daughter? To a *mother-daughter* event?"

"Lyla Tremont is taking her granddaughter. I thought Eloise might enjoy spending time with Megan."

She probably would, and for that reason, as well as others, Lennox wouldn't say no. Still, it took her a moment to swallow down her protests. She hated every moment her little girl was with Monty's family.

"Yes. Of course. I'm sure she would."

"What is she screeching about?" Eve frowned, finally hearing and acknowledging Eloise's concert.

"She's singing," Lennox answered. "El!" She took a few steps toward the kitchen. "El, Grandma McArthur is here."

"Gramma!" Eloise's excited voice barely sounded before the blonde streaked through the door and stopped just short of throwing herself at Monty's mother. She did that with Lennox's parents and Jaxon, jumped them and climbed them like trees. Lennox wasn't sure Eve McArthur permitted Eloise to *hug* her.

"Hello, Eloise." Eve nodded like she was speaking to a maid. "Would you like to go to lunch with me next Saturday?"

Lennox held her breath, praying Eloise wouldn't ask if they were going to McDonald's.

Her daughter simply stared up at Eve with those big dark eyes and nodded. Eloise didn't really have a grasp of time yet, so she wouldn't be sure when Eve was talking about. Nor would she like being in a museum, being told to be quiet, to behave like a lady.

But she might enjoy seeing Megan Tremont.

And Lennox had agreed to letting Eloise spend some time with Monty's family. In exchange for his parents not dogging her every step or trying to take her to court as an unfit mother. Or hiring a hit man to get rid of her.

She wasn't an unfit mother. Her parents often reminded her of that. Told her the McArthurs didn't have a leg to stand on in court. But Lennox hadn't wanted to gamble. She wouldn't put it past them to manufacture evidence to prove she was unfit to raise Eloise.

"Hello, Mrs. McArthur."

Eve shifted her gaze to Collins, now standing in the kitchen doorway. She wore an oversized smile, because she knew Eve McArthur didn't like her. Lennox wanted to hiss at her, to tell her to tone it down. Lennox didn't play with matches. Or pit vipers.

"Colleen." Eve nodded, most likely calling Lennox's friend the wrong name on purpose and turned back to Lennox. "I will pick her up at nine. She should wear a dress and her patent leather shoes."

Rather than argue that nine was too early for lunch, or that Eloise hated the patent leather shoes, Lennox nodded. She couldn't get the woman out of her house fast enough.

"And please watch what you leave laying around for my—"

"Eloise, how about a cookie? Since you ate all your dinner."

Eloise peeked at Collins and then looked at Lennox.

"You can have a cookie," Lennox told her. "Eve, I told you the book was for a class."

"I thought you were studying nursing."

"I am, but I also have to have gen ed classes and a few electives."

"The tripe colleges teach in today's world is disgusting."

Lennox remained silent. She could argue that it was a literature class, but it wouldn't matter to Eve. If she wasn't reading autobiographies or true *literature*, Eve wouldn't approve—exactly what they had talked about in class yesterday, the perception of horror as lowbrow entertainment.

"Have her ready at nine."

"I will."

13

BOOKER

"Seriously? You're acting like a child."

Booker rolled his eyes as he crossed the parking lot. Sunday wasn't a usual gym day, but he had gone anyway this morning. It was that or lay in bed and count the squares in the ceiling for the fifth time. Rather than go home after pushing himself at the gym, his car had driven him like on autopilot to the main campus.

Crave had light breakfast sandwiches. He planned to grab one and head home to eat it. Shower. Read for a while. And then go over his plans for class tomorrow.

"Randi, you're the one who pouted and refused to speak to me the rest of Christmas break, if you recall."

"Because you went off on me like some jackass jerk—"

"The one they all said I am. Is that what you're thinking?"

"Book." She sighed. Booker felt her frustration all the way down the phone line.

"It's fine, Randi." He pulled the door open and stepped inside, relishing the warmth in the coffeehouse. His shorts and sweatshirt had been fine for the gym, but Killdare U's campus was like a wind tunnel in spots. The walk across the parking lot had been miserable enough he had almost jogged.

But, if he was going to play tough guy, he couldn't let on that he was cold.

"I texted you the other night."

"I know. I was busy."

"Right." Her sarcasm was loud and clear. "Doing what?"

Booker hoped she could hear the indie folk rock playing in the coffeehouse. Too bad there was only one person in line in front of him. It would be nice if she heard conversation and believed he was out with other people. Maybe then she would get off his back.

"I was at a bar the other night," he answered absently, eyes on the menu.

"With someone?"

No, but she didn't need to know that.

"Yeah. Few people from school."

"Good."

Booker rolled his eyes. She sounded so excited, he almost felt guilty for lying to her.

"I just want you to be happy, Book."

"And I keep telling you it's just too soon."

"I hope you don't mean Ashley."

He did, and he didn't. "I'm thinking about a mini vacation this summer."

"That sounds like a good plan."

It wasn't a plan. He hadn't given it a thought until the words tumbled out of his mouth. And yet, now that he'd said it, it did sound appealing. Get out of town. Get away from academia and rumors. Maybe he would go to the Grand Canyon; he'd never been.

"Where are you thinking?"

"Grand Canyon," he answered without hesitation.

"Nice."

The woman in front of him moved, and he stepped up to the counter.

"Gotta go, Randi. My turn to order."

"Okay but call Mom."

"Did." He ended the call and ordered a veggie and egg delight breakfast croissant with a black coffee all in one breath.

"Did you want that for here or to go?"

Booker stopped himself before answering. A quick glance around the place told him it wasn't crowded. He had no idea if that was an anomaly, or if Crave was always this dead on a Sunday morning. But staying, enjoying his breakfast around a few other human beings, sounded good to him.

"For here."

"You got it, Dr. Gannon." The girl nodded at him as she ran his credit card. "Let me get your coffee."

The door opened behind him, a rush of cold air stirring the hair on his legs. He shivered and second-guessed himself. Maybe he should have just gone home. Chatter behind him drew his attention. A small voice, like a little kid, and a voice that was already familiar to him. He knew without turning around that it was Lennox who had just come in. The girl at the counter—it wasn't Kara, and it bothered him a bit that the girl knew who he was—handed him his coffee.

"If you want to grab a seat, I can bring your sandwich out to you."

Booker almost snapped at her. He didn't want or need favors. Somehow, he managed to keep his mouth shut. Maybe they did that with all food orders. How did he know? Was it worth causing a scene over?

"Thank you." He nodded and headed without looking back to find a table.

If he had planned better, he would have carried a book with him. He used to while away the hours in the student union with a book and a drink when he was a kid himself. And he had spent a lot of time in coffee shops with books and students at his last job.

That had turned out ugly, but Booker reminded himself he hadn't been convicted of anything. He hadn't done anything *wrong*. And nothing about sitting here in Crave to eat his breakfast was suspicious.

He hadn't expected it. The guilt, the shame, that accompanied those sorts of accusations. Even when he was innocent.

Seated by the fireplace, he scrolled his phone while he waited for his sandwich. No social media, but he still had his email account on his phone. He scanned the subject lines in his inbox, but nothing stuck out as needing immediate attention. If there were newspapers around, he could at least look at headlines. But Booker craned his head around and looked at all the spots where there might be papers and saw only a few used paperbacks.

"Mommy!"

The excited shriek caught his attention. When he turned to look in the direction it had come from, toward the counter, he saw Lennox holding a little blonde. The little girl was peering down at something Booker couldn't see, but Lennox was watching the little girl.

With adoration.

Booker might be out of touch with people. But he had family that cared about him, and he was familiar with the look on Lennox's face. As he watched, her lips curved upward, and she said something to make the little girl look at her.

"Can we stay here?"

He didn't hear Lennox's answer, but he assumed she must have said yes, because the little girl squirmed to get down.

When her feet hit the ground, she scampered toward the seating area, meeting his eyes.

"Hi." She had her mother's smile. Maybe it was a tad more friendly, a bit more dramatic, but the resemblance was uncanny.

"Hi."

"I'm Eloise," the little girl announced.

Booker nodded, impressed with her name, and not at all surprised by it.

"El." Lennox called as she approached the seating area. Eloise had already climbed up to perch on the loveseat opposite Booker. Lennox laughed softly, but the sound faded, and her face froze when she turned to see him sitting there. In her hands, she held two mugs, most likely both filled to the brim with something hot.

"Let me help." He stood and took the mugs from her, ignoring the look on her face that advertised her intention to say no. "Eloise introduced herself to me."

He set the mugs on the table and sat down again.

"What did I tell you about talking to strangers?" Lennox turned to look at her daughter. Even Booker wanted to cower at the *mom-look* on her face.

"But he talked to you, Mommy." Eloise tipped her head. "So, you know him."

"But you don't," Lennox reminded her.

"You can sit," he told Lennox. She jerked her gaze back to

him for a second, sighed with frustration, and then sat by her daughter.

"What's your name?" Eloise asked him.

"Booker."

The little girl giggled.

"Eloise, that's impolite."

"It's a silly name, Mommy." She shrugged and looked at him again. "I like books."

"I do, too."

"Here you go, Dr. Gannon."

Booker looked over his shoulder as the girl from the counter approached him with a tray.

"You're a doctor?" Eloise frowned now, as if deciding her mom might be right, and he might be scary.

"I'm a doctor of philosophy."

"What do you check?" She frowned and shook her head.

Lennox laughed softly. "He's a professor, babe. The doctor in front of his name means he's smart, and he went to school for a long time."

Eloise studied him with suspicion for a moment. "My mommy is going to be a nurse."

"I know." He nodded. "She told me."

"Are you her teacher?"

"I am, but not in nursing stuff."

Lennox cleared her throat as she nudged the little girl with her elbow. "Blow on your hot chocolate." She looked up at him, seemingly unnerved to find him watching her. "Um. We should find our own table. Eloise likes to come here after church sometimes."

"Church," he repeated.

"Mmm." She nodded. "El, let's go over—"

"You don't have to." He shrugged as he put the tray down on his corner of the table. "You don't have to move."

"I'm sure you don't want a chatterbox bothering you on a quiet—"

"It's fine."

He didn't mind. Once upon a time, he wanted kids. He thought he and Ashley would have at least two or three. And he still figured Randi would eventually get married and have kids. The idea of being surrounded by family had always appealed to him.

Now, though, it didn't seem likely that he would have children. He found himself drawn to the little girl, to her innocence.

The thought—the way it could be misinterpreted—made him nauseous.

Especially considering that he was drawn to her mother. To what seemed like innocence but still felt like a challenge each time she looked at him. He should pack up and go home.

14

LENNOX

Something about seeing Dr. Gannon in the coffeehouse dressed like he was unnerved Lennox. She had noticed him immediately, almost before even really looking at him, as if her body was attuned to his presence.

Which was ridiculous.

Standing behind him in line, she had tried her best not to look at his legs. Or his butt. But the athletic shorts he wore practically begged for her attention. For looking so slender, so fit, in his suits, his calves were surprisingly thick and hard, like he spent a lot of time on a bike. The shorts were long and loose, but that didn't mean her eyes didn't automatically trek right up to his butt. To the elastic in the waistband of the sweatshirt he wore.

Didn't mean her mind hadn't wondered for a just a second what he had on beneath the sweatshirt. Tank top? A short-sleeved tee that clung to sculpted shoulders?

Thankfully, Eloise had been too busy talking to realize Lennox was staring. The incessant chatter had finally drawn Lennox's attention from the completely off-limits professor in front of her back to her daughter. It wasn't like she was interested in him. Lennox told herself it was more like an odd curiosity, like when Eloise had seen her kindergarten teacher at the taco truck last fall. She had been floored to realize Miss Smith had a life outside the classroom.

While Lennox knew Booker Gannon had a life—after all, she had heard a lot of talk about that life—it was still a bit disconcerting to see a man normally dressed to the nines slumming it in athletic attire.

She had all but held her breath as she chatted quietly with Eloise, while waiting for Dr. Gannon to order and move on. The last thing she expected was for Eloise to bop right over to him and climb into a seat near him so she could talk his ears off.

Lennox sipped her mocha and sneaked a peek at her professor from under her eyelashes. He was oblivious as he unwrapped his breakfast sandwich. Eloise had scooted back so far on the loveseat that her little legs went straight out, her sparkly purple Cons sticking straight up at the edge of the cushion.

Part of her was intrigued as hell by this new side of Dr. Gannon. Part of her was very aware of the fact that he knew her name, that he had already called on her a lot in just two classes, and that he had even sat and talked to her in Crave the other day. She teetered between a little thrill in her belly that he had noticed her and a little knot of dread working its way from her belly into her chest because he was now talking to Eloise.

As curious as she was about him, Lennox didn't want him anywhere near her daughter. Never mind that none of the rumors she had heard about him had anything to do with little girls or boys. Something about exposing her innocent little girl to a man who was single, *interested in girls* to say the least, and noted for being cruel and rude made her want to snatch Eloise from the loveseat and run.

Not to mention the McArthurs. True, the likelihood of any of them walking into Crave—ever—was less than the likelihood of a barking cat. Lennox could just imagine the scene that would ensue if any of them saw her with Booker Gannon. And undoubtedly, they knew who Booker Gannon was simply because she was attending Killdare University, and she was Eloise's mother and legal guardian.

Lennox glanced at Eloise when she scooted forward on the loveseat.

"Need a drink?"

Eloise nodded. Lennox watched her, though she felt Dr. Gannon's eyes on her. Eloise slipped off the cushion, plopped her feet on the floor, and leaned forward to blow on her hot chocolate. While the barista hadn't filled the mug to the top, it was still too full for a five-year-old to handle. Lennox held her breath, eyebrows at her hairline, as she watched her little girl lean way over and take a sip without picking up the mug. While it wasn't a good display of manners and Eve McArthur would be embarrassed, Lennox decided it was probably a good move.

She pushed aside the memory of Monty McArthur leaning over to put his mouth on a shot glass. Straightening with the glass in his lips, shooting the liquor—Lennox didn't remember what it was—and wiping the back of his hand over his grinning mouth as he set the glass back down. What would Eve McArthur think about her son executing that move?

What would Eve McArthur think about a lot of things her son had done during that three-month-period when Lennox was dating him?

"Mommy?"

"Hmm?" She blinked, hating that she was still caught up in thoughts of the McArthurs. Every girl lost her virginity, and probably a lot of girls lost their virginity to assholes like Monty McArthur. That part wasn't the bit that had scarred her.

Wasn't realizing she was pregnant or having Eloise, either.

It was Eve and Joseph McArthur showing up, uninvited and unannounced, at the hospital when she was giving birth. Lennox still had no idea how they knew she was in labor. They knew things about her that her parents hadn't known. How fun to have Eve explain to her mom about the night Monty had stripped her naked in the hot tub and fingered her until she thought she would be permanently bowlegged.

Never mind that she liked it. Why couldn't it have been between her and Monty?

"Can I play a game on your phone?"

Lennox wanted to say no. She wanted Eloise to shoot her hot chocolate like a coed at a frat party. But the drink was still much too hot. And maybe a game would keep her distracted, so she wouldn't bother Dr. Gannon.

"For a little bit." She leaned forward to slide her phone from her back pocket and handed it to Eloise. Again, she felt Dr. Gannon watching her as she leaned over Eloise to watch what game she chose. Normally, her first choice was either *Duolingo ABCs* or some monkey math game. Today, though, Eloise picked a game with building blocks that Lennox's dad said reminded him of *Tetris*. The video game and apps had skipped a generation; Lennox had never been into those games. If she had time to play, she wanted to be outside, reading a book, or watching cartoons.

When she finally relaxed on the loveseat again, she found herself staring right back at Dr. Gannon. He had finished his sandwich and was now sitting idly with his arms folded over his chest. The pose pulled the sleeves of his shirt tight on his upper arms, but what really bothered Lennox was that he looked like a college student the way he was sitting, the way he was dressed.

Alarm bells went off in her head. Not because she thought he would join her on the loveseat and put his arm around her to cop a feel. But because she had no business seeing him as anything other than a professor.

One she would do well to keep her distance from.

"Do you speak Spanish?" Eloise asked. So much for keeping her preoccupied. Lennox clenched her teeth together and sucked in a deep breath through her nose.

"Not well," he answered with a shrug when Eloise peeked up at him.

"Do you have kids?"

"No."

"Do you—"

"Enough." Lennox dropped a gentle open hand on Eloise's head. "Either you play, or we need to get home."

"But my hot cocoa!" Eloise twisted her neck enough to look up at her.

"We'll get it in a to-go cup."

Eloise rolled her eyes at her, but she tipped her chin back down so she could look at Lennox's phone.

"Ready for class tomorrow?"

She reached for her own mug and glanced at Dr. Gannon when she sat back.

"Yes."

"What did you think of class Friday? The Gothic discussion?"

Ready to answer about the reading for tomorrow, Lennox hesitated and back stepped to the discussion on the Gothic.

"Honestly, I think it's interesting."

"Gothic? The discussion of what the Gothic genre is?"

She narrowed her eyes and considered his question for a moment. "Yeah. Because it's always interested me. Gothic books, movies. Settings. And so, I think it's fascinating that all the reasons I'm drawn to it are the actual discussion of what it is."

"The excess of emotion."

Lennox nodded.

"The aesthetics of fear. The promotion of violence and se—"

"Yes." She cut him off with a glance at Eloise.

"So, am I to assume you like horror movies?"

"Sometimes."

"Vampires in particular? Or all horror?"

Eyes on Eloise, Lennox shrugged. "Depends."

"Count von Count is a vampire," Eloise announced without looking up.

Lennox sighed and reached for Eloise's mug.

"I'm gonna get a to-go cup for you, babe." She patted her daughter's leg. "We've got stuff to do."

Dr. Gannon watched her as she stood, a small smile on his face.

15

Booker

It seemed possible that bad dreams might come with the territory. But Booker wasn't scared of vampires or dark, creepy-looking castles. Then again, that didn't mean he wasn't afraid of *anything*. Pretty, sexy coeds were at the top of his list of things to fear and distrust.

Nothing happened in the dream. Well, the wind blew, and a half-dead tree limb rubbed on the stone wall of a castle or southern mansion or something. Booker had walked the main hall in that damned building for what felt like miles, knowing somehow that Lennox was at the end.

But she was nowhere in the dream.

And yet, the feeling that she was going to be there, the feeling that if he kept walking, he would eventually see her, bothered him more than if she had just been part of it. He woke up pissed off at the world, specifically her, for showing up at Crave two seconds after he did. Jesus. He had to deal with her in class three days a week. He had seen her twice recently in Sidecar, which was his escape, and now he had bumped into her twice at Crave.

He didn't need that, for damned sure.

Surly and ready to snake his fingers around the throat of the first person who had the nerve to talk to him this morning, Booker carried his travel mug of coffee up the steps of Palmer Building to the third-floor lecture hall.

Why the hell would he dream about her anyway? He had never once dreamt of Sofie or Reese. And given all the stupid things that had happened, *that* would make sense. Lennox had poured her daughter's hot chocolate in a paper cup and taken the little girl by the hand. She had mumbled a goodbye to him, but Eloise had looked up from her mother's phone and flashed him a sweet smile.

"Goodbye, Dr. Book."

Her words had delighted him. And Booker was damned sure nothing in his life had ever delighted him. He had left Crave not long after Lennox and her daughter. He went home and showered. Drank more coffee. Worked on his presentation for class today, added a few things, and edited a slide or two. To make sure his sister stayed off his ass, he called his parents again and spoke to them on speaker for a good half hour. Luckily, they were both talkers, so they filled in most of the phone conversation with their own stories, and Booker had simply answered a few questions— yes, the second semester had started. Yes, it was going well. And yes, he had been at a bar the other night.

Randi must have hung up with him yesterday and got their parents on speed dial before he had ordered his coffee.

While he had remembered the look on Lennox's face when she was studying her daughter, and he was amused by Eloise calling him *Dr. Book*, he didn't lay awake when he went to bed, thinking about Lennox. He watched football. Read for a while. And watched an old black and white horror movie before going to bed.

That might explain the creepy building in his dream. The night scape. The wind and the tree limb. But not the knowing that if he walked that main hall long enough, he would find Lennox at the end.

The door banged open behind him as he set his bag and mug on the desk. Irritated that she was here already, encroaching on his space, *in his brain*, Booker whirled around to snap at her, only to find it was Josh who had come in. The tall guy trudged up the stairs to his row, eyes on his phone, and ignored Booker.

Fine by him.

Booker took his laptop from his bag and booted it up. Kara and Rupe were next to arrive. Both nodded silent greetings at him. Booker simply stared back. Kara turned in her seat to look at Rupe and started a conversation about a party over the weekend. Before long, Josh put his phone down and chimed in. Booker stood behind the podium, elbow on the wooden top, chin in his hand, and watched the lecture hall fill in slowly.

Was she not coming today? After him reminding them how important it was to be in class, that it was part of their grade, she was going to blow him off? Pissed off at her all over again, he straightened and dropped his hands to the podium. He glanced at Josh and wrapped his fingers around the edges.

Who was Eloise's father? Was it a college kid? Someone on Killdare's campus? Booker didn't give a damn who it was, but the thought of Lennox sleeping with someone like Josh made his blood pressure climb. Josh was probably damned good at talking a girl out of her panties. But Booker would bet the kid didn't know a damned thing about how to please a woman in bed.

Not that it mattered.

Lennox trailed in with two minutes to spare. She looked flustered today. Her hair was pulled back in a messy twist, but several strands had slipped loose and now curled around her face. She wasn't wearing a coat over her Killdare University sweatshirt—Booker did a double take, wondering if it was Josh's. Or some other student athlete's.

She flashed a brilliant smile at Kara and Rupe as she slipped into her seat and swung her bag down to the floor. What the hell was that about? They'd had a somewhat normal conversation yesterday, and now she couldn't be bothered to look at him?

"Who read the assignment?" Booker called. The buzz of conversation stopped immediately. Every hand in the room went up. He highly doubted everyone had completed the reading, although it was significantly shorter than most things they would read this semester. Tucking his hands into his hip pockets, he stepped out from behind the podium. "Who wrote it? You? Who wrote what we read for today?" He pulled his hand from his pocket and knocked his knuckles on the front table. The dark-skinned guy there scrambled to sit up straight.

"John Polidori."

"Who's John Polidori?"

When the guy shrugged, Booker tipped his head up and raked his gaze over the rest of the class. No one raised a hand, but then he hadn't expected anyone to have an answer.

"Let's talk about who he was before we get into *The Vampyre*."

Without waiting for a reaction, Booker walked back to the desk and tapped the keyboard of his computer. He clicked through the introductory slide and stopped at his notes on the Polidori family.

"Remember, I will share the presentation with you." He perched on the edge of the desk. "Why do you think it's important to talk about Polidori's family?"

Rupe raised his hand, but Booker looked at Lennox. The rosy color had faded from her cheeks; Booker assumed it was either from the cold outside or from rushing up the stairs to the lecture hall. She stared back at him without a word, though she quirked an eyebrow at him.

She had rushed out of Crave yesterday simply to get her daughter away from him. Did she really think he was some child-molesting freak? A rush of rage exploded through him.

Until last April, he was a normal guy.

Now people thought he would harm a child?

His rage was for Sofie, for Reese, but now for Lennox, too. Rather than call on her, Booker looked at Rupe and nodded.

"His family, his early life, would have shaped the man he grew into. And therefore, his writings."

Booker nodded.

"You can see that his grandfather was a physician and a poet." Booker glanced up at the slide on the screen as he talked. "What's the significance of *Osteologia* being written in 'ottava rima'?" His notes clearly stated that *Osteologia* was a long poem about the human skeleton written by Poli-dori's grandfather and that "ottava rima" was the meter Lord Byron later used in English.

No hands when he looked back at the class.

"Lennox."

"Because of the relationship that developed between Poli-dori and Byron."

"What kind of relationship?" Josh snapped with a frown in Lennox's direction.

"If you read the notes after *The Vampyre*, you would know," she mumbled.

"Maybe you could share for the class," Booker suggested.

She stared at him for a moment, her face a mask of indiffer-ence. Finally, she spoke again.

"Polidori graduated with a medical degree. He was Byron's physician. They traveled together. In *The Vampyre*, Lord Ruthven or Lord Strongmore and Aubrey's relationship is like Polidori and Bryon's."

"But what kind of relationship was it?" Josh insisted.

"It's implied at the very least Aubrey was in love with Lord Ruthven, but why does it matter?"

Booker stood and cleared his throat. He would rather watch paint dry than listen to Lennox and Josh Stone argue about John Polidori.

"Okay, let's get back to the family history."

16

LENNOX

Lennox wasn't a stranger to sex. Even before she got pregnant with Eloise, she knew the basics. She had dabbled. And there had been high school teachers who got a little flirty and said weird things—not necessarily to her, but in general. Her biology teacher got a little overzealous talking about lips and other parts of the body being made of more sensitive skin, which was why kissing and *other things* felt so good. Lennox didn't mind Mr. Hanover, but she wasn't crazy about thinking of her teacher and kissing in the same sentence.

Reading *The Scarlet Letter* as a junior in high school had been interesting. Mrs. Frazier had delved deeply into discussions on adultery. Discussions on "Young Goodman Brown" touched on evil. *Doctor Faustus. The Crucible.* All the gothic pieces discussed in her English classes all tended toward the weird, topsy-turvy feeling of excitement and shame.

Which, Lennox reminded herself, was exactly what the article Dr. Gannon had assigned about the Gothic had said.

She shouldn't react to the reading material in his class any differently than she had in high school. Talking about the basics of reproduction in biology hadn't affected her. Talking about *The Scarlet Letter* hadn't shamed her. And yet, reading *The Vampyre* and drawing conclusions about the relationship between Aubrey and Lord Ruthven, reading *Carmilla* and understanding the draw, the attraction, between Laura and Carmilla felt almost scandalous.

Ridiculous, considering Lennox was twenty-four years old and had a child of her own. She'd had sex for the first time when she was seventeen, and she had done a lot of things with Monty McArthur. Not that she believed she was worldly, but she had thought she was mature enough to be part of Dr. Gannon's class and not end up with a crush on him.

Especially after all the things she'd heard said about him.

She had no intention of sneaking around, trying to catch his attention or insinuate herself into his life. But still, reading the texts about vampires, the constant reminders of creamy flesh, long necks, the stab of pain in a breast, the rush of blood, and the burning, yet pleasurable sensations that were almost sexual in nature—

Lennox found it hard *not* to think of Booker Gannon when she was reading.

True, what they had read in class so far had been tame. It was old literature, and less was more then. Just the mention of flesh and warm lips was titillating. The things she read now, outside of class, of vampire lords and princes swinging their big cocks around and sinking their fangs into the soft supple flesh of a woman, of the dizzying rush of pleasure those women felt when the vampires drew blood, when they sucked deeply from the wounds they inflicted. The press, the pounding of their cocks deep inside the women's walls—totally different story.

Lennox shouldn't have done it. She should not have searched for the article Dr. Gannon wrote on the *Blood Rite* series. And she sure as hell shouldn't have read the damned thing. He had, *indeed*, read the series, and he written in detail about the scene where Raiah, the demon mother, had ridden the giant cock of Kalyx, with her full breasts swaying as she moved over him. The scene where Zedayah, former friend of Raiah, had laid her down, shoved her thighs apart, and pierced her inner thigh with her own fangs and sucked deeply at the wound, as she drove Raiah to rapture with her fingers.

Thank God, Eloise had been in bed and sound asleep when Lennox read the article. Dr. Gannon's theories on the series, his recounting of the sensuous and sexual scenes, had left her hotter than the actual books. It didn't take a rocket scientist to know it was because she knew Dr. Gannon. Because she had heard rumors about him doing inappropriate things. And even though he was off-limits to her, he was also hotter than any guy Lennox had ever seen. Hot and haughty. Delicious-looking in a suit. She could only imagine what he would look like without it.

It was enough to make her uncomfortable. Banks had jokingly told her once, a few years ago, to hit him up when she wanted to experience some benefits on the side of their friendship. Lennox had had sex twice since she and Monty broke up. Mostly she hadn't cared much in the past six years, but after reading Dr. Gannon's article, she had considered Banks' offer.

She needed someone to scratch the itch.

But she wouldn't use a friend for that. Even if he had offered.

Which left her on edge. Especially around and about Dr. Gannon.

Unfortunately, Collins knew Lennox well enough to read her mind. And while Collins agreed that Booker Gannon was easy on the eyes, she was quick to remind Lennox a hundred times a day that he was a user, that he preyed on young girls, that if she wasn't careful, he might push her for favors in exchange for a good grade. Collins' worry only flustered Lennox more. It was one thing to feel that pull, that attraction, to the man. She'd had crushes that went nowhere before. She simply had to get through the semester without getting on his radar. Lennox would be done with literature credits. Booker Gannon would leave Killdare Springs. End of story.

But talking about it, hearing Collins voice her thoughts, only put Lennox further on edge.

Not to mention, while Lennox couldn't imagine a time when she wouldn't have her guard up around the guy, she had been in his presence enough between a few weeks of classes and the times she had bumped into him at Crave, that she felt like she sort of knew him. He wasn't particularly friendly. He wasn't warm. And he wasn't flirty. Booker Gannon might look like a Greek god, but he had the personality of a brick.

She wasn't sure she believed a damned thing anyone had said about him.

Didn't sexual predators groom their victims? Didn't they feed into a victim's attraction? Flirt? Say leading things that didn't necessarily mean anything, but could? Lennox hadn't seen a hint of that in Booker Gannon.

"Where are you going tonight?" Collins asked from the couch. Eloise was curled up beside her, eyes on the TV. Both were dressed in comfy jammies, ready for a movie marathon. Lennox had told Collins more than once that it was a study night, not a date night, but as usual, her friend refused to listen.

"I think we're just getting dinner. Talking about the test next week."

"What class again?"

"Biology."

"Well, you look pretty..." Collins wagged her eyebrows at Lennox and offered her a lecherous grin.

"You do look pretty, Mommy," Eloise agreed. She flicked her eyes over Lennox and then looked back at the TV, where Scooby Doo was currently chasing a vampire, of all things.

Lennox looked down at her skinny jeans, the heeled boots, and black sweater she'd pulled from her closet. She didn't feel pretty anything other than basic. But she knew what Collins was doing. After reading that article, after considering Banks' offer of no-strings-attached sex, Lennox had texted Collins, who had come to her rescue with a bottle of cab and unending girl talk. The two of them had killed that bottle, opened another, and talked about hot celebrities.

Until Collins had pried it out of her that she had gone down the rabbit hole of sexy things and Booker Gannon and was feeling like a curling iron, plugged in and left to overheat.

Collins met her eyes now and arched her brows. "El and I will be just fine tonight. So you take your time, Lex."

Translation: get laid, even if it's Banks after Sidecar closes. Don't come home until sunup.

Lennox rolled her eyes, but she had to admit as she leaned over to kiss Eloise goodbye, she was tempted.

17

BOOKER

Booker considered breaking his rule tonight. Sidecar was busy, but he was mostly alone at the bar. An older gentleman sat at the far corner nursing an Old-Fashioned. Behind Booker, most of the seating areas were occupied, though the conversational buzz was pleasantly low. The ever-present instrumental jazz was a nice buffer. And yet, right now, he wanted conversation. Didn't give a damn about what—he was almost willing to sit at the bar and discuss bucket list items, classic cars, European travel, sports.

Anything.

After last April, he had cut himself off completely from friends. Maybe that had been a shortsighted move, but on the other hand, if your own wife didn't believe you, who would? He spoke with fellow professors at the university daily, and of course, he had his students. Not that he planned to engage them in conversation, other than what they were reading for class.

But still. Booker used to be a normal guy. With a wife and plans for a future. With friends. Good friends from his own school days. Friends at Artas State, the university where he taught before coming to Killdare Springs. Friends he had made on the golf course. Friends he met through Ashley.

He had shrunk his world from all of that down to himself, his sister, and his parents.

"Need another?"

The bartender with the earring—the one Lennox had slipped in to talk to that one night—stood before him, finger aimed at his glass.

"Why not?" Booker shrugged and nudged the glass forward a bit.

"Got something new," the guy announced. "Twelve-year bourbon from Lockland Distilling in Rodey, Kentucky. Had it?"

Booker shook his head. "I'll try it."

"Perfect." The guy nodded as he slipped away to grab the bottle. "I think it's about time I hit the bourbon trail again." He tipped it over Booker's glass.

"Yeah?" Booker watched the amber liquid splash into the bottom of the tumbler.

"You been?"

"I haven't."

"You like bourbon, you should go sometime." The guy shrugged.

Booker arched a brow as he picked the glass up to nose the bourbon. Maybe he would. Maybe instead of visiting the Grand Canyon this summer, he would pack up and drive south to Kentucky.

The nose on the bourbon was oaky. But Booker picked up a trace of tobacco, too.

"Good nose."

"Mm." The guy nodded. "Wait'll you taste it."

Booker tipped the glass and took a sip. He should have rinsed his glass, but the bourbon was good enough that he noticed the difference between this and his last pour. Notes of sugared wood and that little bit of tobacco coated his tongue, the creamy texture filling his mouth.

"It's good," he agreed as he swallowed and put his glass down. "Good finish."

"Right?" The guy nodded and pointed at him. "Name's Banks if you need something."

"Booker."

Booker took his glass and held it up to the light on the bar. He studied the color of the bourbon and wondered who *Banks* was to Lennox Clarke. Was he the father of her daughter? What had Lennox come in and said to him the other night?

The guy was alright. But the thought of him putting his hands on Lennox burned through Booker like white lightning.

Get a grip.

He had no claim to Lennox Clarke. And he never would.

Didn't stop him from grinding his teeth at the thought of Banks the bartender touching her. The thought of *any* other man touching her. Of her long, slender fingers smoothing over another man's shoulders or arms. The thought of her nails digging into a man's shoulders or back.

As if his thoughts had conjured her, Booker looked up in time to see the heavy black door open, and Lennox walk inside. Her chin was dipped down, eyes seemingly absently looking around, as she listened to the guy on her left say something. The guy spoke animatedly, a big smile on his face. At Lennox's right, a girl had her cell phone pressed to her ear.

It interested him that Killdare Springs had a population upward of 35 thousand people and any number of bars and restaurants. But this was the third time in almost as many weeks he had seen Lennox Clarke here at Sidecar. It wasn't the typical student hangout. Booker thought the average age in the speakeasy was at least thirty-five, if not forty, and yet this girl seemed to frequent this place. Again, he wondered about her relationship with the bartender.

The trio waltzed past the bar; Lennox still completely unaware of him there. Fine with him. However, Booker did note that she didn't stop and speak to Banks, nor did Banks call out to her. Lovers' quarrel?

Booker lifted his hand to pinch the bridge of his nose. This was getting to be a habit. A problem. Wondering and worrying so much about one young woman's sex life was weird and pointless. Not to mention, he had no idea how old she was. While she wasn't jailbait, she *was* his student.

Funny, though, that she had gotten under his skin like she had. Booker hadn't exactly sworn off women, but with the fiasco with Sofie and Reese and then Ashley leaving him, he had simply lost interest in the opposite sex. Lennox was the first woman he had paid any attention to since last year. Maybe it was a good sign. Maybe it meant the timing was right, that he and his dick were coming back from the dead. But the woman was wrong.

The woman was definitely *way-the-fuck* wrong.

He took another sip of his bourbon and saw Banks' face light up suddenly. Booker swung his gaze over his shoulder, not surprised to see Lennox smiling back at the bartender. She and her two companions had claimed a small cocktail table in the far corner where a waitress approached them.

Booker had seen the waitress before. The dark-haired woman was attractive, sexy, and closer to his age, maybe older. Her long lean legs went on for miles. The sexy stilettos and tiny skirt had probably stolen away the breath of many men. The dark blouses, open deep enough to flash anyone who cared to look the curves of her breasts and the black lace bras, had no doubt sent more than one man home with a hard-on.

Unless she worked the back alley, too, and took care of that situation before those men headed home. It was an unfair thought, and he knew it. But Booker had learned the hard way that life isn't fair. The waitress had been friendly to him, but she had never approached him, nor had Booker seen her get inappropriate with any customers.

Then again, Booker tended to sit at the bar, back to the seating area, and mind his own business.

Not tonight, though. Like he was connected to a power supply, he was keenly aware of Lennox's presence behind him. The hair on the back of his neck stood on end. His dick remained mostly comatose, but his heartbeat was kicked up to fight or flight mode.

If anything, it gave him hope that one day, maybe soon, he would feel the-fuck-and-forget mode again.

LENNOX

"Do you want me to wait around?"

Lennox, at the bar now, tipped her head back to look up at Erick Bonner. Lia had come to Sidecar with them after dinner, after studying until they all felt like they had scrambled eggs for brains. But she had ended up ducking out after one drink to go to her boyfriend's house. Collins had been texting Lennox all night with updates on what she and Eloise were doing, as well as threats to not come home until well after midnight. Knowing Collins, she would sit Lennox down the second she did walk in the door and pump her for details about every facet of the night.

Including the nonexistent sex.

Lennox and Erick were just friends. She wasn't into girls, and Lia had a boyfriend, anyway. Still, it had been a good night. Relaxing, even with the intense studying and quizzing each other. The drink she had just finished was good. She knew Eloise was in good hands, and now she had time to sit and talk to Banks for a while.

"No. It's okay."

Erick narrowed his eyes at her. "How're you gonna get home?"

"I can get a cab." She shrugged off his concern.

"Lex." Erick groaned.

"You're not responsible for getting me home."

"Your car's at the restaurant."

"I can give her a ride."

Lennox swept her hand out in a Vanna White gesture as Banks approached them on the opposite side of the bar.

"You know him?" Erick asked suspiciously.

"He's my best friend's brother," she answered.

"Don't you close at, like two a.m.?"

"Erick. It's fine." Lennox rested her hand on his chest and patted him. "Promise. I'll be fine."

"Okay. We're gonna kill it on that test."

"Of course we are."

Lennox jumped off the stool and threw her arms around him in a quick hug. Erick leaned in, wrapped his arms around her, and gave her a hard squeeze. Lennox lifted her head to look up at him, but she found herself looking at Booker Gannon over Erick's shoulder. He stared at her unabashedly, his face blank, from his stool around the corner of the bar. A low hum of electricity curled through her blood. Heat, lust, unfurled low in her belly. Her nipples hardened under his stare, making her grateful she was wearing a sweater, so Erick wouldn't notice.

Jerking her gaze from Dr. Gannon's, she looked up at Erick with a smile.

"Night."

"Night." He nodded and dropped his hands. "Call me if you change your mind."

"Thanks." She watched him walk away, Dr. Gannon's intense stare burning her. With a glance at him, she sat down again, her cheeks flushing in the dimly lit room.

Definitely shouldn't have read his article on the *Blood Rite* Series.

Adding liquor on top of those already uncomfortable, unwelcome feelings had been a big mistake.

"Want another drink?" Banks asked her.

She nodded, lifting her hands to rub her forehead. "Water, too, please?"

"You got it."

Eyes closed, she wondered if Dr. Gannon was still looking at her. If she should go over and speak to him. Should she sit down by him? What was the protocol? *Was* there a proto-col? Hell, no, there wasn't. He was a professor; she was his student. End of story.

"Collins with Eloise?"

Lennox blinked and looked at Banks. She snatched the glass of water he put in front of her and took a long drink.

"Yes. They were watching *Scooby Doo* when I left earlier."

Banks smiled. Lennox watched him go through the motions of mixing her a vodka cranberry drink and vowed to herself to sip it, to be sensible.

Nothing about tonight felt sensible.

"Here you go." Banks nudged the mixed drink over the bar to her. "Gotta make my rounds. I'll be back."

She nodded as she picked up the glass and slipped the tiny straw between her lips. Something made her turn her head toward Dr. Gannon. She took a pull on the straw as their eyes met. He dipped his gaze to her mouth as she set the glass down, swallowed, and licked her lips.

What the hell was she doing? She should have just left with Erick, Collins' lectures about getting laid be damned. She had seen the McArthurs in here a time or two, always when she had been with Collins. But who said that door wouldn't open any minute, and they wouldn't walk in and see her sitting here alone like a barfly? Tipsy and making eyes at her professor.

Dr. Gannon picked up his glass and stood. Lennox tried to catch her breath, but her heart was now beating up in her throat. If Dr. Gannon *were* a vampire, he would see the rapid flutter of her pulse under the skin on her neck. If he were a vampire in the *Blood Rite* series, he would be able to scent her arousal. Lennox hated reading that line, *those words*, over and over in vampire romances. And yet, right now, she was living it.

"What's a girl like you doing here?" Dr. Gannon sat down on the barstool next to her.

"A girl like me," she repeated, mostly because all rational thought had faded, and the only information in her brain was Dr. Gannon's theory that Raiah was an unstable, vengeful demon ruler who used her sexuality to control everyone and as a result ended up exposing her tender underbelly to everyone who hated her. Her sexual needs, her ecstasy at her enemies' hands, had been her undoing.

"Mmm." Dr. Gannon nodded.

"What am I?" she asked him. "What is a girl like me?"

"I don't see many college students here." He looked around the bar and then back at her pointedly.

"Not long ago, there were three of us in here."

"This is the third time I've seen you in here since the semester started."

"You're keeping track?" She arched her brows in surprise.

"You still haven't answered me." He tipped his head and stared at her curiously.

"I was here with friends," she answered with a shrug.

"And they just left you here."

Lennox laughed softly. "It's okay. I know Banks."

Dr. Gannon turned his attention to his glass as he twisted and turned it in his hand.

"And how do you know Banks?"

Lennox swallowed down the flash of irritation. Why was he quizzing her? If this was Dr. Gannon outside the classroom, the rumors had him dead wrong. He was boring, borderline harpy and parental, and nosy besides. Her belly might be churning with anticipation, her nipples could probably cut glass right now, but it sure as hell had nothing to do with Booker Gannon being flirty or sexy.

"He's my best friend's brother."

"Mmm." He nodded, lifted his glass to finish his whiskey, and then stood again. "Goodnight, Lennox."

19

BOOKER

Booker slipped a book from the shelf as his phone buzzed in his pocket. He resisted a groan as he tucked the book under his arm and pulled the phone out to look at it. A text from Randi. At least this one was about an uncle they hadn't seen for a while and not Randi harping on him to get out more.

The university library wasn't his favorite place to be, not since he was bound to run into at least one of his students here, if not more. But he had come to do some research for the film and lit class for the following week. He could probably walk into the Killdare Springs Public Library and not worry about bumping into anyone he knew. But then, he wasn't going to find what he needed for class at the public library, either.

Book still under his arm, Booker moseyed over to a gray leather armchair, eyes on his phone. Randi's text was to inform him that Uncle Steffan had passed away the night before. Steffan was their dad's eldest brother. Booker and

Randi had been close to him when they were kids, but Booker hadn't seen him in years.

What was he supposed to say to that? Was Randi going to suggest he cancel class and catch a plane to Sacramento to be at the funeral? He set the book on the floor between his feet and then ducked his head and scrubbed his fingers through his hair. Sometimes he wished he could rewind the past year and do it over. Sometimes he wished he could rewind about five years and make a whole lot of changes.

And some days, he was just exhausted, and he wanted to win the lottery and pack up and vanish from this life. Go off the grid and find a little peace.

Hard to do, considering he didn't gamble. Not even a buck or two on a lottery ticket.

Before he could decide what to say to Randi, another text came through.

He would send a card to Aunt Jennette. But no, he wasn't going to cancel class and fly out to the funeral. Booker wouldn't forget that their son, his cousin, had snubbed him through the last year, as if he had done the things he had been accused of. Booker had no desire to rub elbows with family members who believed all the bullshit things said about him.

Let's just send flowers.

Booker gushed out a deep breath, relieved that Randi had read his mind. Randi had stood behind him through all the ugly stuff, everything. As much as she frustrated him, he would do well to remember that she was on his side.

Works for me.

He set his phone on the book, still on the floor, and rubbed his hands over his face. Regardless of what he thought of his cousin, he should call his dad.

"Dr. Gannon?"

He suppressed another groan, this one irritation with himself for being here like a sitting duck.

"Yeah." He dug his fingers into his eyes and rubbed for a moment and finally dropped his hands to find Lennox watching him curiously. She had a book in her hand, her backpack slung over her shoulder.

"Are you okay?"

Her words shocked him. No one, outside of his parents and Randi, had asked if he was okay in the last year. No one had asked how he was doing.

"Yeah." He sighed. "Just got a text from my sister. My uncle died last night."

He snapped his mouth closed hard enough to break his teeth. Why had he said that? He didn't share anything with his students. Not anymore.

"I'm sorry for your loss," she said quietly.

"Thanks." He mumbled it, eyes on the shelf behind her. Hard to look at her after going home last night from Sidecar and wondering about her. Thinking about her announcement that the bartender there was her best friend's brother. Thinking about her as a mom versus his student. Wondering who the father of her daughter was.

Wondering why it mattered to him.

Worried she might try to ask him something, to pry, he took another deep breath, picked up his phone and book, and went on the offensive.

"Where's your daughter today?"

Lennox shrank back from him instantly, as if he had threatened her. She was pale, no makeup today. Blond waves framed her face, but she reached up to tuck a chunk behind her ear as she turned away from him.

"Um." She shook her head. "She's with her dad's family today."

Booker winced. He hadn't meant to be an ass, just to deflect her from asking him something more.

"Are they close?"

Before he could berate himself for another personal question, she shrugged and glanced at him.

"I dunno." She pressed her lips together. "It's complicated."

Booker stood and tucked his phone in his pocket. "I'll see you later. Going to get some coffee and go home."

"Me, too." Her answer sounded like a confession. Had she really planned to go over to Crave? Or had she just said that so she could follow him? Booker laughed to himself at his arrogance. She wasn't interested in him. And it didn't matter.

"Great." He shrugged. "Let's walk together."

She stared at him for a moment, teeth worrying her lush lower lip, and finally she nodded and turned to lead him back through the stacks. Booker gave her plenty of space at the checkout counter, but he watched her pull her student ID from the front pocket of her backpack. She didn't live in the dorms. He doubted she lived on campus, since she had a kid. So where was home?

He checked the book out he had been carrying, surprised to find her waiting for him in the vestibule of the library. Booker stepped in front of her at the door and pushed it open for her. After last year, he had sworn he wouldn't do that. He wouldn't open a door for a woman. Wouldn't engage a woman in polite conversation. Wouldn't find himself alone in an elevator with a woman.

Her word against his hadn't worked out for him in the past. He wasn't about to let another woman hurt him again.

But his parents had taught him to respect women.

Lennox smelled like springtime, some fresh, floral scent. Booker breathed deeply as she slipped by him. She wasn't wearing a coat, just a Killdare University sweatshirt with her leggings. The elastic on the sweatshirt covered her ass today, but Booker took a moment to notice her delicious-looking thighs.

"Did you tell me you're from Killdare Springs?" he asked as he trotted to catch up with her, only because he couldn't follow her and not look at her legs.

"Yeah." She shivered and hunched her shoulders as a brisk wind whipped around across campus. "Lived here all my life."

"Do you like it?"

"It's okay." She glanced at him. "Not going anywhere for a while. Not exactly rolling in cash."

"Your parents live here?"

"Yeah." She cleared her throat. "Yeah. They help a lot with Eloise."

"How old—?"

"Eighteen."

"Is your daughter?"

Lennox looked away, but Booker noticed the flush in her cheeks.

"Five, soon to be six."

He caught himself before he could say something about how cute she was, afraid it would be taken the wrong way. The fact that he had to live this way, to think before he said something completely innocent, that someone would truly believe he would hurt a child, made his head hurt.

"Were you close to your uncle?"

Booker jerked his gaze from the trees to find her looking at him. He wondered what his face looked like to invite such a question. He considered blowing her off, but just as quickly, he found himself answering her.

"Randi and I were close to him when we were kids," he said with a shrug. "He lived in Sacramento. We went out to stay with him and my aunt for summers for a while. But." He cleared his throat. "It's been years since I've seen him."

"Eloise's father wants nothing to do with her," she announced, head turned forward, away from him. Booker wondered what she was looking at. "But his parents... They do."

She looked uncomfortable. Booker wasn't sure what to say. He couldn't imagine having a child and wanting nothing to do with him or her. He and Ashley used to talk about their future, when they would have two kids and a dog—a boy and a girl and an Aussie. Part of him wished they would have had a baby before things got bad. Because the possibility of Booker being a father now was less than zero. But the other part of him, the sane part, knew it was good they hadn't dragged a child through their ugly divorce.

"Are they good people?" he asked as they neared Crave.

Lennox turned to look at him, brows arched in disbelief.

"Um." She licked her lips. "They're the McArthurs," she answered as if that should mean something to him.

20

LENNOX

Butterfly wings fluttered in her belly as she stepped up to the counter to order her drink. Lennox had worried that Dr. Gannon might offer to buy her coffee; she didn't want him to. But now that he was standing behind her in line, she was hyperaware of him behind her. Was he watching her? Was he looking at her ass? Her legs? Did he like what he saw?

Didn't help that she couldn't shake the words in his article —his conclusions about Raiah using her sexuality for power and in the end losing power, because of her need for sexual pleasure and even affection. The idea of Dr. Gannon reading those books, thinking about him reading about the threesome between Raiah and two of the vampires she had turned, made her weak in the knees.

Flustered and embarrassed to be stuck in this thought pattern, she gave herself a mental shake as she paid for her drink and stepped aside. She had ordered a to-go cup, but now she wasn't sure if she should just walk out or stick around and walk out with him? Would people talk? Were they already talking? She had seen Dr. Gannon a few times on campus since class had started, but they were always in public. Never touching.

But that probably didn't matter. People were vicious with rumors and careless with the truth.

Dr. Gannon turned to her with his paper coffee cup; she held her breath, wondering what came next. Wondering who the hell she was if she was going to let him get to her like this. Even if he wasn't the sexual predator he was rumored to be, even if there wasn't misconduct at his last school, he was her professor. Not to mention, she had to watch herself around town because of Monty's parents.

"You in a hurry to get out of here?" he asked her.

Lennox opened her mouth to answer him. This was her chance to slip away. She should say yes. But she had already told him Eloise was with her grandmother. She didn't work today. She had nothing to do but go home and try to study while she wondered what Eve McArthur and Eloise were doing.

"No." She shrugged.

When he wandered past her to the seating area, Lennox assumed she was supposed to follow him. He led her to a corner table in the back of the small room. Several tables right through the center of the room were taken, and the cozy chairs by the fireplace were occupied, too.

Lennox hesitated when he sat down. On one level, a plain table and plain chairs probably looked more harmless than the cozy seats by the fireplace. On the other hand, sitting at a two-top table with him would put her much closer to him. She didn't want to consider why that made her anxious.

He looked up at her when he was sitting, and she was still standing. Feeling stupid now, Lennox moved to take the chair across the table. She let her backpack slide to the floor at her feet and put her cup on the table. To avoid having to look at him right away, she took her phone from her bag and checked for messages.

Naturally, there were none.

"I don't know who the McArthurs are."

"Consider yourself lucky." She met his stare as she put her phone on the table.

"How'd it happen?"

Lennox took a sip of her coffee and eyed him over the cup.

"How did I get pregnant?" she asked with a laugh. "The same way all women do."

Dr. Gannon laughed softly and shook his head. "Not what I meant."

"We were dating, I guess." She shrugged. "Why do you get to ask me personal questions?"

"You're answering me," he reminded her.

That buzz of awareness, of attraction, skittering around in her body was a distraction. She fisted her fingers, wishing she could will it away.

"Monty and I dated for a few months. And I ended up pregnant."

"Were you in love with him?"

"No." She held his stare for a second and finally looked away. "No. And he wasn't in love with me. When I told him I was pregnant, he said he didn't want a kid. Didn't want a permanent relationship with me. And that was that."

"How did his parents get involved?"

"You've never heard of Joseph McArthur?"

Dr. Gannon shrugged. "New to Killdare Springs, remember?"

Lennox cleared her throat. "New to Killdare Springs? Or visiting?"

"Fuck if I know," he mumbled.

His quiet rumble of what sounded like a confession surprised her. Lennox flinched when he met her eyes.

"Sorry." He sighed. "Shouldn't have said that."

"Are you and your sister close?"

Dr. Gannon stared at her for a long, silent moment and finally nodded.

"Why?" he asked.

"Why what?"

"Why would you ask that?"

Lennox frowned. "Why would you ask me how I got pregnant?"

"Did you ask because you wonder how my sister can be close to me after what I supposedly did?"

Lennox tried to swallow, but her mouth was dry.

"Everyone needs someone in their corner," she finally answered.

Dr. Gannon's bitter laugh chased a chill up her spine.

"Joseph McArthur is an attorney here in town," she told him. "They have more money than...I'd say God, but I can't even use his name in a sentence with them. You wanna talk about vampires?" She shrugged as she clenched her teeth.

Jesus, shut up, Lex.

"Let's talk about vampires," he suggested. "I'm guessing you've read ahead."

"Actually, I haven't," she admitted. "Had a big bio exam that I was concentrating on."

"When you were out last night? At Sidecar."

"We had dinner and studied together," she said with a nod.

Dr. Gannon picked up his cup and lifted it to his mouth. Lennox studied his long fingers. His thin lips on the cup. His piercing green eyes looking right through her.

"Who's your favorite fictional vampire?"

She wouldn't say Raiah, even though Raiah had always been her favorite. She didn't want to start a conversation about the sexuality in the *Blood Rite* series.

"Dracula." She shrugged.

"Bullshit."

"What?" She tipped her head with a frown. "I'm entitled to whatever favorite fictional vampire I want to choose."

"Agreed." He nodded. "But you're lying."

"I'm—? I'm lying?"

"You are."

"Okay, then, who is my favorite fictional vampire, Dr. Gannon?"

"Call me Booker when we're not in class."

"No."

Their eyes met. Lennox swallowed hard, desperate to look away, certain he could see into her soul. And yet, she wouldn't back down. If she gave an inch here, Dr. Gannon might take more.

And worse?

Lennox might give more. Until she'd given him enough rope to hang her.

Dr. Gannon nodded. "Right." He picked up his cup and drew in a deep breath. "See you Monday, Ms. Clarke."

21

BOOKER

"Josh." Booker rested on the edge of the desk and nodded at the kid. "*Carmilla*. What're your thoughts?"

"I mean..." The kid shrugged. "It's boring."

"What do you mean boring?"

Josh looked around the lecture hall, like he wanted support. Booker noticed that Rupe wouldn't turn to face his friend. Kara rolled her eyes. Booker swept his gaze over Lennox, but he didn't let himself catch her eye. He was still pissed off about Saturday at Crave.

They'd had a normal conversation, and normal conversations were few and far between for him these days. Booker had let his guard down, just a bit. Some of his students at his old school had just called him *Gannon*. Even Sofie and Reese had called him *Gannon*. Hell, *Ashley* had called him *Gannon*.

While it was his legal surname, Booker didn't want any new acquaintances linked to those memories in his head. And likewise, he wasn't comfortable in a coffeehouse situation with one student or a group of students addressing him as *Dr. Gannon*. It made him feel old and stodgy. So he had asked her to call him Booker.

Her simple, flat refusal spoke volumes.

He hadn't slept much all weekend. He had gone for a long, harsh run Sunday morning. When that didn't put her or her cool, calm face out of his head, he had showered in ice-cold water. The cold had made his body hurt. He wasn't chasing away a hard-on. Didn't wrap his hand around his cock and work it while he pretended he wasn't thinking about Lennox.

Her face became Sofie's became Reese's became Ashley's as he stood under the icy needles, his head on the shower wall, eyes squeezed closed. Images flashed through his mind on fast forward. Ashley handing Sofie a seltzer. Sofie's bright red lips parted in a big, happy smile. Reese's lithe body in the air as she put up a perfect jump shot.

When the shower didn't push the thoughts away, Booker had dressed and climbed into his car and driven. To nowhere. And everywhere. He drove the streets of Killdare Springs. He drove the outskirts. All the way to Springfield for no other reason than to outrun the nightmare in his head.

Only to come home and have that fucking nightmare right there on his shoulder, in his head, his heart. In his empty house.

"I like that it's about a lesbian vampire," Josh said finally. "But..."

"Oh, I see." Booker nodded. "It's not titillating enough for you?"

The class burst into laughter at Josh's expense. Booker didn't care.

"That's what you're getting out of the story?" Lennox leaned forward to ask Josh.

"What else is there?" He shrugged.

Booker wanted to stop her. To look at her and freeze her mouth shut. And yet, he wanted to hear what she had to say.

"It's not about lesbians." Lennox rolled her eyes.

"Um, pretty sure Laura's got a thing for Carmilla." Josh shot Booker a look before turning to Lennox.

"Yeah, but it's about the magnetism of the vampire creature," Lennox told him. "It's not porn for your pleasure."

"No shit." Josh held his hands up as if in surrender. A low roar of laughter followed his words.

"Vampires are sensual," Lennox continued. "But the story isn't written just as something to turn *you* on."

"Isn't it?" Booker tipped his head. "Isn't that what we said about the Gothic? That it calls to that base desire? That need for something a little salacious? Maybe forbidden?"

Lennox narrowed her eyes at him.

"But I don't think LeFanu wrote it with college guys in mind."

"Obviously," Josh mumbled. "I need a little more detail in my porn."

"Hold that thought, Josh." Booker held up his hand and looked back at Lennox. "Are you arguing that women should be allowed to feel that sexual desire, too? Because remember in that time period, women *weren't* allowed to show their sexuality. And homosexuality was considered immoral."

When Lennox didn't answer, Booker shrugged and straightened. He tucked his hands in his pockets as he paced the front of the room.

"You're right, Lennox, in your comment that vampires in general have that magnetism that draws people to them. But in this particular story, yes, Carmilla is a female vampire with only female victims."

She looked away first. Only then did Booker turn back to Josh.

"And no. Josh, you're not going to get detailed sex in a book written in the Victorian age. For that time, *Carmilla was* scandalous. Now, are there books written in our time with more detailed sex? Of course. But you have to remember the culture and the age when you look at literature."

"So, what's the point of the story then?" Lennox asked.

"Anybody have an answer for that?" Booker watched the class and finally tapped the keyboard to advance to the next slide. He heard someone mumble something about society.

"I think it's a message about female sexuality and society's...uncertainty about it."

"Their fear," Booker corrected Kara.

Aware of Lennox's gaze on him, Booker finished the lecture without calling on her again. Still angry when class was over, he took his time packing his laptop up.

"Dr. Gannon, you got any recommendations on those current vampire books?" Josh and a few other guys laughed. "Something with lesbian vampires?"

When Booker looked up to answer Josh, he noticed Lennox lingering in her seat. He took a quick breath and shifted his focus back to Josh.

"What are you, Josh? Fifteen?"

"Twenty." The kid totally missed Booker's sarcasm.

"'kay. You're twenty. Don't worry about lesbian vampires. Go get laid."

"Man, I'm tryin'," the kid said with a smirk.

"Maybe if you weren't such a dick," Lennox mumbled. Booker snorted. "Just sayin'." She shrugged when Josh glanced at her.

"Goin' to Crave?" he asked her.

"No."

Josh and the two guys waiting on him shuffled out the door leaving Booker alone with Lennox. He stared at her for a moment and then turned back to the desk to pack up his belongings.

"Really?"

"Really, what?" he asked without looking at her.

"You poked into my personal life two days ago. Remember that? And then you just got up and walked away, and now today, you treat me like an idiot in class?"

"I didn't treat you like an idiot, Lennox. You're too sensitive. You know damned well the story *Carmilla* is about female sexuality." He picked up his bag. "Grow up. You have a child. You obviously know how attraction and sexuality work."

She laughed softly and raised her eyebrows. "Okay. And this is all because I refused to call you *Booker*? Am I getting that right?"

"Have a good day, Lennox—"

"And if I called you *Booker*? What next? Come hang out in your office? Maybe we could—"

"Stop right there." He looked at her over his shoulder. "You don't know me. Don't presume that you do."

22

LENNOX

"What's wrong with you?" Collins asked from Lennox's kitchen table. Lennox glanced at Eloise, bent over her homework paper, crayon in hand. Sometimes the letter and number worksheets she brought home irritated Lennox. She would rather give Eloise real life lessons than have her copy numbers or count or trace letters. On the other hand, there were times she was grateful Eloise was busy with something and didn't notice things.

Like when she was in a bad mood.

Or when Collins called her on the bad mood.

Lennox shook her head. "Not a good day."

"Work okay yesterday?"

"Work was fine." Lennox nodded. Waitressing wasn't her favorite thing and not her idea of a career, but it paid her bills, her tips were good, and she liked her coworkers. "Pax let me out early."

"Of course he did. He's sweet on you. So what happened today?"

Shrugging off the comment about her boss, Lennox loaded the last of the dinner plates in the dishwasher, dropped a soap pod in the door, and pushed it closed.

"Just." She shrugged. "Dr. Gannon made me look like a fool in class."

"How?"

Lennox glanced at Eloise. Collins nodded at the subtle reminder she couldn't speak freely.

"Done, Mommy!" Eloise put her crayon down. "Can I play now? Before bath time?"

"Yeah." Lennox nodded and tousled her daughter's hair when she zipped by her.

"Spill." Collins stood and crossed the room. Lennox sat and watched her friend grab the open bottle of wine from the counter and take two glasses from the cabinet by the window over the sink.

"We read a story about a lesbian vampire. And Josh had to comment on it. It pissed me off. So I reminded him that vampire stories are *all* about carnal lust and that LeFanu didn't just write this story to get him off."

Collins snorted. "Remind me again why you're studying vampires. What does that have to do with nursing? And should I be nervous?"

Lennox laughed softly. "No. It's just a lit class."

"But why vampires?"

"I think we're supposed to take away new thoughts on society and politics and race, blah blah blah when the class is over. Just Dr. Gannon's bent, I guess."

"And sex? With vampires?"

Collins sat down again and splashed wine into both glasses before pushing one at Lennox.

"Would you have sex with a vampire?" Collins asked her.

"There are days when I would," Lennox said with a grin. "It's been a long time."

"I hear that." Collins nodded. "I told you to have some fun last weekend."

"That's not me." Lennox shrugged. "I can't just hook up with someone."

"Banks is always willing to volunteer."

"I don't wanna sleep with Banks."

"What's wrong with him?" Collins frowned.

"He's like a brother, Collins." Lennox took a drink. "Would you sleep with him?"

"Eww."

"I had a dream about Dr. Gannon the other night." She eyed the glass suspiciously as she set it down. "God. Have you ever had a dream that was so...vividly detailed...that you swore you would never share it with anyone?"

"Only for the truth to slip out of your mouth after one drink of wine." Collins waggled her eyebrows. "Do tell."

"He kissed me."

"And?"

"That's it. He kissed me."

"And that's so scandalous you wouldn't have told me if I hadn't plied you with truth serum?"

Lennox sighed. "It was just...I still remember...*everything*. The way he looked at me. The cold air on my face. The *heat* of his mouth on mine. The slide of his *tongue* over mine. He tasted decadent. Like expensive chocolate and wine."

Collins rested her elbow on the table and propped her chin in her hand.

"We were outside Sidecar. I was leaving, and he followed me out. Cornered me. Pressed me into the wall. I remember tipping my head back and looking at the sky. It was velvet black with like...seven stars...and then he was looking at me. Eyeing my neck. Like he wanted to kiss me there. Or maybe bite me."

"Jesus, Lex," Collins groaned.

"And then he leaned in and slid his fingers under my chin and his lips over mine. I touched him—my hand on his shoulder—and dug in to hold on."

"You sure this was a dream?"

"Yeah." Lennox nodded. "I did see him last Saturday at Sidecar. And he did talk to me. But he didn't follow me out. He didn't touch me. No kissing."

"So, you're attracted to him."

Lennox slumped in her chair. "I am." She ducked her head

and whispered her confession. "That scares me. Like what if Eve knew that?"

"She can't just *take* Eloise from you."

"I know, but she could try. She could turn my little girl against me."

"Lex, you're a good mother. You have a great support system. Monty's name isn't even on her birth certificate. There's *nothing* Eve can do to you."

"Yeah, well, Eloise isn't yours to lose," Lennox reminded her friend. "I won't risk it."

"So you're never going to live again, because you're afraid of Eve McArthur?"

"I don't need to live again. I have Eloise."

"You do, and we love her to bits and pieces, Lex. But you're entitled to more. You can have love, too."

"Maybe we should talk about you, Collins."

"I'm not the one having hot dreams about a certain professor."

"He's your age."

Collins snorted. "I'm not going after the guy you're having hot dreams about."

"He just." She shook her head. "He gets under my skin."

"And that makes you mad," Collins said. "Because he makes you feel things that are out of your control."

"I don't know if I'd go that far."

"I would." Collins shrugged. "Please go out with Banks. Let him show you he's not your brother."

"Collins."

"Lex, he's crazy about you. And he's definitely safer than Booker Gannon."

"Maybe I'll bust out some tip money and purchase a nice battery-operated boyfriend."

"You don't have one?" Collins yelped.

"Shh!" Lennox lunged over the table and grabbed her friend's arm. "No. I don't."

"Every woman should have at least one sex toy in her nightstand."

"I'll take that under advisement."

"Mommy?" Eloise called from the living room.

"What, El?" Lennox narrowed her eyes at Collins in a warning and carried her glass to the doorway. "What's up?"

"Will you read to me?"

"Of course. Pick a book."

When her phone buzzed the next evening after work and she reached for it, Lennox noticed Banks' name on the screen. She hesitated, knowing Collins had told her brother about Lennox's dream kiss with Booker Gannon. Just over twenty-four hours later, Banks was calling to suggest they go out. With a sigh, she leaned sideways to snatch the phone from the coffee table and pushed her laptop away.

"That's the last time I tell Collins my secrets," she said by way of a greeting.

Banks' laugh trickled down the phone line. She heard piano jazz in the background, but it was the clinking of glass that told her he was at work.

"Seriously, Lennox? You're having dreams about the campus tool, but you won't go out with me?"

"Dammit." She scooched her way down the couch to rest her head on the arm. "It was a dream. I can't control what I dream."

"Seems to indicate that you're hot for your teacher."

"Have you ever had a dream so out-of-left-field you can't explain it?"

"Sure, but in my experience, a kissing dream means you're attracted to the kisser."

Lennox laughed and closed her eyes. "Nope. Not true. Because Collins once told me she had a dream about kissing your cousin's husband."

"Alex?"

"Yep."

"Eww. Yeah, no." Banks sounded disgusted. "That's just wrong."

"Well. Maybe my dream means I hate going to his class."

Banks made a noncommittal sound, said something to someone at the bar, and then to Lennox, "Or maybe...Hear me out. Maybe your dream just means you need to get out. Go out on a date."

"Banks."

"I'm not saying you wanna go out with the good professor. But just out."

Lennox lifted her hand and pinched the bridge of her nose. "I don't have time to date."

"You do. What do you say? Let's just try dinner. Just you and me."

"Because when it comes time for a goodnight kiss, it'll freak me out. Because you're like a big brother, Banks. And I don't wanna kiss my big brother."

"I dare you." His voice held a hint of teasing, but she knew the challenge was real.

"And when you try to kiss me goodnight, and I back away? What then?"

"Then you come back to Sidecar with Collins, and everything's back to normal. No harm, no foul. Come hang out with at the bar. Just you and me."

"I'll think about it."

"Okay. I'll accept that. You think about it, and I'll see you next time you come in for a drink."

"Bye, Banks."

She ended the call but fired off a text at Collins before putting her phone down.

No more truth serum around you, Traitor.

Lennox dropped her phone on her belly and propped herself up far enough to retrieve her laptop and pull it close again. She lay still for a moment, but the house was quiet. Eloise had gone to bed an hour ago; Lennox had forgone her assigned reading and dug into the rabbit hole of Booker Gannon information online. No news articles. But she'd found more articles he had written published in journals—scholarly and not-so-scholarly. None were as carnal or adult in nature as the first she had found about the *Blood Rite* Series. And still, she saved them all for the evenings, after Collins or her mom or whoever was gone, and Eloise was in bed, and she was alone. Like a guilty pleasure. Reading Dr. Gannon's articles was a link to him that made her feel a connection.

Which explained the kiss dream and invited more, more in quantity and heat. She definitely would not share that admission with Collins or anyone else.

Her phone buzzed, but Lennox took her time picking it up to check Collins' reply.

Anything to keep you outta trouble.

23

BOOKER

He wasn't surprised this time when he saw Lennox enter Sidecar. Not even when he realized she was alone. She climbed up on the barstool at the far end of the bar, unaware that he sat in the shadows around the corner. Banks wasn't bartending tonight, so even though Booker wanted to look away, he couldn't. What was she doing here alone if her friend's brother wasn't here?

She ordered a drink from the woman behind the bar and engaged in small talk. But when the bartender moved away to check on other customers, Lennox sipped her drink and kept her eyes on the door. When she sat up ramrod straight each time the door opened, Booker realized she was meeting someone here.

He hadn't said much to her the rest of this week in class. She hadn't volunteered anything in discussion. She was bright enough to know the underlying theme in *Carmilla*, as well as the rest of their reading material. Maybe Josh had simply set her off.

Eyes on her phone now, Booker studied her profile. Strong cheekbones. A straight, aristocratic nose. Plump lips. She was smiling now. Was she watching TikTok videos or texting with someone?

The door opened again, but Lennox didn't look this time. Booker did. Banks crossed the room and flashed her a smile when she did lift her chin. They exchanged a greeting, but Booker was too far away to hear it. Banks stood at the end of the bar, head bent close to hers, talking.

Was she meeting *him*? Or had he just happened to come in while she was waiting for someone else? Booker glanced at the bartender when she stopped in front of him.

"Doin' okay?"

"Can I get a double pour of the twelve-year Lockland?"

"Absolutely."

He could leave. Go home and catch a movie. But he was intrigued now. As wrong as it was, Booker was ready to settle in and watch Lennox. When his glass appeared in front of him, he picked it up without looking at it and took a small sip.

Banks slid his arm around Lennox's shoulders and pulled her close to kiss the top of her head. Booker waited for Lennox to shove him away. When she didn't, he put his glass down and spun it in slow circles on the bar.

Instead of shoving him away, Lennox, still laughing, turned on the barstool and looked up as Banks moved in closer.

Booker let go of his glass when the guy cupped her chin in his hand and kissed her. Square on the mouth. Open mouths. Tongues. Booker finally looked away. What the hell? She had told him this guy was her best friend's brother. Was she fucking him? Did her best friend know?

Not your business.

He huffed out a sigh and took another drink. Nope. Wasn't his business. Except that he wanted to fuck Lennox Clarke. Watching her kiss that guy brought his dick to a full throttle hard-on in less than two seconds.

Jesus.

Letting go of the glass yet again, Booker dipped his head and covered his face with his hands. He wasn't sure if he should celebrate—his dick had been useless for so long—or be ashamed that watching one of his students kiss someone turned him on like real porn apparently did for Josh Stone.

They weren't kissing anymore. He could see them from the corner of his eye. But they were still close, and they were laughing. Were they lovers? And if they were, why the hell were they doing this here? In public?

Booker glanced at them again. He pictured Lennox with her blouse unbuttoned. Parted. The swell of her breasts over a lace bra.

All imagination.

He had never seen her wear anything provocative.

Imagination was good, though. Fuck, just looking at her lips was enough to create some vivid fantasies.

She snatched her phone up suddenly and put it to her ear. Booker felt a pang of sadness, loneliness, when she threw her head back and laughed. Was she aware that he was watching her? Was this all a show for his sake?

Banks took her phone and started talking to the caller.

Sofie had worn low cut shirts all the time. Showing as much of herself as she could get away with. He had seen her tits a few times and not because he was particularly looking to see them. Reese tended toward tiny little cutoff shorts that left her ass cheeks peeking out. Booker had overheard the two of them in conversation with his wife, talking about guys they had picked up, things they did with those guys.

Booker gritted his teeth as he remembered hoping that Ashley wouldn't say something about him, about their sex life, to the girls. They had all gotten too close, and they tended to overshare.

A gruff bitter laugh escaped him.

He had looked. If girls were going to put it out there, they had to expect men were going to look. Fuck that. Men, women. If you paraded your tits or ass around like that, *people* looked. Didn't mean he acted on it.

"Fancy seeing you here."

He looked up when Lennox slid onto the stool beside his. The hard-on was gone; his dick was lifeless again. But a wave of anger roared through him as he looked around the bar. Banks was nowhere to be seen.

"Were you putting on a show for me?"

Lennox narrowed her eyes at him. "What?"

"Making out with your best friend's brother. Was that for my benefit?"

Wouldn't be the first time.

Lennox laughed, but it didn't ring true. She sounded a little hurt.

"No." She shook her head. "No. It wasn't for your benefit, Dr. Gannon."

"So, you make a habit of fucking around in public places."

"Char?" she called. The bartender turned with a smile. "Can I get a drink?"

"Sure."

Booker watched the woman mix Lennox a vodka cranberry.

"I don't fuck around," she said quietly when the bartender delivered her drink.

"No? What was that then? Didn't you tell me he's your best friend's brother?"

"Why?" She turned in her seat and drilled him with her stare. "Why is this your business?"

"Why did you walk over here to talk to me after the lip lock with the guy?"

She stared at him a moment longer and finally turned away.

"Collins has tried to set me up with him since the beginning of time. And I keep saying no. It would be like dating a brother."

"What changed your mind?"

She took a drink, suddenly intent on avoiding his eyes.

"I haven't dated anyone. For a long time." She shrugged. "So, I gave in."

"So, you're talking to me while you're on a date with him?"

"No. We're just gonna hang out tonight."

"That's a date."

"Banks suggested a kiss." She licked her lips and hesitated. "If I thought the kiss was good, I would go out with him."

"How was it?"

"Like kissing my brother." She laughed softly. "I don't know why I feel compelled to explain myself to you. Banks is talking to someone he knows over there. I saw you over here and thought I'd say hi."

"You knew what the theme of *Carmilla* was."

She shrugged. "Josh pisses me off."

"Maybe so. But he was right."

"Josh was upset because there was no graphic detail about lesbian sex. *Josh* was hung up on Carmilla and Laura. Not the *bigger picture* of female sexuality."

"You slept with him." He arched an eyebrow at her. "Didn't you?"

Lennox opened her mouth to say something, but she apparently thought better of it. Instead of speaking, she took a drink.

"Say it," he ordered.

"Yeah. If I say what I'm thinking, you'll flunk me." She slipped off the stool and pulled cash from her pocket. "Or is that where you have a suggestion for me for extra credit?"

She tossed a ten on the bar and walked away.

24

LENNOX

"Okay. *Uncle*." Banks put his arm around her waist and tugged her close for a squeeze. "We're better as friends. But I'm not sorry I kissed you."

Lennox still shook with anger at Dr. Gannon, but she managed a smile for Banks and his friends.

"Banks." Lennox slipped her arm around him and leaned in. "Don't make me feel guilty."

"Not my intention." He kissed the top of her head again. "Just know I'm here for you. Whatever you need."

"You deserve someone who feels the same way for you."

He nodded. "And until then, I am at your disposal."

Lennox laughed.

She knew the guys gathered around the small table in the back of Sidecar. But her talk with Dr. Gannon had left her twitchy and buzzing with anger. She had almost told him to fuck off. Maybe he had baited her on purpose. So she would speak her mind, and he could threaten her grade.

As much as the idea of seeing Booker Gannon naked intrigued her, she had no intention of being forced into a situation like that for her grade.

"You okay?" Banks nudged her knee with his.

"Yeah. I think I'm gonna go, okay?"

He stared at her for a moment and then nodded. "I'll walk you out."

"You don't have to."

"I want to." Arm still around her shoulders, Banks nudged the guy standing next to him. "I'll be right back. Gonna walk Lennox out."

"You're leaving?" The guys called after her. "Buy, Lex."

"See ya guys." She looked back over her shoulder and waved.

She felt Dr. Gannon's gaze on her as she and Banks walked past him, but she didn't look. She didn't flinch. She only led Banks around the bar and outside.

"Shortest first date ever," Banks announced when they were outside.

She laughed softly. "It wasn't a date, date."

"I know." He grinned. "If it was, it would be the shortest relationship ever. For me. First date. First and last kiss. And a breakup."

Lennox winced. "I suck."

"No hard feelings."

"Jeez." She laughed and dropped her head forward to rest on his shoulder.

Banks nodded. "Maybe I should be sorry I couldn't deliver for you."

"It's not you—"

"Oh, God. Not that line. Go home. Be safe."

"I will."

"Text me? When you get home?"

"Okay." She hugged him quickly and then stepped back. They stared at each other for a moment and finally, Banks turned to go back inside. Lennox looked at her phone as she walked to her car. She texted Collins an eye roll emoji.

"Don't you know that's not safe?"

She froze when she heard Dr. Gannon's voice behind her.

"What's not safe?" She turned to look at him. He moved slowly but with a purpose as he approached her. No swagger but at the same time, arrogance painted his features.

"Looking at your phone while you walk to your car in the dark."

"Thanks for your concern," she said quietly. "But I can take care of myself."

"Can you?"

Still walking right toward her.

She took a step back. Light from the bar sign and the street-light on the corner painted the lot, him, in shades of gray. Eyes locked with his, she slammed her mind closed, refusing to think about the dream when he had kissed her.

On a night just like this.

He stepped closer to her. Lennox stepped back and found herself pressed to the side of her car. Dr. Gannon moved again, closer still. Lennox told herself she didn't feel the heat of his body that close to hers. She was imagining it.

He stared at her for a long moment, his green eyes a raging storm and his face carved of stone. Lennox thought of that heat, the heat of his open mouth on hers in her dream.

don'tlookdon'tlookdon'tlook

She dipped her eyes to his lips, thin and bloodless. Imagined him smoothing them over her neck. Opening them, his hot breath on her skin. The nip of his teeth on her neck, under her ear. Lust rippled through her, rendering her boneless.

When she forced herself to drag her eyes from his mouth, she tipped her chin up and warily met his eyes. His intense stare burned through her and left her raw, exposed, like he was reading her mind. Undressing her in his.

He lifted a hand but stilled it when she flinched. Relief and disappointment warred in her belly when he let it drop back to his side. He dragged his gaze over her face, her lips, and down over her shoulders before meeting her eyes again.

Without a word, he turned away from her and walked without a care in the world toward a black SUV.

Lennox collapsed against her car, weak in the knees. Energy, lust, something that felt incredibly good but not remotely enough, slammed through her like a train. Eyes on him as he climbed into the vehicle, she gasped and then panted.

She felt like he had kissed her.

But also, *still* desperate for that touch. The feeling of his hot, wet tongue on hers. That carnal sensation of his body invading hers.

Trembling, she finally managed to straighten and open her car door. But once inside, she locked the doors, turned the key, and sat for a moment. Her heart still fluttered, and her body felt foreign or disconnected, like she couldn't command it to move. Nipples beaded painfully hard, she dropped her head back on the seat and wondered about Dr. Gannon.

Had he assaulted those two girls? Had he simply seduced them? Wasn't there a difference? Or did she just need to believe that, so she didn't feel like a fool?

The black SUV crept through the parking lot past her car. He didn't even look her way.

25

BOOKER

Maybe he would have to quit going to Sidecar.

That made him angry.

But he couldn't keep going there, if he was going to see Lennox Clarke there all the time. Watching her kiss that guy had messed with his brain. When she left the other night, it had been a tossup between following her and going after Banks.

Wasn't like the guy had taken advantage of her. Booker couldn't justify knocking his teeth down his throat with the excuse that he had come onto Lennox, unwanted. Nope. His only reason for considering it was that he was jealous as fuck.

Jealous.

Hot for Lennox.

Which was the biggest part of the problem.

He had nowhere to go with those feelings. Booker had followed her out of the speakeasy the other night fully intending to kiss her. Show her what a man who desired her could make her feel. Thank fuck he had come to his senses.

Then again, if she hadn't flinched when he damned near stroked her lips with his thumb, he would have. He would have kissed her.

All the times he'd watched Sofie and Reese around his wife, all the skin he had seen when the girls were around, all the innuendo—none of it fazed him like being in Lennox Clarke's presence.

Which meant exactly nothing.

He was ten years older than she was. And he was her professor.

Never mind that he had seen her slide her tongue into that guy's mouth. That she was no stranger to sex, since she had a kid. It wasn't like he would be stealing her innocence. And yet, it hadn't been a year since Sofie and Reese accused him of sexual misconduct. Since that video surfaced and talk of assault sprouted up all over campus.

If he sniffed around Lennox Clarke, his ass would be fired from Killdare University, and he would be an unemployed piece of shit.

Never mind that he wasn't. Never mind that he had never touched Sofie or Reese. Never mind that he had loved his fucking wife, and the three of them together had railroaded him out of his job, his house, his life.

He sure as fuck couldn't make that mistake again.

But that left him with nowhere to go. The only place he could ease his tension, his anger, now was the gym. He had gone to the liquor store Sunday and stocked up, so he could drink at home. Alone. And stay out of trouble.

The solitude would drive him fucking crazy within a week, but by God, he would try it.

By Wednesday, he was past thinking about lewd actions with one of his students and ready to throat punch anyone who came within a mile of him. He had sucked down a few cocktails every night this week, and he'd played some instrumental jazz, and he'd watched three ridiculously cheesy movies. By Friday, he would hate the house he was living in.

They had moved on from *Carmilla*; he had introduced the subject of their cultural artifact presentations—finding vampires and references to vampires and lore in everyday life—and started *Dracula*. Discussion flowed freely; Booker was pleased with the class at least. But it was just another reason to stay the hell away from her. The lively debates in the film and culture class were reigniting his passion for teaching, for literature. He had no reason to believe so, but he wanted to play his cards right and hope that he might be offered a permanent position at Killdare University.

After class Wednesday, he headed to his office, a small entourage walking with him, Josh and Rupe leading the charge. Booker used to have students surrounding him all the time at Artas State. He had a good repertoire with them; he related to them, and he genuinely liked the give and take of conversation with college students.

He loved the moment when something clicked for them, but he was just as grateful for the times they taught him something.

Except for Sofie and Reese's lesson. He could have done without that one.

"You ever go out?" Josh asked him as he put his bag on his desk. The office was small, but adding four college guys made it feel like a glorified closet. Booker perched on the edge of his desk and folded his arms over his chest. He had. He'd gone out with students at Artas a few times when he knew they were of age.

Unethical? Maybe. But if pressed, he would have to admit, he had enjoyed those times. Even if it had led to the girls hanging around his wife, around the house.

"No."

"Man, you should go out with us sometime."

Booker eyed Rupe with a frown. "Professors don't go out with students."

Josh arched his eyebrows at him. The look unsettled him. These guys believed he had done things with Sofie and Reese. Hell, who knew? Maybe that was admirable to them. Maybe it made him cool.

Time for a change of subject.

"You guys thinking about your presentations yet?"

"Nope." Rupe leaned against the door frame.

"Get outta my office and get busy." Booker waved them all out the door. They laughed, like they were all buddies, and called goodbyes as they filed out. Booker remained where he was for a moment, listening to the echoes of that laughter in the room.

Remembering the kids he had taught before.

He had genuinely cared for them. And most of them had turned on him, pointed the finger, spread the gossip.

A light tap on his door snapped him out of his memories. Lennox stood in the doorway looking uncertain. Booker straightened slowly and move to stand behind his desk. Maybe he wanted protection from her.

Maybe from himself. Around her.

"I didn't."

"Didn't what?" he asked, doing his best to sound annoyed. Apparently, he failed, as she stepped into his office. She dropped her bag on the loveseat and turned to him like she was ready to square off.

"Sleep with Josh Stone."

Booker winced. He shouldn't have said that to her.

"He tried." She shrugged. "We went out once. And then one night last year, we were studying. Drinking. There were other people around. He copped a feel under the table. I got up because..." She arched her eyebrows helplessly. "Not into him, right? He followed me outside. Thought I was sending him a signal."

"Fuck," he mumbled and sighed. Had Josh forced her? Had he unknowingly stepped in a pile of steaming shit he wanted nothing to do with? "Did he hurt you?"

Her soft laugh was cold with sarcasm.

"No. He stuck his tongue down my throat, and I put my knee in his balls. I think he got the message."

Booker clenched his fists and reminded himself to breathe.

"I just wanted you to know that." She reached for her bag. "Since you asked."

"It was a rhetorical question."

"It was kind of a douchebag question, Dr. Gannon. I'm not sure why you feel the need for all the digs. I show up at class, and I contribute, and my grades are good."

Booker snorted.

"Me? Dig?"

"I said what I said."

"Okay." He nodded. "See you Friday."

He met her eyes and waited her out. When she finally turned to leave, he deflated, relieved to see her go. He planned to follow her out and close and lock his door after her.

But once at the door, she turned to look at him.

"You weren't at Sidecar Monday."

Booker, at the end of his rope, stalked out from behind his desk and grabbed her wrist. She gasped softly when he pulled her back into his office.

"What're you doing?" she whispered.

"What're *you* doing to *me*?" He crowded her, standing close enough to hear the soft panting of her breath. Eyes locked with his, she stared at him with—

Desire.

Fuck.

He knew that look. He knew the struggle painfully well.

Just outside this open office door, students roamed up and down the hall. Conversation and laughter drifted in to them. Anyone could walk in on them. Other students. His colleagues.

And yet he couldn't let her go.

Booker loosened his grip on her arm, satisfied that she wouldn't run out on him. His damned dick throbbed, awareness of her, of her nearness, stealing his breath away. He lifted his hand, startled to realize he was shaking, and cupped her chin.

"This." He smoothed his thumb over her lips, pressing the plump, warm flesh to her teeth. "This. Can't. Happen."

Eyes wide with wonder, Lennox answered with a small shake of her head.

"Ever." He leaned closer. Rested his forehead on hers. "Never."

Lennox finally jerked her chin, but Booker refused to let go. She licked her lips, the tip of her tongue over his thumb pounding through him and straight to his dick. Shocked and ready to mount her like an animal, he dropped his hand and stepped away from her.

He turned his back to her, hoping she hadn't seen the bulge in his pants. Booker drew in a deep breath and held it as he waited to hear her leave.

26

LENNOX

Lennox made it to the restroom down the corridor and ducked inside on trembling legs. The door on the last stall banged open and a tall girl walked out without looking at her. Lennox hung back and watched her wash her hands. When she left the room, Lennox hedged up closer to the sinks, to the mirror.

Her cheeks were flushed, and her eyes were glassy and wide.

Dr. Gannon had touched her. Just her face, but still. He knew she had been thinking about him. But the way he had touched her, the desperate sound of his voice—it made it pretty obvious he felt the same way.

Right?

Lennox looked down at the sink. She leaned sideways and let her backpack slide from her shoulder to the floor. Her heartbeat pounded in her throat, her ears, like a drum. She rested her hands on the edge of the sink and spread her fingers, watched with wonder as they shook.

What the hell was she doing? It wasn't like he had threatened her. She was stumbling into this with her eyes wide open. No idea what her next move should be, what she wanted to happen, she reached for the faucet and turned on the cold water.

She was interested. Of course she was interested. The man was so intense; she longed to feel that intensity directed at her, the way it had been just minutes ago in his office.

But she couldn't. It couldn't happen. Maybe this was part of his game, how he played. Maybe he wanted to push her until she was begging him. Maybe that last little move he pulled was meant to drive her right back into his office, and maybe when she didn't fall for it, he would start docking points.

Nothing else made sense. If Dr. Gannon had been asked to leave the last school where he taught because of inappropriate behavior, if that behavior had led to his divorce, he clearly had no morals. If he had done it once, she doubted he would hesitate to do it again.

She might not be the only one.

Dread, colder than the water she ran over her hands, pulsed through her. Of course she wasn't the *only* one. Would a guy like that, a guy that looked like that, settle for her? Hell no. He probably hit on girls all day long.

And Lennox had been stupid enough to fall for it. *To think he might be into her.*

She turned the water off and gripped the sides of the sink with both hands. Water dripped to the floor as she stared at herself in the mirror again. The churning in her belly was angry now; she was angry with him, but even more so with herself.

"Get it together, Lex." With a deep breath, she took a step back from the sink and reached for her bag. Slinging it over her shoulder, she wiped her hands on her jeans and headed back out to the hallway.

She had to work this afternoon after class. Lennox usually went to her mom's to visit with her and hang out with Eloise since she wouldn't see her until bedtime tonight. But she couldn't do it right now. She was visibly upset, and her mom would pry it out of her. Lennox might have been stupid enough to think for a minute that Booker Gannon was interested in her, but she wasn't so stupid she planned to tell anyone that.

And if Eloise overheard her, she would repeat it, innocently but still. That would be a problem. Lennox would never be able to take her into Crave again, because if they ran into Dr. Gannon again, Eloise would tell him her mom thought he was hot. Without a clue as to what that meant.

She would go to the library and read until her next class. She hated to lie to her mom and Eloise but telling them she had to study was harmless. Lennox hurried down the stairs of the Palmer Building and straight across the lobby to the main doors. Outside, shivering in the cold, she rushed over to the library. Once inside, she stood for a moment just to warm up.

Winter could go away anytime, but unfortunately, they still had the rest of February and March to get through. Both months could deal some nasty weather before spring officially arrived. Even after that date on the calendar. In Midwest Illinois, Lennox had seen snow in spring a time or two.

Finally making her way into the library, she passed the turnstiles and headed for a faraway reading corner. She wanted somewhere quiet, but she also didn't want to be seen. Not by fellow students or Dr. Gannon, should he be here.

Lennox found a cushioned armchair on the far wall and dropped her bag at her feet. She shrugged out of her coat and dropped to sit, relieved to be off her feet, but irritated to find she was still buzzing with...

Adrenaline.

Excitement. Desire.

She was *attracted* to him.

Giving herself a mental shake, she unzipped her bag and pulled her book out. Not a schoolbook. Something she was reading for pleasure.

Pleasure.

Interesting word. She sat back in the chair, book in hand, and thought about the press of Dr. Gannon's thumb on her lips. That touch was more sensual than any other she'd experienced. She wondered about the press of his mouth to hers, his hand somewhere else.

"What're you reading? That for class?"

She sighed as she met Rupe's eyes. Of course someone had found her. She never came to the library at this time of day; she would usually be at her mom's.

"Nope." She turned the paperback over so Rupe could see the cover.

"*Vermillion*?" he asked with a frown. "What's it about?"

"Vampires."

"So it is for class."

"No. It's not."

Rupe shrugged. "Have you started on your presentation yet? For Gannon's class?"

"No."

"When do you do your comm presentation?"

She arched a brow. "End of the month, I think."

He nodded. "Hey. That Wisconsin kid is having a party this weekend. You should come."

"Why would I want to go to that Wisconsin kid's party?"

Lennox liked Rupe; she considered him a friend. But it was hard to sit here and talk to him and pretend she wasn't jittery over what had happened in Dr. Gannon's office. She was still a little short of breath from rushing over here, and she could still feel the tremble in her hands. She hoped Rupe didn't notice.

"It'll be fun." He shrugged. "You haven't been out with any of us since the semester started."

"I have a kid, remember?"

"Yeah, but you went out with us last semester a few times. And last year."

"I'll think about it," she lied with a smile. She had no intention of going to any parties this weekend, but she would do whatever it took to get Rupe to leave her alone.

"Good."

"Hey." Josh appeared behind Rupe. Lennox stifled a groan and tossed her book on the small table to her left. "You guys read that next article yet for Gannon?"

"No." Rupe frowned as if to say *are you kidding me?*

"Bet you did." Josh tipped his head at Lennox. He pissed her off more than not, but most of the time, Lennox tolerated him.

"I did." She nodded and continued when he rolled his eyes, "but I have to work tonight and tomorrow night, so I wanted to get it out of the way."

Something made her jerk her gaze up over Josh's shoulder. Her eyes met Dr. Gannon's as he walked by them. He nodded at the guys, looked back at her, and then at the book she had set aside. But thankfully, he kept walking.

"He's pretty cool," Rupe decided.

"Did you *see* that video?" Josh asked them.

"How'd you see it? I don't even know what school he was at before."

"Somebody I know had it and forwarded it to me."

Lennox flinched and then slid her hands under her thighs so the guys wouldn't notice her cross her fingers, hoping they were oblivious to her feelings. *There was a video? Of Dr. Gannon? With someone?*

Jesus.

Her heart exploded a little bit at the thought of getting a glimpse of him in action. To get a peek at his thighs, his shoulders.

Wow. She was ridiculous. A video of her professor with students was going around, and instead of being disgusted by it, she wanted to *see* it?

"That girl's got some big titties," Josh said with a grin. "You hot for him, Clarke? Not sure he'd be into you."

"No." She lied around the stab of fear and arousal in her belly. "And no."

"Let's get something to eat," Rupe suggested to Josh. "See you in comm?"

Lennox nodded when she glanced at him. She picked up her book as she watched them walk away, a sinking feeling swallowing her lungs and her belly as it slid lower.

A video of Dr. Gannon and girls? How the hell had he gotten this job if that was the case? Thank God Rupe hadn't directed the food suggestion at her. She might have vomited at his feet.

27

BOOKER

He should be happy. That little scene in his office must have scared Lennox Clarke away. If he wondered before if she was stalking him, trying to accidentally bump into him everywhere he went, now he had to assume she was trying to avoid him. Other than class, Booker hadn't seen her in two weeks.

And he had caved and gone back to Sidecar.

Not just for the liquor and the jazz. But because he wanted to see *her*. Even if it meant watching her fuck around with someone else. Booker *needed* to see her. He wanted her to approach him at the bar and brazenly order a drink. To give him that look like she either wanted to tell him to fuck off or fuck her.

Booker wanted to fuck Lennox Clarke, and he wasn't sure what to do about that.

The thought scared the hell out of him.

He had heard his name that day in the library, when he had seen her with Rupe and Josh. Interesting to him to find her tucked away in the library with the guy she claimed to dislike, talking about him. He hadn't stopped to talk, not even to eavesdrop. But he had noticed the book she was reading.

He read it last summer.

More vampires. More violence. More blood and sex.

Booker knew those books were hot right now, but picturing Lennox reading them intrigued him. He even considered rereading it, devouring the carnal scenes and wondering if she was reading the same scenes when he was.

His phone buzzed on the bar in front of him. Assuming it was Randi, he took his time picking it up to look at the text.

Ashley's name on the screen was a surprise.

An unwelcome surprise.

FYI. Going to Montreal next week.

Booker frowned at his phone wondering why she thought he would care. He reached blindly for his glass. Maybe she had sent the text to him mistakenly. Maybe it was for the new boyfriend. Just about to put the phone back down without responding, he saw the dreaded three dots bobbing, indicating she was typing.

He held his breath while he waited. The dots disappeared. And appeared again. And again. Like she was typing and deleting.

Thought you should know, they found that video on some kid's phone the other day.

Booker sucked in a sharp breath. It wasn't like it would ever go away. And no matter that he wasn't *in* the video, that he was *nowhere near the girls* when the video was made, didn't mean a damned thing to anyone.

Someone climbed up on the barstool next to him. Booker smelled her fresh scent and looked up with a severe frown. Lennox met his eyes. He looked back at his phone. Should he ignore Ashley? They hadn't exactly parted amicably. On the other hand, it seemed like she was trying to warn him. Like there was anything he could do about it.

"What do you want?" He dropped his phone on the bar and took a drink. A steady throb started behind his right eye.

"I read your article."

He had wanted her here. And like he had willed it so, here she was. Part of him wanted to drop his hand to her thigh and slide his fingers up to what he knew would be sinful and heavenly. Part of him wanted to chase her off.

"And?" He shrugged, assuming she meant something he had assigned the class.

"Why does her sexuality have to make her weak?"

Jesus. Was she drunk? She was referring to the article he wrote about the Blood Rite *series.*

Booker looked her in the eyes. Hers were bright and clear, the depths of blue almost intoxicating. He didn't smell alcohol on her.

"No, seriously. I want to know why women are always weak. Why do men always assume agency and sexuality makes women weak? Why can men use sex to demonstrate their dominance, but when women do the same, it's a weakness?"

"The author of the *Blood Rite* series is a woman," he reminded her.

"But *you* read it that way."

"Do you disagree with my conclusion?"

She huffed out a frustrated sigh, obviously because she did agree with him.

"I hate how women are treated in literature and film. Either they're depicted as evil, crazy, or weak."

"Did you ever stop to think that's why I'm using the literature I am? That it might be one objective? For you all to walk out of my classroom with the understanding of what film and literature have done to belittle women?"

Lennox lowered her gaze to the bar. The screen of his phone was face up, Ashley's text still visible. But Lennox didn't appear to be looking at it.

"Char," she called. The bartender held a hand up and nodded at Lennox.

"Or do you just assume that I get off on reading and talking about women and sex?"

She snapped her gaze up to meet his eyes.

"That weak women turn me on?"

"Weak women seem to make some guys hot and bothered. A damsel in distress. Women being battered in thrillers—"

Char appeared and slid a drink in front of Lennox.

"Where's your daughter tonight?"

Lennox stared straight ahead as she took a drink.

"What does that mean?"

Booker opened and closed his mouth, unsure what to say.

"Are you suggesting I'm a bad mom?"

"Jesus Christ," he muttered. "You're defensive."

She laughed softly, but she looked anything but amused.

"Eloise is at her grandmother's for the night."

"Your mom or his?"

"His." She huffed out a sigh. "It's her first sleepover with the McArthurs. I was at home, trying to study. And I'm a fucking wreck worrying about her. So rather than climb the walls, I thought I'd come for a drink."

"The girl you're here with sometimes? She your best friend?"

"Mmm." Lennox nodded. "Don't worry. I'm not going to sit here and twist my hands with worry and cry on your shoulder all night."

"I don't think I suggested you would."

"So." She cleared her throat. "How many?'

"How many what?"

"How many girls have you cornered in your office? Like you did with me?"

Booker groaned and scrubbed his hands over his face.

"Fuck."

Maybe he needed to leave academia.

"So, what? This is where you threaten me?" he asked as he dropped his hands to his lap. "What do you want? If I don't...what?" He stared at her, fury building inside him. "You'll go to the dean and tell him I assaulted you. You're already getting an A, Lennox."

When she didn't speak, he tipped his head and shrugged.

"Or are you just one of those girls?"

"What girls?"

"Fuck it." He shook his head and slid off the stool. She watched with wide eyes as he tossed cash on the bar, snatched his phone, and turned to walk away.

28

LENNOX

Lennox set her drink down and caught Char's attention.

"Be right back."

"Sure." The woman nodded and waved her away.

Heart racing, Lennox followed Dr. Gannon past seven tables, two occupied by older couples—no one she knew, thankfully. She'd apparently gone and lost her mind to follow him out of here, to search him out in the first place. No idea what she planned to do when she got out to the parking lot, her body vibrated with nervous energy as she finally pulled the door open.

Not seeing him in the parking lot, panic slammed into her so hard, she took a step backwards. Afraid he was already gone and afraid she would actually *find* him, Lennox walked a few steps into the lot and looked around. She wandered to the sidewalk and looked down the street.

There he was. Standing beside his SUV, hand on the door, looking toward her. Like he was expecting her to follow him. What had he been accusing her of back there in the bar? She had mind fucked herself over Booker Gannon since he had cornered her in his office. Since it hit her that she was looking at him through rose-colored glasses, feeling flattered that he had noticed her, when in fact she was probably one of a dozen.

Since Josh had referenced a video.

Terrified to approach him but unwilling to walk away and go back into Sidecar without whatever confrontation was about to happen, Lennox took a few steps toward him. Shivering more from nerves than the cold, she made her way slowly down the sidewalk until she stood just in front of his SUV. Dr. Gannon dropped his hand from the door and stared at her silently.

She had lost her nerve. Frozen there on the sidewalk, she simply watched him watch her.

When he didn't move, she slid her foot back, ready to turn tail and run.

"I can't do this."

He spoke so quietly, she wondered if she heard him right. If she was making it up in her head. He took a step toward her, still muttering under his breath. Lennox thought she heard the word *game*.

She didn't want to be a game. It wasn't as if she had expectations. If something happened between them, it would be a one and done.

But she didn't want to be a *game* to him.

She swallowed hard, shaking more the closer he came.

"What're you doing to me, Lennox Clarke?" He stopped toe to toe with her, so close she could feel his breath on her face. She wasn't much of a whiskey drinker, but she could smell it on his breath. What would it taste like on his lips? His tongue?

He lifted his hand and cupped her chin again. The way he had done that day in his office. This time, he didn't touch her lips, though. He only studied them intensely. Lennox let her gaze roam over his face, noticing the deep groove between his thick, dark eyebrows. The severe frown didn't click with the idea of her being a game to him. A conquest.

She gasped when he dragged his thumb over her mouth. Gently at first and then with pressure, almost painful. He leaned in close enough that she felt his five o'clock shadow on her face. The warmth of his skin on hers. His mouth at her ear, she heard his unsteady breaths.

"Lennox."

He pressed his cheek to hers, the stubble scratching her, making her belly seize with need. She was wet for him, too desperate for his next move to be embarrassed. He drew back to look her in the eyes; Lennox mewled a protest at the cold air on her cheek in his absence.

Dr. Gannon leaned closer to nuzzle her nose with his. His lips lingered at hers, the nearness of his hot mouth driving her wild with need. Still, he didn't kiss her. Afraid to move, afraid she would break the moment, that he would walk away, she stood still and dared only to breathe.

His fingers slid over her cheek and back into her hair, drawing a shiver up her spine. Eyes still locked with hers, he moved his mouth, as if to kiss her. Need ripped through her belly straight to her core as she mimicked him. Kissing, but not.

Finally, fingers digging gently into her skull, his thumb pressing now into her cheekbone, he brushed his lips over hers and lit a fire in her throat, her lungs. The flames spread quickly, the fire of lust scorching her. Lennox whimpered when he tipped his head back just slightly. He dragged his gaze over her face again, lingering at her mouth.

Another almost-kiss nearly brought her to her knees, but he rested his free hand on her waist and slowly pressed his mouth to hers. His lips were soft and warm. Lennox lifted her hands, not to touch him, but to hold on, afraid she would break if he demanded more. More afraid she would break if he didn't.

She parted her lips at the gentle stroke of his tongue and felt the heat of that touch wrap around her and slide over her shoulders, her belly, her hips. The whiskey on his tongue when he stroked hers was decadent and intoxicating. Lennox fisted her hands on his arms, gathering his wool coat in her fingers. Damning it for being in her way. She wanted to feel the hard muscle under his shirtsleeves.

The heat of his skin.

His mouth devoured hers in a slow, deep kiss. Lennox, uncertain what it meant, what happened next, kissed him back boldly and swept her tongue inside his mouth, desperate to sample every bit of him.

When he broke the kiss, he rested his forehead against hers and closed his eyes. Panting, neither of them could speak. Lennox had no idea what she would say if she could.

"Goodnight, Lennox."

With his hand still cupping the back of her head, Dr. Gannon brushed his lips over her cheek and stepped back. Cold air rushed in to fill the emptiness he left as he walked back to the driver's side of the SUV and pulled the door open.

Her body still vibrated with pleasure and desire as she stood and watched him climb into the vehicle and drive away. She watched his taillights all the way down the street until he turned, and the SUV was out of sight.

"Jesus." She hissed, reminding herself to move. To look around. Raising a hand to her lips— to remember his touch, to hold that memory there or to touch herself because his lips had been there, she didn't know—she turned to look the other way down the street. There was no one around; she was on fire out here alone, desperate for him to come back and finish what he had started.

A vicious shiver wracked her body. She couldn't go back inside. Not now. She would just have to text Char and let her know she had to leave. Banks would cover the drink; she would pay him back. That wouldn't be a problem.

Class next Monday would be a problem.

29

BOOKER

Since his gym wasn't a twenty-four-hour fitness place, Booker had nowhere to go with himself. His body was jammed with emotion—rage at himself, rage at Sofie and Reese, at Ashley. At Lennox. Grief for the life he had lost. His marriage. His hope for children with Ashley. His plans to grow old with Ashley. His professional reputation. Even the people who had supported him—all four of them and *three* were *family* and probably felt like they had to—had to see him differently now. Even if they didn't believe he had sexually preyed on Sofie and Reese and God knew how many other girls had decided to get involved in story time, they had to assume something had happened. Something he had said or done had led to Sofie and Reese targeting him.

Guilty until proven innocent, he supposed. And forever scarred.

If he was being honest with himself, he would have to admit it was more than rage. More than a need to find some peace of mind, some sort of future that didn't involve the hate that filled him now. He wanted Lennox Clarke.

Like he'd never wanted anyone.

Booker had loved Ashley. Loved. Her. Desired her. Cared for her. All the above.

But he hadn't been on a six month fast from women, from sex, when he and Ashley met. And right now, he was beginning to wake up and remember what it felt like to want. To need. To need to *feel human contact.* To need to bury himself balls deep in a hot woman and feel her nails dig into his back. He wanted the heat, the burn, the pain.

The release.

With Lennox Clarke.

And she was so fucking off-limits, he had no business thinking about her. He shouldn't have gone back to Sidecar, because he knew there would be a possibility he would see her again. He shouldn't have engaged with her tonight. He shouldn't have put his fucking hands on her. Definitely shouldn't have kissed her.

Because now the phantom-like feeling of her soft, silken hair on the back of his hand drove him crazy. Because the taste of her on his lips, on his tongue, only reminded him how starved he was for more. The sound of her whimpers, the desperation in her kiss when she kissed him back—and *fuck, yes, she kissed him back*—told him exactly what she thought about while he lectured about lust and sexuality, and she stared at him with those stormy eyes.

He needed to move. He needed to pound the fuck out of something. And if it couldn't be Lennox's pussy, he needed to pound the fuck out of a punching bag. He didn't have one. He didn't have a damned piece of workout equipment in the rental house. The gym was closed until seven tomorrow morning. He could go out for a run, but he wasn't sure that would fix what he was feeling.

Why had fate put Lennox Clarke in his path? Why now? If he'd met Lennox last year, before the shit hit the fan, before he and Ashley split up, she wouldn't have affected him. Booker had never considered cheating on Ashley. Nothing would have made him cheat.

Maybe now it didn't matter. He was single. Unattached. Why couldn't he just say fuck it and take Lennox to bed and be the monster the dean at Artas State insinuated he was? Why not give in and make every fucking rumor out there true?

Booker laughed out loud, the sound ringing bitter in his cold, empty kitchen. He grabbed the bottle of bourbon he'd picked up at the market the other day, twisted the cap off, and took a long swig straight from the bottle. It wasn't him. Drinking hard liquor straight from the bottle. He had never been that guy.

Maybe it was time to turn over a new leaf.

Kicking off his shoes there by the island counter, he carried the bottle to the living room. If the kitchen was cold, the living room was dark and almost dank looking. Booker set the bottle on the Midcentury Modern style coffee table— the house was a hodge-podge of styles that would delight his mom and sister—and leaned over to turn on the hurri-cane lamp on the end table.

He could do without that. The lamp reminded him of one his ancient piano teacher had in the foyer of her house, where he would have to wait until she finished the lesson before his. While he liked the piano, he hadn't liked the old bat or the lessons at all. Ironically, Ashley had found a smaller hurricane lamp at an estate sale and brought it home to put in their living room.

With a sigh, Booker flopped down on the sofa and rested his elbows on his knees. He tipped his head down and rubbed his neck.

He couldn't do it. He *wasn't* the asshole, lecherous, old man people thought he was, and even having that reputation couldn't make him be that person. Lennox was his student. He shouldn't be talking to her. He sure as fuck shouldn't have kissed her tonight. But she had been all-in outside of Sidecar. If he had suggested she come home with him, she would be here now, and he would have her upstairs in his bed making up for lost time.

But what if she thought there would be something more? What if when Booker ignored her on Monday in class, she decided to fuck with him? To hurt him. Would she do that? As much as she seemed to dislike, *fear,* her daughter's father and his family, would she do anything to draw that kind of attention to herself?

Booker lifted his head and reached for the bourbon. He took another long pull, cringed as he swallowed, and put the bottle back down. He stared for a moment at his laptop there on the coffee table and finally leaned forward to pick it up. Dropping back against the couch, he propped his feet on the table and crossed them, careful not to knock the bottle over. Never mind the mess, he might need the juice to get through the night. He opened his laptop and typed punching bag into the search bar. Fuck it. He would find a place to put a bit of exercise equipment here so he could do something constructive with this angry energy until he worked Lennox Clarke out of his blood.

30

Lennox

He looked like hell.

Small comfort.

Lennox had climbed the steps of the lecture hall without a backward glance. But once she was settled in her place, backpack on the floor, and laptop out, she gobbled him up. Booker Gannon looked like hell. The skin under his eyes was dark with bruises that suggested he hadn't slept any better the last few nights than she had. The normal five o'clock shadow had grown to a rough scruff. She assumed it was unkempt for him, but she liked it. His wavy hair was mussed at eight in the morning, like he had already been dragging his fingers through it. And the top button of his dress shirt was open, his tie loose and crooked.

Like he'd had a long day.

Already.

She watched him pick up his travel mug and take a drink. As if he could feel her heavy stare, he lifted his gaze and met her eyes. His face was stone as he dragged his eyes over her and continued on to look at Josh, who beat her to the room today.

What the hell?

He was just going to blow her off? After that desperately fierce, greedy kiss Friday night, he was going to ignore her. Pretend it didn't happen. It wasn't like she expected him to run to her the second she stepped into the lecture hall and throw his arms around her. She didn't even expect him to say hi. But a smile, maybe a nod, would have been nice.

"What'd you do this weekend, Stone?"

Josh kicked his feet out under the table and sank back into his chair.

"Kegger at Keale House."

"And you don't look as hungover as I feel," Dr. Gannon muttered.

Lennox rested her elbow on the table and propped her chin in her hand. Was he hungover? Had he been out partying? Had he gone back to Sidecar? She sure as hell hadn't gone back the rest of the weekend. She wasn't sure she was ready to run into him again. And she hadn't wanted to see Banks. Not after the way Gannon had kissed her.

She wondered if he had gone home alone Saturday night.

Or was he hungover because he was drinking alone? For a different reason? Maybe to forget something?

Josh's laugh was like fingernails on a chalkboard, but Lennox refused to react.

"Well. You're not a frat guy anymore, Dr. Gannon," Josh reminded him. Lennox closed her eyes for a moment at the thought of Booker Gannon as a student, in a fraternity. He had probably slept with every girl who crossed his path. Granted, she had been to a few parties, both before and after Eloise. And she hadn't been Little Miss Innocent since she was fifteen or sixteen.

But she still felt sick thinking about who he might have been with.

And yet, here she was. Pining for him already. Wanting to *be* one of those girls. Which was ridiculous. She wasn't sexy. She hadn't worn a bikini since she got pregnant. She didn't have matching lingerie sets. She didn't sleep naked. Her pjs were flannel or fleece with silly patterns like coffee cups or bumble bees. She didn't wear a ton of makeup. She couldn't afford manicures.

And even though she obviously knew how to have sex, she wasn't a sex kitten who would ever bring Booker Gannon to his knees.

She still wanted him. She wanted to be all of those things to him.

"Good thing," Dr. Gannon said with a laugh. "Those kinds of parties would kill me now."

Lennox opened her eyes. Gannon had turned his back to them. He was setting his laptop up for his presentation. She looked her fill, drinking in the way his trousers hugged his slender butt and thighs. His suit coat was slung over the desk, like he had yanked it off and thrown it there when he came in. Once his introductory slide was up on the screen —they were starting *Dracula* today, and apparently, they would be discussing Bram Stoker first—he slipped around the desk and reached for his mug again.

"What'd you do this weekend, Lennox?"

A tidal wave of hurt and irritation nearly drowned her, but she stared at him calmly.

"Nothing exciting." She wasn't sure how she managed, but she kept all inflection out of her voice. Hopefully, he would think she hadn't been into that kiss. Maybe he hadn't realized she had been ready to shuck her clothes and offer herself to him right there on the sidewalk.

Right, Lennox. Because you're so suave, and Dr. Gannon's naïve.

He held her stare for a long moment, only looking away when the door opened, and a bunch of her classmates entered the room.

"Dr. Smythe was at Keale House," Josh announced. Rupe slid into his seat with a laugh. Lennox assumed he had been at the party, too. Kara twisted in her seat to look at Rupe, but she looked past him and rolled her eyes at Lennox. "You need to come out next time."

"Oh, man." Rupe laughed. "He was hammered."

"You were hammered," Josh told Rupe. "Smythe goes out with us all the time."

Lennox didn't know Dr. Smythe. She wondered if Dr. Gannon did. He simply stood at the podium, mug in hand, watching everyone settle in. How did Dr. Smythe get to party at a frat house and not end up in hot water? But Dr. Gannon—

Wait.

Was she *defending* him? She didn't know if the rumors were true or not, but based on what happened last Friday night, it seemed plausible that Dr. Gannon had slept with his students. Feeling stupid yet again—she was attracted to him, but that didn't give her any reason to think he *wasn't* an arrogant prick who played games with coed students— she swallowed hard and reminded herself she had to be careful, too.

As Collins reminded her often, she was a good mom. She knew that. No one could love Eloise more than she did. But Eve McArthur watched her closely, just waiting for her to fail so she could swoop in and steal Eloise one way or another.

"Has anyone read *Dracula*?" Dr. Gannon put his mug down. "Not like last night. But before this class?"

She would leave immediately after class. No stopping to chit chat about anything. Because she was pissed. And hurt. And damned if she was going to let him see that.

31

BOOKER

After drinking himself into a stupor Friday night and again Saturday night and struggling to drag his ass out of bed Sunday, struggling to peel his tongue from the roof of his mouth, and wishing he could turn the sun off or at least down, Booker had gone to the gym Sunday. And worked out until he had to stumble into the men's room and puke.

Only to splash water on his face, rinse his mouth out, and go right back out after it again. Treadmill. Weights. Punching bag. He had ordered one the other night. Ordered other shit, too, apparently, after drinking too much. An email had informed him that the dog harness, twelve pack of toothpaste, and six copies of *Vermillion* that he had ordered would be delivered Thursday.

Seeing Lennox Monday in class had been harder than he thought it would be. She hadn't done a damned thing to make herself more noticeable. Dressed in skinny jeans and a flannel over a Drake t-shirt, she'd had one side of her hair tucked back behind her ear. Booker had counted four tiny diamonds in her ear, two in the lobe and two in the shell.

She hadn't tried to avoid looking at him, though. And that had unnerved him. She'd stared at him so fiercely, he felt chastised. Like a junior high kid caught with his hands in a girl's pants. And then that absolute bored flat tone when she told him she hadn't done anything exciting over the weekend. She could have said she'd gone out Friday. She could have said she'd had fun. Josh wouldn't have read a damned thing into that.

Spooked about what she might do now that he had crossed the line, knowing he already had a strike against him because of that damned video, Booker had gone to the gym Monday after class and stayed too long.

He went back Tuesday.

Wednesday.

He was sick of gym rats. And sweat. And the smell of rubber equipment. Hip hop and trance music. He wanted cold beer and wings. A night with friends, with the guys. His friends had either slipped away or outright sided with Ashley. There were two or three left, but they lived in Artas, not Killdare Springs. And he hadn't met anyone in Killdare other than his students and that Banks guy.

Not like he was going to suggest a guys' night with a dude that had his tongue down Lennox's throat not too long ago. He'd been wrapped up in thoughts about that— comparing the way she had kissed that guy to the way she had kissed him outside Sidecar—when Josh and Rupe stuck their heads into his office and told him they were going bowling.

And asked him to go. Before he could beg off, they told him Tito's—the local bowling alley—had the coldest beer in town and damned good bar food. Instead of a flat out no, he told them he'd think about it.

He did. He was still thinking about it. In the parking lot, in the driver's seat of his SUV, outside Tito's. Wasn't like there was any harm in going in there. He didn't plan to buy anyone alcohol. Neither Josh or Rupe was attracted to him and vice versa. Wouldn't be any girls with them.

Fuck it.

He got out of the SUV, closed the door, and beeped the lock. He would go in and have a beer or two. Maybe a burger. And then go home. Surely that didn't constitute sexual misconduct. How in the hell did Adam Smythe party all the time at a frat house and not get banished from the campus?

Booker took his phone from his pocket and shot Randi a text as he crossed the lot to the door. She had mentioned finding time to come and visit him. Booker wasn't sure how he felt about that. He wasn't in the right frame of mind for company, but he hated the way things were with his sister right now.

Going bowling.

He tugged the door open and shrank back as a wall of heat hit him. Stepping inside, he unzipped his coat and looked around. The music playing was 80s. It was a nice change from what he'd been hearing at the gym. The bowling alley was relatively small—only twenty lanes. Looked like only seven or eight were occupied. The place looked ancient. The orange and white seats by the lanes were chipped and stained. No computers for scoring. Just a little table to sit at while tallying each ball and keeping score.

"Dr. Gannon." Josh gave him a nod as he approached him and Rupe. Not bowling, they were at the bar, apparently devouring a plate of wings. His stomach growled.

How far he'd fallen. Josh's greeting had sent a little jolt of happiness through him. It had been so long since anyone had been happy to see him. Anywhere. Other than Christmas. And that didn't count, because it was his family. And not even because they were family, but because his parents were giving, compassionate people, and they *might* be courteous or forgiving to Satan if they met him.

"Hey, man." Rupe slid backwards off the cracked black vinyl stool and reached to shake his hand. "Whaddaya want?"

Booker shook his head and pulled his wallet from his pocket. "You're not buying my beer."

"Have some wings." Josh shoved the basket at him. "If I eat more, I'm gonna die."

A silver-haired man approached from behind the bar and asked what he could get him. Wondering if he was Tito, Booker asked for a beer as Rupe returned to his stool.

"What do you do here, man? D'you know people? Didn't you just move here last summer?"

Technically, he hadn't *moved* moved here. Not permanently. But he didn't want to get into that.

"Go to the gym. Sidecar."

"Sidecar," Josh repeated with a look at Rupe. "That the place Lennox goes? With her friend Collins?"

Rupe nodded. Booker bit his tongue.

"You seen her friend Collins?" Josh asked him.

The old man slid the bottled beer over the bar to him. Booker nodded his thanks and handed him cash.

"I have."

"She's hot."

Rupe snorted. "Josh, she's like fifteen years older than you."

"Still hot." Josh shrugged. "Lennox and her are together all the time."

"She's got a kid," Rupe reminded him.

Before Josh could say more that Booker didn't want to hear, he looked around. "Thought you guys were bowling."

"We are." Rupe nodded. "Had to eat first. Thursdays is half-price appetizers."

"Gotcha." Booker helped himself to a wing and sank his teeth into the meat. The tangy hot sauce was music to his ears.

"Did you ask Kara if she was coming?" Josh nudged Rupe, bottle in hand.

Booker watched the exchange curiously. If Kara showed up, he would head out. But he had to admit, it was good to get out of the house and not go to the gym or campus.

"Yeah. She said she had to finish an accounting assignment first."

Blue-haired Kara was studying accounting?

Booker tipped his bottle up to keep from expressing his surprise.

"Gonna wash my hands," Josh announced as he stood and walked away.

"What do you think?"

"Of what?" Booker shook his head, uncertain if Rupe was talking about Josh, the bowling alley, or the Quiet Riot song playing.

"Kara."

Damned near choking on his beer, Booker lowered the bottle and blinked at Rupe.

"What?"

Rupe shrugged and looked away.

"Oh. You got a thing for her."

"Kind of." Rupe nodded.

Booker liked her. She was cute. Smart. And she participated in class discussion, which Booker thought made her interesting. And yet, he wouldn't say a word of that out loud. "Ask her out."

Rupe shrugged again, but he scrambled to his feet again just a few seconds later. Booker looked over his shoulder to see the object of Rupe's crush walk in. After a quick look around, she saw them and flashed them a big smile.

Yep. One beer, and he was out of here.

"Hey." She hugged Rupe as only college kids, specifically

college girls, did and then grinned at Booker. "Josh didn't think you would show."

"Came for one beer."

"Fun. You're not gonna bowl?" She frowned.

"I'd blow you all out of the water."

She snorted. "You probably would. Although, I have a beautiful gutter ball."

Rupe laughed.

"I asked Lennox to come." Kara shrugged out of her coat and tossed it on Josh's stool. Booker hoped he didn't visibly flinch, but he sure as hell felt it. "She had to work."

"Where does she work?" he asked before he could stop himself.

"The Garage."

"What's that?" He directed his question at Kara as Rupe ordered her a beer. Booker didn't know if she was of age. Yet another reason to get the hell out of there.

"Dive bar," Kara answered. "She waitresses. Tends bar in a pinch. Makes good tip money."

"She works a dive bar, and she's got a kid at home?"

He was showing too much interest.

"And she's a full-time student?"

"Yeah. She doesn't work a lot of late shifts. Every now and then she will. But her boss is hot for her, so he gives her the best hours."

Booker swallowed a mouthful of bitter beer. His phone buzzed. He pulled it from his pocket, grateful for an excuse to look away from Kara.

Good for you. Watch out for the gutter.

Too late for that, Randi, he thought as he downed the last of his beer. He couldn't run out just yet. That would look weird.

"C'mon, Dr. Gannon. Bowl with us." Kara nodded at the lanes behind them.

32

LENNOX

"I think he threw six strikes in a row," Kara announced with wide eyes.

"And Kara threw six gutter balls in a row," Josh teased. Kara, seated beside Josh on the loveseat by the fireplace, stuck her tongue out at him.

Lennox sat on the hearth, the heat on her back like her coat was in flames. She had been cold just minutes ago when she had come into Crave to grab a quick coffee before class. Kara and Josh had waved her over, both rattling about their bowling night. Lennox had hated to miss it; she hadn't gone out with her friends for fun for a while. Now that she knew Dr. Gannon had been with them, she was a little bit sick with envy.

"Sounds fun." She yawned and stood. "I'm gonna go on over to Palmer."

"Suck up." Josh ducked when Lennox swatted at him.

She slung her backpack over her shoulder and offered Kara a smile.

"I get it." Kara nodded. "He's easy on the eyes."

"Gannon?" Josh snorted. "Seriously? You're hot for him?"

"Josh." Kara sat forward and drilled her finger into Josh's chest. "Just because I think someone might be easy on the eyes, doesn't mean I have to be hot for him."

Lennox laughed and smacked Kara's hand in a high five as she walked by the two of them. Josh said something else, but Lennox headed across the coffeehouse to the door. She was pissed. She had been miserable since that night Dr. Gannon kissed her. A week ago tonight. And he was out partying it up with her friends now. Had kissing her been like trying on jeans? She didn't fit him just right, so he was moving on to the next pair?

She stalked up the steps at Palmer Building, slowing as she neared the third floor. The anger now buzzed like bees, her belly churning with nerves. She took a deep breath and sipped her coffee again. Probably not a good thing. She was shaking already. No breakfast. Too much caffeine. And nerves and yearning and hurt all mixed in there, too. At the landing, she stood for a moment to pull herself together. She couldn't go charging into the lecture hall, fueled with anger and jealousy. She would look stupid. Immature.

She was *being* immature. Jesus, what would she do if she had slept with him only to be relegated to nothing special the following Monday?

And if she saw that, saw her own behavior, damned right Dr. Gannon would see it, too.

And if he saw it, he wouldn't ever be interested in taking that kiss any further.

"Jesus." She sighed and shook her head. Counted to three. And pulled the door open to find the carpeted corridor empty. Good. A few more minutes by herself to get her rapid pulse under control.

That thought brought vampires to mind. She hadn't had time to finish reading last night. Well, she'd fallen asleep with her face in her book. And woke up with Eloise beside her in bed.

She took another deep breath and then forced herself to step inside the lecture hall. Dr. Gannon was sitting on his desk. The rest of the room was empty. Naturally.

"Heard you had to work last night."

"I did." She nodded as she put her cup on her table and let her backpack slide to the floor.

"Heard your boss is hot for you."

She snorted and ended up laughing out loud. "I suppose he is. He's also old enough to be my grandpa."

She slumped into her seat and stared at him. Dr. Gannon simply stared back. She sipped her coffee, assuming he was thinking about asking her if she had slept with him. After all, he had asked about Josh. And he had asked her about kissing Banks.

"Wouldn't stop some guys."

"I know that." She nodded.

Dr. Gannon wrapped his hands around the edge of his desk. "How's your daughter?"

"She's good. Keeps asking me when she can go to Crave to see Dr. Book again."

His laugh sounded tender and genuine. Lennox tipped her chin down and rubbed her fingers over her forehead. Stupid, stupid, stupid, she reminded herself. He wasn't a tender man. And he sure as hell wasn't genuine.

"When can she come and see me again?"

Lennox jerked back as if he had swung at her.

Dr. Gannon hung his head and grumbled something. When he looked up at her again, he seemed upset.

"Sidecar. Tonight."

Stunned by his command, she froze for a moment. Before she could respond, three people trailed through the door. Dr. Gannon stood and paced to the window. He propped a shoulder on the wall and stared absently, like he was a million miles away. Lennox ignored her fellow students as they filed in, and kept her eyes on Dr. Gannon. On the gray trousers and black button-down shirt he wore. His face. He'd shaved, to her disappointment. She liked the five o'clock shadow, the scruff, more than his baby face.

While she was lost in thoughts of what that stubble, that scruff, would feel like on her neck, her breasts, Booker turned and caught her staring at him. Rather than look away, he held the eye contact as he moseyed back to the podium. Lennox crossed her legs, desperate to ease the ache at her core. Dr. Gannon dragged his gaze down past the table that hid her waist from him. But when he saw her feet, one higher than the other, he arched a brow and jerked his gaze back to her face and looked her in the eyes again.

33

LENNOX

"What are you doing?"

Lennox, white knuckling the closet door, glanced to her bedroom door when she heard Collins. Eloise must have let her in; Lennox had been staring into her closet for what felt like two decades, trying to decide what to wear. She looked back at the closet without answering, figuring that was Collins' greeting since it was obvious what she was doing.

"Eloise says she's going to Grandma's."

"Yeah." Lennox cleared her throat and rubbed her free hand on her leggings. She was sweating. She'd been nervous since Dr. Gannon had said those two words to her. Directly to her. Before anyone else was in the lecture hall with them.

Sidecar. Tonight.

"Like, your mom's? Or Eve's?"

"Mom's."

"Okay." Collins nodded. "Because you're going...where?"

"Out."

"Gathered that." Collins leaned on the wall by the closet as Lennox reached for a black blouse. She eyed it for a second and then dropped her head back and groaned. "But I have a date, so I know you're not going anywhere with me."

"You have a date?" Lennox flashed her friend an excited grin. "With whom?"

"Some guy I met through work," Collins answered. "Name's Jeff. I'll tell you more after the date."

Lennox chuckled at her friend's policy. Collins didn't talk about dates until after the fact. So she wouldn't jinx them, or so she said.

"Who are you going out with? I know it's not Banks. Because he works tonight."

"I'm not going out with anyone in particular."

"Lex." Collins sighed and shook her head. "You're going to Sidecar hoping to see Dr. Gannon."

Lennox looked at her friend but said nothing. She reached into the closet again and fingered the same black blouse.

"Aren't you?"

"Sort of." She nodded.

"What does that mean?"

"He told me he would be there," Lennox hedged. She couldn't tell Collins that Dr. Gannon had ordered her to be there. The words were delivered like an ultimatum, but Collins didn't know he had kissed her. That secret had been burning holes in Lennox all damned week. She was dying to tell someone. But she couldn't tell Kara. Not since she was at Killdare with her, since she was in Dr. Gannon's class. She couldn't tell Collins, because her friend would give her the same damned lecture her mother would.

"He asked you out?"

Lennox cleared her throat again and laughed to herself. *Collins thought* that *would be bad?*

"No." Not technically a lie.

Collins straightened and looked out the bedroom doorway. Checking on Eloise. Lennox braced herself as her dark-haired friend turned back to her and launched into mom mode.

"Spill it."

Lennox swallowed hard. "If I spill it, will you help me pick out something to wear?"

"Lex, you know what he is."

"*I don't know*, Collins. I've heard rumors."

"That must be true if he's hitting on you."

"He's not hitting on me." Lennox dropped her hand to her side and slinked over to her bed. She perched on the end and leaned back to rest on her hands.

"So, you're meeting him at Sidecar to talk about literature?"

"I'm twenty-four years old," Lennox reminded her. "I'm independent. I'm not in a situation where he can hurt me."

"What does that even mean?" Collins threw her hands up.

"Shh!" Lennox frowned and looked over her friend's shoulder as she stepped away from the door to sit down by her.

"I have a good GPA, Collins. I get good grades. He can't hold that over me."

"Maybe, maybe not." Collins shrugged. "But that doesn't mean he can't hurt you."

Lennox sat forward and leaned into her.

"How's he gonna hurt me?"

"You're already defending him." Collins gave her the side eye.

"And what? You think that means I'm gonna—? What? Fall for him?"

"That's exactly what I think. Use your head, Lex. This has all the makings of a thriller movie. Tall, dark, and hand-some visiting professor. Suddenly single with a cloud of doubt that follows him everywhere. Sweet, innocent, pretty girl who hasn't hooked up in at least two years, if not longer. He's gonna use you—"

Lennox took a deep breath. "I don't even know where to start."

"Take your time. Maybe he'll be gone by the time you get ready and—"

"I'm not innocent."

"Lennox—"

"I have a child, Collins—"

"You have a child, yes," Collins agreed. "You're not a virgin. But you're innocent up against someone like Booker Gannon."

"So, you're not worried about who he is. You're worried I'm gonna fall for him and stalk him when he tells me he's never gonna have feelings for me."

"Well, there's that." Collins nodded. "Also, we don't know if any of those rumors are true."

"Pretty sure he's not a vampire."

"He was *accused* of assault. At the very least, he's probably guilty of sexual misconduct."

"There's no proof—"

"Lennox!" Collins snapped. "Use your head! What if he gets you alone and suggests you blow him? What if you say no, and next week, suddenly, your grade tanks? What if you're alone with him, and you change your mind, and he rapes you?"

Lennox stood and paced her bedroom, taking a quick glance out the doorway to see Eloise still on the living room floor surrounded by toys.

"What about those other girls? What about his *wife*?"

Lennox cleared her throat and shook her head.

"What aren't you telling me?" Collins stood. "Have you already slept with him?"

"No." Lennox sighed. "No. But he kissed me. Last weekend."

Collins opened her mouth to reply but closed it without a word. Lennox knew her well enough to know she was hurt that Lennox had kept it from her.

"I don't even know where to start." Collins arched her brows as she tossed Lennox's words back at her.

"I didn't tell you, because I knew I would get a lecture."

"With good reason."

"Maybe." Lennox licked her lips. "Look. He told me one day last week...that it can't...that it can't happen."

"What can't happen?"

"The two of us together."

"Did you suggest it should?"

"No!" Lennox yelped. "That's what I'm saying. It feels like there's something there, Collins. And he acknowledged it. He feels it, too."

"Of course he does." Collins tipped her head. "He's a predator. And he wants you. And he will play whatever role necessary to get you in his bed. Where he'll chew you up and spit you out. Just like he's done with who knows how many other girls."

Lennox pressed her lips together, eyes on the floor at her feet.

"Can you *really* sleep with him? If there's even a chance that he did it? That he talked two girls into bed with him and—"

"I didn't say that." Lennox shook her head. "I didn't say I was going to sleep with him. I said I was going to Sidecar."

"I don't want you to go." Collins shrugged. "Stay home. Let your mom take Eloise. I'll cancel my date. We can—"

"I'm going to Sidecar," Lennox interrupted her. "Please trust me, Collins. Have you ever known me to do something stupid?"

"What about the McArthurs?"

"I'm not doing anything wrong going to Sidecar to get a drink."

Collins lifted both hands and dragged her fingers back through her hair. "At least if you were dating Banks, I would never have to worry about him hurting you."

"No, but imagine if I shared details about having sex with him. How big—"

"Lennox."

"His heart is," Lennox said with a small smile. "How giving he is."

Collins chewed on her lip and rolled her eyes.

"Besides, I don't want you to cancel your date. Go and have fun."

Lennox watched her friend turn her attention to the closet.

"I'm gonna give you the benefit of the doubt. I don't trust that man as far as I can throw him."

"Such a dumb saying."

"Don't distract me." Collins frowned. "Maybe you know him better than I do. And you're right. You have good judgment. Monty McArthur notwithstanding. And at least you got that beautiful kid out there out of *that*."

Lennox nodded agreement even though Collins wasn't looking at her.

"I wanna know everything." Collins turned now and paralyzed her with an intense stare. "*Everything.* Tomorrow. If you have a drink and talk about *Dracula* or Edward from *Twilight* until dawn, I want to know. If you hash through the rumors about him and walk away, I want to know. If he threatens you, I want to know. If you sleep with him, I want to know."

"Why?"

"So you have an army if shit gets real."

"An army of one."

Collins shrugged.

"Fine."

"Wear jeans. And this." Collins pulled a gray cashmere sweater from a shelf in the closet. "Stay who you are. You don't change a damned thing for him. Got it? And if you get yourself in a situation where you need help, you call me. Or you call Banks. Got it?"

"Jesus, Collins, I've been around him for weeks now. He's not going to—"

"No arguments."

"Of course." Lennox shrugged.

She watched Collins head back out to the living room to talk to Eloise. After a lecture like that, after the reminders that Booker Gannon could be dangerous, Lennox was certain Collins didn't need to worry about anything. She'd banked the flames in her and turned the heat down so low, Lennox wasn't sure she would be warm in the sweater Collins had picked out for her.

34

BOOKER

Booker picked at the broken corner of his phone case, eyes on the door across the room. Every now and then, he remembered he shouldn't be watching the door. Because if Lennox showed up, he would visibly deflate with relief, and if anyone was watching him, it would be obvious he had been waiting for her. No need to advertise that he was watching that door with bated breath, wondering if she would come. That he was giddy with relief if and when she did show up.

He'd only been sitting at the bar for a half hour, but it felt like hours. The whole damned day had dragged on and on. At school, in the classroom and his office, he had closed that door of thought and shoved Lennox out of his head. Doing this—playing this back-and-forth game with her— was completely against the rules and so dumb of him, he wished he had someone here to talk him out of this. There was no one. If Randi were here, she would ride his ass about it until he came to his senses. But she wasn't, and Booker wasn't about to get into this with her over the phone. So the best he could do was at least close Lennox Clarke out of his head while he was on campus and focus on the job.

When he got home earlier this afternoon, he had given in. Let himself wonder if she would come. What she thought about his demand that she meet him at Sidecar. If she had told anyone—he had to hope not, but he assumed she did. He went over what to say to her once they were sitting side by side or face to face. Well, he tried. But he was blank. He had no idea what to say. He needed to tell her, again, that *nothing* could happen between them.

But Booker wanted to feel the warmth of her skin, her cheek, against his. He wanted to taste her lips again, because there was no way she tasted as good as he remembered. He was hungry for that little mewling sound she made in her throat, for the grip of her fingers on his shoulders.

Hours later, sitting at the bar, he still hadn't figured a damned thing out.

He wished her friend Banks wasn't working tonight. No matter the direction tonight took, no matter what they discussed, doing so under Banks' watchful stare would be uncomfortable. Aware that he had been watching the door again, he dipped his head and flipped his phone over to look at the screen. Unfortunately, there were no text messages to occupy his brain for a few minutes. No voicemails. Sure, he had emails he could look at, but he would rather not get dragged into actual work while he was sitting here, wishing for things he couldn't have.

"Playing *Minecraft*?"

Her voice was a cool breeze on a balmy night. Though she surprised him—she must have slipped in the second he looked at his phone—he didn't give any indication of it.

"What's *Minecraft?*"

"Seriously? It's a video—"

"I know what it is," he interrupted her with a glance.

She rolled her eyes as she eased onto the barstool next to him. Since he wasn't sure what tonight was about, he knew Lennox had no idea what to expect. Or that she might expect that they would pick up where that kiss left off last weekend. It had occurred to him she might show up dressed to the nines, like this was a date. Like she wanted to impress him.

He needn't have worried. Lennox looked like Lennox—a dark gray sweater with simple jeans. Her cheeks were flushed, but Booker assumed it was from the cold outside. Her lashes were long and thick, but from what he could tell, she wasn't wearing eye shadow. Her plump lips were a natural shade of pink.

Never mind that she could show up in overalls or a burlap bag and Booker wouldn't be able to look away.

He watched her flash Banks a smile. Booker wondered now what Lennox had done after that kiss last Friday. Had she come back into the bar? Talked to the bartender? Had another drink?

She asked for a drink. Booker caught himself before he told Banks to put it on his tab. That wouldn't look good, no matter what came of tonight.

"What're you drinking?" she asked him when they were alone at the bar again.

He tipped his glass to peer into it. It was his first pour; he was milking it because he needed a clear head.

"Bourbon." He looked at her, barely holding down the shiver that wracked him when their eyes met. Hers held a hint of challenge, like she was here for whatever game he had initiated, and she wasn't about to give in and lose, whatever that meant.

"What kind?" she asked with a smirk.

Could have been motor oil for all he cared right now.

"Lockland Distilling," he answered. "Somewhere in Kentucky."

"Imagine that."

"You don't work weekends?"

"Sometimes." She shrugged. "But Pax knows I want to be home with Eloise." The bartender came back with her drink; Lennox said a polite thank you as she picked it up.

"How old are you?"

She laughed softly. "Twenty-four."

He scanned the bar again, partly because he couldn't just sit here and stare at her. And partly because he needed to know if anyone was giving them undue attention. The place wasn't crowded yet; it was still early.

"Why am I here, Dr. Gannon?" she asked after a few moments had passed.

"I don't know." He shook his head and waited a beat before looking her way again. "But we have an issue, and we need to figure it out."

"An issue," she repeated.

"Did you tell anyone?"

When she simply stared at him, eyes wide with a look of wonder, Booker sighed and dragged his gaze away. He fiddled with his glass before finally lifting it for a drink.

"I told someone about..." From the corner of his eye, he saw her glance at her phone screen. "A half hour ago. Because she wasn't going to let me out of the house."

"Your mother?"

Jesus. He hadn't considered that possibility.

She snorted. "No. Best friend. Landlord." She shrugged.

"It's inappropriate behavior," he mumbled around the sharp pain in his chest. Booker had never been a by-the-book kid or adult. He got in trouble in school sometimes. Talking in class. Talking back to the teacher. He got busted with a case of beer when he was seventeen. His high school girlfriend's dad caught the two of them making out more than once. He had speeding tickets. He didn't always grade as hard as he should. He had favorites in his classes. And yes, he used to hang out with students.

But he had never done anything *inappropriate* with a student, and it tore him up that he had to say the word. That when people saw him now, it was their first thought.

"Well, as I just reminded you, I'm an adult."

"You're my student," he snapped.

Her silence drew his attention. But she only shrugged.

"The friend you told." He tipped his head. "Will she say anything?"

"No." Lennox frowned. "Is that what this is? You fishing to see if I'm gonna report you for harassment?"

"Are you?"

"No." She took a drink, kept her eyes on the glass when she put it down on the bar.

"And why should I believe you?"

"Well, for one thing, it's been a week since it happened. Two, there's no proof. Three, I'm not gonna do something stupid and drag my daughter through any messes I make."

Booker considered what she had said. All three points were valid, and he figured the last of them was the most important to her. Which meant she wouldn't want anything to happen between them. Nothing other than that kiss.

"So, what changed your mind?" she asked after a few moments.

"About what?"

Her laugh was bitter. "You kissed me a week ago tonight. And then you hardly spoke to me in the classroom. But you decided to hang out with Kara and the guys at Tito's?"

Booker cringed. He didn't need this.

"There's no relationship—"

"Give me a little more credit than that, Dr. Gannon." She sighed. "I know how it works. I don't expect a damned thing from you, but I *am* a student in your class. You can at least treat me the same as you treat everyone else in the room."

She was right. He didn't have an answer for her.

"Moving on to Kara?" she asked quietly.

Frustration surged through him, curled his fingers into fists. He turned her way again to meet her eyes.

"If there's anyone in that room I want." He tipped his head and drilled her with an angry stare. "It's you."

35

LENNOX

His words touched her like a spark and tingled under her skin. Until now, until he had said those words, this felt like a game. One he regretted starting. One he was trying to quit and walk away from. As disappointed as she would have been, Lennox wanted to think she would have let it go. She didn't want to be the crazy stalker girl who wouldn't take no for an answer, as Collins had confessed to worrying about earlier.

Dr. Gannon's last words changed everything.

Or did they?

While he had said he wanted her, it didn't have to change anything. For one thing, even if anything happened, even if it was just another kiss, he could still walk into the lecture hall Monday and blow her off. And while she didn't want to be needy and clingy, she deserved the same courtesy and respect as her classmates.

Lennox swallowed hard, unsure what to say to him.

His words—whether an admission or just the next move in a game he controlled—didn't mean she was going to follow him to the parking lot for a quick fuck in the back seat of his car. She couldn't deny her attraction to him, but as Collins had pointed out earlier, there were other things to consider before jumping into something she could end up regretting.

She wouldn't do anything to hurt Eloise.

And yes, if Booker Gannon had assaulted other coeds, if Booker Gannon had cheated on his wife with his students, she had no interest in him.

Hard to go over all of that while sitting in a public place. No one was close enough to overhear their conversation, but she still hesitated to answer him.

"Did I shock you?" he finally asked her. Lennox cleared her throat as she let her gaze roam over him. He watched Banks mix a drink, and Lennox studied his profile. He could be a model; his face was made for a camera. "Ready to walk out?"

"I haven't moved," she reminded him.

Elbows on the bar, Booker dropped his head forward and reached to rub the back of his neck.

"We can't do this here."

"Mmm." She wanted to agree with him. But on the other hand, where were they safe to have this conversation? Dr. Gannon straightened and looked at her again.

"Where's your daughter?"

"With my parents," she answered, dragging her eyes away from him. "She likes to spend the night there sometimes."

Lennox worried her lower lip with her teeth. Had she tacked that on just to let him know she was free for the night? Maybe. Mostly, she didn't want him to think she had scrambled to push her daughter off on someone else so she could meet him. She didn't want him to think she was desperate for him.

He nodded and picked up his phone. Lennox watched him curiously as he opened the screen and tapped a notes app. Using only his left thumb, he typed something and then dropped the phone on the bar. Lennox flicked her gaze up to his when he gave it a casual nudge with his finger. He raised his eyebrows.

She looked at it quickly and then back at him. It was an address. Lennox had to assume it was *his* address. She studied it for a moment—721 Sylvia Rise—and then looked at him again. Was this too practiced? Was this something he did for fun? Sneaking around with students? Casual hookups?

She knew where Sylvia Rise was.

Dr. Gannon picked his phone up again, deleted the address, and then looked at the home screen.

"Nine?"

Lennox swallowed. It was just after seven. She couldn't wait until nine to do this—whatever *this* was. The anticipation would kill her. She would talk herself out of it. Or she would be so nervous by the time she drove to his place that she wouldn't be able to move.

She shook her head and glanced around the bar. Booker watched her take a drink.

"No?"

"Too far away."

His frown was severe. "Sylvia Rise? It's walkable."

"Nine."

"Mmm." He nodded when he understood. "Come when you're ready," he told her. Lennox watched him snatch a few bills from his wallet and drop them on the bar. "Good-night, Lennox."

"'Night, Dr. Gannon." She watched him walk around the bar and head to the door. Glass at her lips, she finally tipped it up for a drink. He didn't look back. Rather than look around right away, Lennox tipped her chin down and studied her phone. She'd sat at this bar with friends, but she'd sat here alone a few times—enough that it wasn't weird for her to be here now by herself.

She didn't know much more now than she had when she talked to Collins earlier, so she wouldn't check in yet. Instead, she scrolled social media, heart in her throat, as she wondered what the hell she was doing.

Booker Gannon was the sexiest man she'd ever laid eyes on, no question. Monty had been good-looking, but he was also seventeen when they dated. Seventeen and horny and dumb when it came to sex. Lennox never mistook what they had for love. And she wouldn't mistake whatever happened between herself and Dr. Gannon for love.

But she imagined he would be more fun, more interesting in bed, than Monty had.

But did she want that? Did she want to be used that way?

"You okay?"

Lennox glanced up as Banks paused in front of her. It felt weird to talk to him right now, because he had seen her with Booker. And he knew she was attracted to him. And it was possible Collins had texted him to tell him to look out for her tonight.

"Yeah, I'm good." She nodded. Smiling, she waited until he was talking to another customer before letting her thoughts wander back to Booker.

He was reserved; there were times when he thought no one was looking that he appeared vulnerable. A little bit broken. It was entirely possible that it was part of his act, but again, Lennox felt like she'd caught that look when he wasn't aware that she or anyone was watching him.

Her fingers and toes tingled, and her heart beat so hard it rattled her ribcage. But she made herself wait until it was almost eight before she paid for her drink and walked out of the speakeasy. The place was packed by then, and no one paid attention to her as she walked out.

She considered walking to his place. Sylvia Rise was a nice neighborhood. And it would probably be better not to have her car around his house. On the other hand, Sidecar *wasn't* in the best of neighborhoods, and she had to get out of here before she could get to Sylvia Rise. Besides, she might want her car close if she wanted to get away from him fast.

As arrogant or reserved—however she thought of him—as he was, Lennox didn't get the sense that he was dangerous. He might seduce her; after all, she was ninety-five percent willing. But she didn't believe he would raise a hand to her. Or force himself on her.

And if he did? She would defend herself. She'd put a few guys in their places since she was eighteen.

A Billie Eilish song blared when Lennox started her car. Not in the mood for music, Lennox drilled her finger into the power button to turn the radio off. She took a moment before she put the car in drive. Smoothed her hands over her thighs. Thought about Eloise. About Monty and his family.

Monty had left town for college. On schedule. He had graduated and moved to Denver. He had no contact, no relationship, with Eloise. Lennox figured he'd probably slept with a dozen more girls during his college years. He might be married now. Might have another kid. And Lennox walked the straight and narrow because she feared his parents.

Her phone buzzed and made her jump.

"Easy, Lex." She took a deep breath as she reached for it. Even though he didn't have her number, Lennox's mind jumped to conclusions. What if it was Dr. Gannon? Telling her he changed his mind?

What if it was? She would just have to go home, wouldn't she? She wasn't going to beg. It wasn't necessary.

The text was from Collins.

U ok?

She responded immediately with a simple yes, set her phone on the passenger seat, and pulled forward out of her parking spot. The speed limit was twenty around the speakeasy, revving up to thirty as she neared the next corner. Lennox was careful with her foot on the gas. No need to drive over the speed limit and get a ticket. She used her turn signals conscientiously, laughing at herself as she did so.

She'd never done this. Well, she had never met a teacher with the possibility of having sex with him. But she'd never *driven somewhere* to meet *anyone* for sex. Or the possibility. Sex had always come during a date or at the end of a date. This felt different. *So* different. Every nerve ending in her body burned with need, with anticipation.

Maybe the danger made him more enticing.

Then again, Dr. Gannon had the body, the face, the voice— she didn't need danger to be this hot for him. She slowed when she turned left onto Sylvia Rise, eyes on the east side of the street. Spotting the old Victorian with the numbers 721 to the left of the door, she drove on to the corner, turned on Eighth, and parked there. Tucking her phone in her pocket, she closed the car door gently, beeped the lock once, and then slipped her hands in her coat pockets as she walked back toward his place.

When she neared his address, she realized he was sitting on the porch steps, waiting for her. She slowed as she approached him.

"C'min." He stood and nodded back at the door.

Just because she was going into his house didn't mean a thing, she reminded herself as she slipped past him to the door. Dr. Gannon touched her lower back—maybe in a polite ushering gesture—sending flames erupting through her. Even through her coat and sweater.

If he touched her—*really* touched her—she would probably shatter in two seconds and make a fool of herself.

36

BOOKER

Booker watched Lennox look around the entry hall and over his shoulder into the living area. She was the only person to enter the house other than him since he had moved in last August. Her lips tipped up in a smile of appreciation; it was hard not to be impressed with the place. The house had been well-loved and cared for. And Booker kept it clean. Not for occasions like this, but because it gave him something to do.

"Here." He stepped closer to her and slipped his fingers under the collar of her coat. She shrugged it off without comment and watched him hang it on the coat tree in the corner of the entry way. He cleared his throat, aware that she was probably just as uncomfortable as he was. Contrary to popular belief, he didn't know how to do this. Seduction, yes, but that had been with his wife.

Not a student.

Not someone he would have to see in his classroom come Monday morning.

"Want something to drink?"

"Yes, please." She flicked her gaze over his and nodded. Booker headed down the short hall to the kitchen, relieved when she followed him.

"Soda? Beer?" He peered into his fridge. If he had thought ahead, he could have stocked up with vodka and cranberry juice for her. Then again, maybe that wasn't such a good idea.

"Um." She shrugged when he looked at her over his shoulder. "Beer."

Relieved she asked for a beer, he grabbed two and closed the door. Lennox watched him twist the tops off the bottles and took the one he offered her. He took a long drink, put the bottle down, and dragged his fingers back through his hair.

"You're worried about your daughter."

"More about Monty's parents." She shrugged.

"Do you date?"

"Not much. Went out with Josh once. Before the studying fiasco. Went out with a guy when Eloise was a baby. That was a disaster."

"And what? When you date, his parents—what? Follow you around?"

"No. But something tells me they wouldn't approve of this."

"*This*." Booker lifted an eyebrow curiously.

"Yeah."

"And where is he?" Suddenly hot, Booker hooked his fingers in the collar of his sweater and tugged it off over his head. He tossed it on the counter and smoothed down the gray t-shirt he wore under it.

"Monty?" She laughed softly. "Um. No idea. He was seventeen. A year behind me in school. Once I told him I was pregnant, I didn't deal with Monty anymore. I dealt with Eve."

"Eve."

"His mom."

"So you don't talk to him?"

"He was a basketball star." She leaned her elbows on the island and met his eyes. "Told me he didn't want a kid. Wouldn't deal with a kid. The next thing I know, I get a call from his mother. She tells me if I have an abortion, she'll destroy me. Take away any hope I have of ever going to college. She'll blackball me in any career I choose. She and Joseph showed up at the hospital when I was in labor, demanding to see the baby. Demanding visiting rights, threatening me. I was only eighteen. I was afraid they could really do it. Take her."

"So you were saddled with a pregnancy and a baby, and he got to keep playing?"

Lennox opened her mouth, but she was slow to answer. "I wasn't exactly ready for Eloise, but I can't use *those* words now. And as far as Monty, I think I'd rather he knew his daughter, and that I didn't have to deal with his parents. But I can't change anything."

"What does your daughter think about her daddy?"

"She doesn't know the story," Lennox said quietly. "And I dread the day she asks, and I have to tell her."

"And you think being here with me jeopardizes her somehow?"

Booker stepped around the island to get closer to her. Lennox stared at him for a long moment, finally looking away when she spoke.

"Sometimes I feel like everything I do puts her at risk or puts her and I at risk of his parents stepping in."

"Like what?"

"Eve saw my books for your class. She thinks it's awful that I'm studying vampires. Imagine if she knew the vampire stories we study are symbolic of female sexuality. Or homo-sexuality."

Booker smiled and nodded. "Scandalous stuff."

"And yet not enough for Josh Stone."

"I'm rereading *Vermillion*." He stepped closer to her. Lennox pushed her bottle back to the middle of the counter and turned to face him.

"You've read it?"

He nodded.

"Is it good?"

"Yes." He lifted his hand and stroked his fingertips over her cheek.

Lennox swallowed hard. "You do that in my dreams."

Her words, delivered in that thick, butterscotch voice, were electric in his veins. He moved closer still, their middles pressing together now. Booker's cock was hard, ready to take her. She had to feel his excitement. Lennox tipped her head back and looked up at him.

"I love your lips."

He hadn't meant to say the words out loud. But when he did, she gasped softly. Booker lifted his other hand and cupped her face. With his fingers spread over her cheeks and his thumbs at her lower lip, he leaned closer to kiss her. A soft, gentle press of his lips over hers.

"I think about your lips on me every fucking minute of the day," he confessed and moved to rest his cheek against hers.

"Dr. Gannon—"

"Booker."

"Booker."

His name on her lips unraveled him. He kissed her again, this time with greed, desperation. Booker swept his tongue inside her mouth, thrilling when she met his tongue with hers, thrust for thrust, sliding and curling over his.

"Have you done this before?" His throat tight with emotions, his voice was no more than a whisper.

"Booker?" She drew back to look at him.

"I mean...with...someone like me."

"With a professor?"

He nodded.

"No." She shook her head and let her eyes roam over his face, down over his shoulders. He hesitated to move, unwilling to move away. Afraid to move forward. If she had said yes? Would he be more comfortable crossing this line?

Booker groaned his approval when she reached for him. Her mouth was on his; her tongue stroked his. Her teeth nibbled on his lower lip.

"I want to strip you down and fuck you right here on the counter, Lennox Clarke." He circled his fingers around her neck and made her look up at him.

Breathing hard, eyes locked on his, she arched her eyebrows and waited.

"I can't," he whispered. "I can't do this."

Lennox whimpered and dropped her head forward to rest on his chest.

"Why?"

"You know why, Lennox."

"Did you do it?" she asked. "Did you do what they said? Am I just one of many?"

37

LENNOX

"No." He backed away from her and dropped his hands to his sides.

"No?"

"No." He sighed as he turned his back to her.

"Because as much as I want this." She struggled to catch her breath. "I can't."

"Jesus." He dropped his head back and growled. "I did not do it. I have never touched a student." Lennox flinched at his sarcastic laugh when he twisted around to look at her again. "Except you."

She folded her arms over her chest.

"What about the video?"

"Have you seen it?" he asked quietly.

"No. But I know there is a video." She licked her lips. "Josh had it on his phone the other day."

"Who the fuck does he know that he got his hands on it?" Booker paced the length of the island counter, turned, and paced back to the other end. "I am not *in* that video."

"That doesn't make me feel any better."

"Why? Because it's in my bed?"

Lennox clapped her hand over her mouth when the half laugh, half sob slipped out.

"Look." He shook his head. "Fuck. I don't have the video. And I don't want to go looking for it."

"Why is there a video of coeds in your bed?" she whispered. "If you didn't sleep with them?"

"I guess because they wanted to fuck me," he answered. "One way or another."

He stormed down the same path again and swung his hand out to snag his beer. Lennox eyed him silently.

"You don't believe me, do you?" he asked as he tipped the bottle up for a long drink.

She *wanted* to believe him. She was ninety-nine percent certain she believed him. And the ache in her core was pushing her over the edge to absolute certainty.

Lennox closed the distance between them slowly. Giving herself time to chicken out. To turn and run. The look on Booker's face was one of torture. Where was the smug liar's face, if he had harassed or assaulted the girls on his last campus?

Again, Collins' misgivings, her warnings, came back to her. He could play any role to get what he wanted. But why would he go to this length for *her*? Lennox wasn't a smokin' hot girl who showed a lot of skin and played flirty games with anyone. She was a single mom with little experience when she got right down to the bones of it.

Maybe it was exactly that—her naiveté—that he was attracted to. Collins had alluded to that, hadn't she?

"I do," she said when she stood toe to toe with him. "I don't think I'd be here if I didn't."

Booker narrowed his eyes at her, his brown bottle still in hand. "Do you wanna know? What—"

"Not right now."

The yearning on his face was enough to drive her to her knees. Booker reached blindly to put his bottle down and then cupped her face again.

"Are you sure?"

"Yes."

"Lennox, you get what I'm saying? I want to fuck you sense-less. I wanna be balls deep inside you." He held her chin still, refusing to let her move. "I wanna make you come so hard, you forget your name."

Mouth dry, she could only nod in response.

"Not my name." His whisper was gruff. "I want *my* name on your lips. I want you screaming my name. Begging me for more."

"Please." She covered his hand with hers.

He nodded as he leaned in, close enough to kiss her. Lennox lunged for him when he missed her mouth and started to pull away.

"Upstairs." He shook his head. "I want you in my bed. I want you naked in my sheets."

He took her hand in his and led her back to the front of the house, to the staircase tucked away on the other side of the entry way. Heart ready to explode, she raced up the steps behind him, mindful of her phone and keys still on the counter in the kitchen.

Didn't matter.

She wanted this to happen. And she didn't need any texts from Collins to interrupt them.

He led her into the first of two rooms, to the side of a queen bed, where he pulled the comforter back.

"I wish I had satin sheets for you." He turned and reached for her. Considering she had been ready for him to spread her legs and take her on the kitchen counter, the white cotton sheets looked fine to her. Rather than undress her immediately, he kissed her again. One hand in her hair and the other on her face again, he sipped from her lips, flicked his tongue over them, and nibbled his way from her mouth to her ear.

Lennox found herself hanging on as he fastened his mouth on her neck and sucked on her skin. The idea of his teeth on her, of him feeding from her, made her mad with lust. She gripped his shoulders to hold on and pulled him closer, grinding her middle against his. His cock felt like steel against her belly.

"Don't hurry," he insisted. "I need my mouth on every inch of your body before I put my cock inside you, Lennox."

"I need you," she panted as she licked a trail down his neck. Booker eased back to look at her when she straddled his thigh.

"Let me," he argued. "Let me do it."

Lennox nodded as he gave her a gentle push. She took a step, the back of her knees hitting the bed. She kicked off her shoes as Booker unbuttoned her jeans and tugged at the zipper. Painfully slow, he eased the denim over her hips. Slipped his hands inside her panties and cupped her butt cheeks before pulling away to look at her again. Before she could open her mouth to ask for more, his lips were on hers again. His tongue stroked hers.

She wanted to stop him, to ask him to touch her, when he only kissed her again. The roll of his tongue inside her mouth, the tip of his tongue on the roof of her mouth, mesmerized her. Lennox sobbed out loud when she felt his fingers between her legs. He rubbed her core through the scrap of silk that was soaked before she had even walked into his house.

"You like that?" His voice was low at her ear, his breath warm on her skin. "Do you want me to touch you here?"

"Yes."

"Like this?" He slowed the touch, barely moving his hand. Lennox whimpered and shifted so she could rub herself on him.

"Faster."

"Faster?"

"Oh, God, please, Booker."

"If I let you come now, will you be a good girl and let me kiss you all over?"

"Yes." She met his eyes, the heat in his stare burning through her like a torch.

"If I let you come now, can I put my face between your legs and lick you until you come again?"

"Oh, God." She shivered and nodded. "Please."

"Hold on, Lennox." He tugged on her earlobe with his teeth. "Hold onto me."

She dug her fingers into his shoulders, harder and harder still, as he stroked her hard and fast. Waves of pleasure slammed into her instantly. Knees weak, she tipped her head back, still holding onto him.

"Booker," she whispered as he slowed his hand, still touching her but drawing out the pleasure, the heat, the tingles radiating everywhere at once. "OhmyGod. I can't...I can't stand up."

"Lay down." He guided her back to the bed and tugged her jeans off as she laid down. She watched as he whipped his t-shirt off and tossed it aside. He unbuttoned his jeans but abandoned that when he caught her eye.

Lennox wanted to look. To take in the six pack abs and the firm biceps and pecs. She wanted to study the tattoos on his upper arms. But he looked at her like she was candy, and he had a sweet tooth. He needed to eat, and she wanted to be devoured.

Booker propped a knee on the bed and crawled up by her.

"I've thought about this every fucking night since you walked into my classroom that first day."

"Me, too," she whispered.

He flicked his tongue over her upper lip and ducked his head to nip at her breast, her nipple, through her clothes.

"Are you wet for me like this when you're in class?"

Lennox lifted her hips when he stroked his fingers over the scrap of silk again.

"Yes."

"You sit up there looking so fucking cool and collected, it makes me crazy. I wanna drag you down to my desk and bend you over and take you from behind."

Lennox arched her back when he nipped at her nipple again. She wanted her sweater, her bra, gone, out of the way. But Booker was teasing her, enjoying the game. His cock pressed at her side painfully hard. He slipped his fingers inside her and hooked them as he pressed his thumb to her clit.

"Did Monty do it like this?"

"No."

"No?"

"No." She shook her head as he worked his fingers in and out of her walls, fucking her with his hand.

"Have you ever been fucked like this, Lennox?"

"No."

He worked magic between her legs as he pressed his face between her breasts. The slide of her silk bra over her distended nipples was sharp, harsh enough to be painful. But the anticipation of his hands there, his tongue and teeth on her nipples, her breasts, made her blind with need.

"That's two," he whispered. "And I still haven't heard you scream my name."

"I can't breathe," she gushed as he pulled his hand away from her and slid it up under her sweater.

"I wanna suck on these." He met her eyes as he tweaked her nipple.

Lennox licked her lips and nodded. She arched her back, hoping he would push her sweater up, take it off her.

"Do you want me to?"

"Booker."

"Or would you rather I suck here?" He slid his knee up between her thighs.

"Both."

"Both?" He grinned. "You are greedy, Lennox Clarke. I'm not sure I would have guessed that about you."

"Please?" She lifted her hand and combed her fingers back through his hair.

"Please what?"

"Booker." She sobbed. "God, I want you everywhere. I need you to consume me."

"Hmm." He pushed her sweater up and bared her navel. "You're not naked enough yet."

Lennox pushed against him to sit up. She pulled the sweater off and dropped it. Booker's hands were on the hook of her bra before the sweater hit the floor. He plucked the silk from between her breasts and filled his hand as he took her mouth for a long, slow kiss. Wallowing in the feel of his cool sheets on her back and the heat of his skin on her belly, Lennox closed her eyes as he kissed his way down her neck. She ached for him, moving with him, wanting everything as he kissed a trail over each of her shoulders, stroked his tongue over her wrists and the palms of her hands.

When he settled between her thighs, she sighed and arched her back again to offer him her breasts. Booker fastened his lips around one nipple and cupped her other breast in his hand, thumbing that nipple.

"The things I want with you, Lennox." He kissed a path from her breast down her belly, flicking his tongue at her belly button. She lifted her hips when his fingers caught the waistband of her panties. Stripped naked before him, she watched him admire her body.

"Spread your legs," he told her. "Let me see you."

38

BOOKER

Booker groaned his satisfaction when Lennox spread her legs and bent her knees. She had come twice; she was slick with her release and arousal. Booker wanted to feast, but he reminded himself to slow down. To make sure she wanted him to do it.

"Did Monty do this?" he asked her.

"No."

"Has anyone kissed you here?" He trailed his fingers up her inner thighs, surprised when she nodded. Interested in who, if not the father of her child, had put his mouth on her, Booker filed it away to ask her later. "Did he make you come?"

"No."

"Did Monty ever make you come?"

"Booker." She sighed and bit her lip.

"Did he?"

"Not really."

"What's that mean?"

"Not without me helping him."

"Mmm." He rubbed his hand over his cock, now trying to burst through his zipper. "Maybe we could do that later."

"I want you inside me."

"I know you do, Lennox." He grinned. "I can smell it on you. You're so fucking wet for me, I could come in my jeans just looking at you."

He lifted her left leg and pressed his open mouth to the sole of her foot. She wiggled when he stroked the tip of his tongue over her arch.

"Booker."

"You said..." He licked his way up her calf and then rested her ankle on his shoulder. "That if I let you come before I could lick every inch of your body. Remember that?"

Lennox, hair spilled out around her like a halo, nodded, eyes locked with his.

"I think you're being greedy." He lifted her other leg and treated it to the same kisses. "However, if you want to touch yourself there while I worship your calves, I wouldn't mind watching that."

Booker had said it as a challenge. He hadn't thought she would do it. And yet, she slid one hand up to pinch a nipple and the other down between her legs. He was used to Ashley's bright red nails between her legs, but this—

Lennox simply and naturally beautiful, her curiosity and her innocence—made his dick throb.

"You win." He grinned as he slid his hands down her inner thighs to press her legs open. She whimpered softly when he swept his tongue over her. He teased her with light strokes, his fingers inside her again. Brushed his face over the delta of curls, planted kisses on her thighs. She whispered his name over and over, each time a little more desperate than before. The squeeze of her walls around his fingers made him desperate to strip his clothes off and bury himself inside her.

Done teasing her, he spread her open and latched on to suck at her most sensitive spot. She jumped, immediately lifting her hips to give him more of herself. He devoured her, not stopping until she was thrashing beneath him, sobbing, and screaming his name.

Booker looked up to see her fists twisting his sheet. Her breasts bounced as she panted, her nipples hard and a deep rosy pink. Slowing the motion of his mouth, he watched her ride out the orgasm, struggling to catch her breath, falling back to earth, to his bed. When she went limp beneath him, he scooted back to stand and stripped his jeans and boxers off.

She watched through slitted eyes as he took a box of condoms from the nightstand.

"You okay?" He crawled up over her and rested his forehead against hers.

"Yes." Her lips tipped up slightly. "Not sure I'll ever be able to walk again, but yes."

"I haven't even put my cock in you yet, Lennox." He kissed the tip of her nose. "Wait'll that's done before you declare you can't walk."

She laughed softly.

"Do you want sex?" He cupped his fingers around her chin and forced her to look at him. "Do you want me inside your body?"

"Yes."

"It's okay." He told her. "If you say no, it's okay."

"Booker." She lifted her hand and stroked her fingers down his chest to his belly and finally, she stroked his length. "I want this."

"Thank fuck." He took her mouth in a kiss. Rather than rush, rather than drive his cock into her immediately and ride her hard and fast, he lingered at her mouth. Long, deep kisses, his tongue making love to her mouth, thrilling at the way she kissed him back.

When he did move to roll a condom on, she spread her legs again and watched him.

"I've thought about this so long, and now I have your taste in my mouth." He moved to lie between her thighs. "Let me control it this time, or I'll come faster than you did. And while I wanna come so bad my dick's gonna shatter in a minute, I want this to last for a few minutes."

"So don't move?" She arched an eyebrow at him.

"Not until I tell you to." He rubbed the tip of his cock over her clit and flicked her lips with his tongue.

She moaned softly as he eased the tip of his cock inside her.

"Lennox."

"I can't moan, either?" She frowned. "You feel so good. I just wanna pull you all the way in."

Booker laughed and put his hand over her mouth.

"No talking, either." Her words were muffled, but damned if her eyes didn't sparkle.

"Do you wanna come again?"

"God, yes." She shivered. Booker watched her nipples harden again.

"Then behave."

Instead, she flicked her tongue over his hand. Booker shook his head and pushed inside her, deeper and deeper, until his balls were tucked up in her heat.

"Not yet." He kissed her cheek. "Not yet."

"Can I just ask you to fuck me?"

"You." He roared with laughter. "You are a little bit dirty, Lennox Clarke. I love it."

"Can I move yet?"

"Are you okay?" He rocked his hips forward. "You're tight as fuck. I don't wanna hurt you."

"You feel good." She pushed his hair off his face, eyes locked with his. "It feels good, Booker."

"Tell me. If I hurt you."

"You're not gonna hurt me," she promised him. "I just need you to..."

He pulled out as her voice drifted away. Pushed into her again, deep and slow. Lennox moved with him, and they settled into a slow, tender pace. Her heat enveloped him. She draped her arms around his shoulders. Her teeth worked the chords of his neck. As he pumped his hips, a little faster and harder, she circled her legs around his waist and locked her ankles over his ass. Sweat gathered on the small of his back. Lennox stayed with him, thrust for thrust, her cheeks pink, her hairline wet with sweat.

Moaning his name, begging for more, she dug her nails into his shoulder and dragged them down his back. She dropped her right hand back to her chest and tweaked her own nipple. Booker watched her eyes roll back in ecstasy. He moved with her to draw her orgasm out, waiting until she was boneless and spent beneath him before thinking of himself. Lennox wrapped her arms around his neck again and squeezed hard on his cock as he pounded in and out of her.

"Fuck." He groaned when his release hit him, bowling him over. Paralyzed over her, he ducked his head to her shoulder and bit her neck as the white-hot pleasure flowed through him. "You are so fucking dangerous, Lennox Clarke."

39

LENNOX

"Why dangerous?"

"Hmm?"

Lennox untangled herself from Booker, from the sheets, and lifted her head to look at him. They had slept a bit and made love again and slept again. She had no idea what time it was. Her phone was still downstairs on the kitchen counter, and odds were the battery was getting awfully low.

She didn't care.

Booker Gannon had fucked her absolutely senseless at least three times; she had lost count after he blew her mind again when he woke her and took her from behind. She didn't feel threatened. She wasn't afraid of him. She didn't care about Monday.

What mattered was this man had done things to her body, made her body feel things it had never felt before, and she wanted more. She wanted as much as he could give her before daylight. Before she had to sneak out and pretend none of it had happened.

"Why am I dangerous?"

Booker lay on his stomach, his left arm up under his pillow. His right arm had been draped over her naked belly, his hand palming her breast.

She kissed his bare shoulder and slid her leg up over his.

While she had touched him, looked her fill, she hadn't tasted him. And she wanted to. She wanted her mouth on him, if for no other reason than for him to look at her lips on Monday, Wednesday, every fucking day they had left together in the classroom and think about her sucking him off.

What would Collins say about that?

"Because you could walk out of here and blow the whistle on me. I've already lost a job. Lost my reputation. Lost my wife."

"Why would you think I would do that?"

"I've been burned before, Lennox."

"The video?" She tipped her head.

Booker flipped over and tucked his right arm under his head.

"Yeah."

"I'm a little scared to ask," she admitted.

"You think I assaulted someone? Do you think I could do that?"

"No." She stroked her thumb over his lips. "But I don't think I could watch you touch someone else."

"Sofie and Reese," he told her.

"Who are they?"

"They were students in my class."

"And were you involved with them?"

"Lennox—"

"I don't think you would assault anyone, but Booker, Jesus. I'd sell my soul to be with you again. After this is over."

He took a deep breath. "We're not together, Lennox. You know that, right? We can't—"

She nodded and pressed her fingers to his mouth. "I know. I'm just saying, I've never had sex like this. I've never had an orgasm that didn't involve my own hand."

"I used to hang out with students." He took her hand and kissed her fingers. "Like the other night when I went bowling with Josh and Rupe."

"And Kara."

He shook his head. "I didn't know she would be there. I wouldn't have gone."

"If I had been there?"

"I would have left," he answered. "It's harder than hell to control myself around you."

Lennox swallowed the knot of emotions. She already wanted more. Booker was as dangerous to her as she was to him.

"There was a big group that I was around a lot. Sofie and Reese were in that group. Ashley would go with me to games. To community events in Artas."

"She's your wife?"

"Ex-wife," he answered. "We were married eight years. Sofie and Reese latched onto her. They were...it was like a girl crush. Ya know?"

"Yep." She stroked her fingers down his chest, but Booker caught her before she could slip her hand beneath the sheet.

"Reese wore her shorts like butt floss. And Sofie didn't own a bra." He shrugged. "I looked. But I never wanted to cheat on Ashley."

"What happened?"

"They got close. I cared about 'em. All the kids. But it was a mistake. I crossed a line with *all* of them. Sofie and Reese started hanging out at our house. A couple of the guys did now and then. They'd have dinner with us. Watch movies. Ashley got close to the girls."

Booker sighed.

"We went out of town one weekend. And told the girls they could stay at our house."

"Oh, no."

"Yeah. They slept in our bed. Made this steamy video together. Made sure enough of my things were in camera range. One of my ties. A framed picture of me and Ashley on the nightstand. A box of condoms. Both girls were completely nude, both all in, and both of them playing to the camera."

"No wonder Josh was gushing about it."

Booker cringed.

"Since I wasn't in the video, everyone assumed I recorded it. It was Ashley that went with me to the dean and proved we were out of town."

"If you proved it wasn't you, why did you lose your job?"

"I resigned. But it was under pressure. Obviously, I had done enough if I made the girls feel that welcome in my house. I was in the wrong for fraternizing with my students. I don't know that they set out to get me in trouble, or if I seriously gave off the vibe that I was interested."

"I'm sorry."

"Ashley couldn't get past the thought that I had led them on. That maybe something had happened at another time. That I didn't want to quit teaching, that I was angry that I had to leave Artas. Things just went from bad to worse."

"And you thought I wanted to hurt you the same way?"

"I wondered." He shrugged. "At first. And now, even if you don't want to, you could."

She sighed and flopped back on the bed.

"What?"

"I dunno. I don't like that you think that of me."

Booker laughed sarcastically. "Try having a whole goddamned town looking at you like you're a sexual predator. I haven't had sex in months."

"Years for me," she answered. "And never like this."

"Stop saying that."

"What?"

"*Never like this.*"

"What? You don't like knowing you blew my mind?"

"It's just gonna make it that much harder when I see you in class Monday."

He shifted to his side and moved closer to her. Lennox lifted her head to kiss him.

"It's not daylight yet," she whispered.

"Lennox, you're gonna be sore—"

She shook her head as she cupped his balls in her hand.

"I want to taste you."

"No."

"No?" She smoothed her thumb over the tip of his cock.

"You know how many times I've heard people on campus say that I've made girls blow me for grades? I refuse—"

"You put your mouth on me," she reminded him. "You made me come three times before you were inside me. Teach me how to make you feel that way."

"Teach you?" he repeated. "Have you ever—?"

"I have, but I don't think I'm very good at it."

"Lennox, you close that hot mouth of yours on my cock, and I'll blow. Simple."

She arched an eyebrow at him. "Please?"

40

BOOKER

Lennox ducked out of his house just before dawn. Booker wanted to walk her to her car, but as she reminded him, that defeated the purpose of her parking around the corner to keep their meeting hidden. He had kissed her one last time at the front door; she had already put her coat on. Her keys were in hand, and reality hung over them, ready to crash down the second she walked out.

He watched her walk down the block. As far as he knew, Sylvia Rise was safe. Not to mention that Lennox Clarke was a bit ballsy and a lot tough, and Booker suspected she could take care of herself. He watched her anyway. Maybe because he didn't want to let her go. Because he wanted to chase her down, throw her over his shoulder, and haul her back upstairs to his bed.

Tough and ballsy as she was, she hadn't tried to hide from him the fact that she was inexperienced. She had a kid, sure, but touching her, kissing her, losing himself inside her, had been a dream. Her body had reacted instantly to his. Booker had never seen a woman orgasm so quickly, so easily. He had seen women fake it; there was no way Lennox had faked shattering and flying apart in his bed each time he had made her come.

She was tight, he had worried he would hurt her. And yet, she had taken him in without the slightest hesitation. She had sunk her short, natural fingernails into his back, his ass, pulling him harder, deeper. Lennox had met his powerful thrusts eagerly, hungry for him to fill her.

Consume her, she had said. She wanted him to consume her.

What if she said something in class?

She wouldn't.

But she could.

When she vanished around the corner, Booker went back to the kitchen. Boxers slung low on his hips, he stood for a moment and stared at the beer bottles they had abandoned for each other.

She could go home and tell her friend. Odds were, she would. If it had been that good for her, she probably would share that with her friend. It was what women did. Ashley had taught him that much. It wasn't to brag, wasn't to tell secrets, but because she wanted to relive it. Make the memories stick.

Lennox could waltz into class on Monday and say something about how he fucked her. She could say it to him before anyone else showed up. Just to mess with his head. And it sure as hell *would* mess with him. Or she could wait until the lecture hall was full, and they were deep in discussions about Dracula and Mina and Lucy, and she could allude to what they had done together.

Or flat out announce to the class how he had fucked her within an inch of her life. How he had even nibbled on her neck and sucked at her skin, as if role playing a scene from their literature.

And because she had said *please*, she could walk into the dean's office and tell him that she had sucked him off in exchange for an A.

At least Booker had her grades recorded from the beginning. There was never any question that she would waltz out of the class with anything but an A.

Sick at the thought of what Monday would bring, Booker went back upstairs and climbed in bed. The smell of sex lingered in the air, and Lennox's scent clung to his sheets. He should feel bad. He had never taken advantage of someone like he had Lennox Clarke. So what if she was a legal adult? She was in a position where she was vulnerable to him, and he had led her here, seduced her, and used the fuck out of her body all night for his gratification.

Sure, she got off several times in the process, but it didn't change the fact that Booker had done it all for selfish reasons. Because he hadn't undressed a woman in nearly six months. Because he hadn't felt that heat and friction since he'd been with his wife. Because he hadn't tasted that lust, that excitement and release in so long, he had forgotten how sweet it was.

Even worse? He had made a big deal of telling Lennox it would never happen again. Like a warning to her not to come nosing around him for more. So far, she seemed to understand that. And *Booker* wanted more. He wanted her naked and in his bed for the next several days. He wanted to come home to find her there, wet, and ready for him, every night. He wanted to fuck her in the kitchen. In his shower. Up against the front door.

He had hoped whetting his whistle, so to speak, would be enough. That one night of pure, selfish, greedy sex would hold him over for a while. And now, he lay awake blinking at the ceiling, worried he could fuck her every night and still never get enough of Lennox Clarke.

41

LENNOX

The problem with her landlord befriending her was that Collins had a key to her side of the duplex. And because they were close, and maybe because Lennox had a key to Collins' side and had used it many times, Collins never hesitated to use that key. They had joked before about just knocking out the wall that separated the house into two units, but neither of them had the money to spring for that kind of construction.

Lennox didn't know how long she had been asleep when she heard someone in the kitchen. Not long, judging by the sand in her eyes as she rubbed them to make them open. She had taken a quick shower when she got home before daylight, put on her comfortable fleece pajama pants, a tank, and climbed into bed, praying she would dream about the things she and Booker Gannon had done.

She knew it was Collins because she smelled coffee. If her mom was here this early with Eloise, her daughter would have pounced on her already. And her mom would insist she get up and dressed so they could all go get breakfast.

Collins would appear any minute in her doorway with two mugs of coffee and demand details. Lennox wasn't sure she had ever demanded details from her friend, but Collins was always happy to share them. Since Lennox didn't spend many nights like she had last night, she never had much to share. Studying with friends and hearing gossip about other students. Tacos. Beer. Drinks at Sidecar. Nothing too exciting.

Until now.

Part of Lennox wanted to keep it to herself. Not because she didn't trust Collins to keep her secret. The only way Collins would blow the whistle on Booker Gannon was if he hurt her. Physically. Or if he decided to bargain sex acts for Lennox's passing grade.

No, Lennox kind of wanted to keep it to herself because she didn't want to share it. Not even a second of it.

"Knock, knock."

With a soft laugh, Lennox sat up when Collins announced herself. She propped her pillow up against the headboard of her bed and leaned against it as Collins entered her room and held out a mug of coffee.

"Thanks." She took a sip and cringed as the scalding hot liquid burned the roof of her mouth.

"I don't even have to ask." Collins put her own mug on the nightstand on the other side of the bed and climbed in beside her. Dressed in her own fleece pajama pants and a loose-fitting sweatshirt, Lennox had to look close to see the years between them. This felt like the morning after a sleepover. With her waves pulled back in a messy ponytail and no makeup, Collins looked as twenty-four as Lennox did, rather than her actual thirty-five.

"What?"

"You're glowing."

"Mm." Lennox rolled her eyes. "Right."

"No. Really. Your hair's all tousled and tangled like you were thoroughly fucked all night long. Your cheeks are flushed. And you're smiling. Even though I woke you up."

"How was your date?" Lennox tipped her head back to rest on the headboard.

"Not as good as your not-date, just-meeting-my-professor-at-a-bar-to-not-have-sex-with-him-night."

Lennox laughed and rolled her head back and forth on the headboard.

"Gonna see your date again?"

"I doubt it." Collins shrugged. "So?"

"You said you didn't have to ask."

"Not for confirmation, no. Just for details."

Lennox closed her eyes and pictured Booker's face. The way he looked at her after he kissed her in his kitchen. When he told her he couldn't be with her. Had it been an act? She didn't know, and she decided it didn't matter. Nothing about last night had hurt her. She had no intention of telling anyone other than Collins that she had been with him. It was a night of consensual sex between adults.

"I didn't know." Her voice was little more than a whisper.

"Know what?" Collins scooted down in the bed to lay on her side. She propped her head on her hand and stared up at Lennox.

"That it could feel that good."

"Oh, boy." Collins' eyebrows shot up comically fast.

"I mean. I messed around in high school. With high school guys. Had sex when I was seventeen. Took me all of four minutes to lose my virginity. And Monty didn't know what he was doing." She shrugged. "God, Collins...I had no idea."

Collins nodded. "Are you okay?"

"I'm good."

"Is this an ongoing thing? Sneaking—"

"No. Just last night."

Collins reached for her, dropped her hand to cover Lennox's. "Are you okay with that?"

"Don't I have to be?"

"Maybe you had to tell *him* that." Collins shrugged. "But you can tell me the truth."

Lennox flinched and sighed. "I like him, Collins. I honestly don't think he's a bad guy."

"Did he tell you that?"

"I'm not naïve," Lennox reminded her.

"I think you are. A little bit. I don't wanna see you get hurt, Lex."

"I'll admit that I hated leaving. That I'm nervous about seeing him Monday in class." Lennox shrugged. "That if I saw him hitting on someone else it would suck."

"That could be a problem."

"I'll live," Lennox assured her. "I mean, he's the one that made that rule. But it's not like anything could happen anyway. Not with Eloise."

"Something did happen, Lennox. Something huge. He touched you."

Lennox snorted. "He touched me a lot."

"Not what I mean." Collins offered her a small, strained smile. "He touched something inside you."

"He did that, too." Lennox grinned. "Please stop worrying. I'm fine. I just hope it's not weird tomorrow."

Collins sighed. "The first time a guy made me feel that good, I wanted to marry him."

"Why didn't you?"

"We broke up." She flopped over on her back and stared at Lennox's ceiling. "We were together. But things were just... blah. I loved him. I think he tolerated me. And I finally decided I was worth more than that."

"I do. Love you," Lennox told her. "You know that, right? I appreciate that you're worried about me, but I'm fine."

Collins looked up at her and nodded. "Okay. What time's your mom bringing Eloise home?"

"I don't know. What time is it?"

"Almost ten."

"No way!"

"Let's go make breakfast."

"I don't have any eggs or pancake mix."

"I do." Collins struggled to sit up. "C'mon. Come to my side. You can sit and drink coffee and tell me all the juicy details while I make you breakfast."

42

BOOKER

Booker felt like a new man. He slept after Lennox left. Dreamt deliciously dirty dreams about her and woke up feeling recharged and ready to take on the day. Crazy; he hadn't felt so good, so energized, since last year at this time. Before everything fell apart. He stayed busy all weekend— moving things around in his place, getting some of his new exercise equipment set up in what was technically a spare bedroom. He went for a run outside. He went grocery shopping. And he reread the required material for class Monday, so he would be prepared.

If he had known a night like that with a girl with lips and tits like Lennox Clarke's would chase all the negativity away, he might have tried to bed her earlier in the semester.

He wouldn't have. The sex with her had been phenomenal, but no, he still couldn't change who he was deep inside. He had to have that time getting to know her, learning to read her, before making a move.

Booker thought about her over the weekend, but he convinced himself it wasn't specifically *her*. That it wasn't her plump lips or her perky little breasts or even how tight she fit him—it was the *sex*. Finally finding that release that he had denied himself since Ashley left.

Hopefully, Lennox understood that it was a one-night thing. He didn't think she would walk into the dean's office today and accuse him of assault. But he couldn't be so certain that she would let things go, that she wanted just the one-night, no-strings-attached sex they had.

Then again, she was so protective of Eloise, surely, she wouldn't make a mess of what they had done.

Would she?

He stopped at Crave on the way to Palmer Building Monday morning. When he saw Rupe and Josh with Kara, huddled by the fireplace, he gave them a smile and a wave. They might ask about his sudden change of mood, but it wasn't their business. Booker wouldn't explain himself to anyone. Not even Randi, and he had talked to her yesterday. He had called her to check in and ask about her plans to visit—brownie points with his sister. And he called his parents and talked to them for a bit. More brownie points. And he hadn't said a word about Lennox Clarke. Nor would he.

The lecture hall was empty when he entered. Booker put his paper cup on the desk, his bag on the chair, and shrugged out of his coat. He wouldn't do it often, but he had dressed down today. The relaxing weekend had apparently spilled over into his Monday morning. Instead of a shirt and tie, he wore a form-fitting, short-sleeved black shirt with gray flat front casual trousers. The tattoos on his arms were mostly covered, but the last he had checked tattoos weren't illegal or even against the dress code in the Killdare University handbook.

Lennox had asked about them. In fact, she had kissed them. Licked a trail up the dagger on his left arm. Kissed across his chest, stopping to suck on his nipples, and then she'd sunk her teeth into the skull on his right arm.

"Careful, there," he mumbled when his dick got the reminder about Lennox's hot mouth all over his body. Since he was alone, he adjusted himself and took a drink, making himself think about class discussion today rather than Lennox's plump lips on his cock. Putting his coffee down again, he opened his bag to take his laptop out, twisting to look when the door opened.

Part of him hoped Lennox would be the first one in the room today so if there were any awkward stares, they could get them out of the way without an audience. Part of him hoped she walked in after at least ten other students, so he wouldn't have to look at her, to look her in the eyes, and deal with any awkward moments.

Kara dropped into her seat with a huff that sounded slightly irritated.

"What's wrong with you?" he asked. He opened the laptop and tapped the power button.

"Got a C on an accounting test."

"Ouch."

"I hate numbers."

"Me, too," he agreed.

"Is that why you're in literature?" She shot him a grin. Her hair was messy, and her makeup already looked old, a little caked. Maybe she hadn't made it home last night. Booker didn't want to know.

"Yes. And no." He shrugged. "I love words."

"When did you know what you wanted to be?"

"You mean when I grow up?" He laughed as the door opened again. Damned if his heart didn't race away when he saw Lennox follow Rupe and Josh in.

"Yeah." Kara nodded.

"I dunno. I was always a nerd." He perched on the edge of his desk, crossed his ankles, and folded his arms over his chest.

"Right." Kara rolled her eyes.

"Seriously. I always loved to read. Loved school. Started lifting weights in high school and beat the shit out of this guy for looking at my sister when I was fifteen. But I still kind of felt like a nerd."

"A badass nerd."

He tipped his head at Kara and let his gaze roam the room as the seats began to fill. Lennox took her time getting settled, but when she did, she stared at him boldly, just as she always did. He wondered if seeing the hint of the tattoos on his arms made her think of the other night. If she had dreamt about the things he had done to her.

"Lennox." Rupe turned in his seat and called to her. Booker wondered how many times her name had rolled off his lips when they were together.

"Hmm?" She flicked her gaze to him.

"My sister's coming in town next weekend. She wants to see Eloise."

Booker had flipped the light switches when he'd come in a few minutes earlier, but Lennox's smile lit up the room.

"I work Friday," she told him. "But I'm free Saturday and Sunday."

"Cool. I'll tell her." Rupe nodded.

"I'm comin', too," Josh told them.

Lennox shot Josh a look, but Booker could still see a ghost of a smile on her face.

"You bring your daughter around often?" Booker asked her.

"Now and then," she answered. "She loves Rupe's sister. And Dr. Rutledge."

Dr. Rutledge?

Why did Lennox's daughter love Matthew Rutledge? Dr. Rutledge was a biology professor or something in the sciences. His office was in the Konrath Building on South Campus. As far as Booker knew, the guy was married and had kids. Maybe that was it. Maybe he had a kid Eloise's age?

"Shoulda been at Keale House with us Friday night, Dr. Gannon," Josh called. Booker dragged his gaze away from Lennox to look at Josh as the kid settled back to lounge in his seat. He held his breath, waiting for Josh to make a dumbass comment that could get him in trouble. "Had a hell of a darts tournament."

Booker hoped his relief wasn't visible.

"Good thing for you I wasn't," he answered. "I'd have mopped the floor with your asses."

Rupe snorted.

"I was undefeated," Josh told him.

"Pretty sure my night at home beat your darts tournament," he said with a shrug. He turned to the door, sweeping his eyes over Lennox, and catching her nibbling on her lip. She'd scraped those pretty white teeth over his ass cheek at one point Friday night while she'd had her fingers wrapped possessively around him. She was a fast learner; he'd give her that.

Booker stepped behind the podium and thought about Kara'a accounting test. He didn't like numbers. Didn't like accounting. Didn't care for Cs. Resting his elbows on the podium, he scrambled to list other things he didn't like, to keep those sexy thoughts of Lennox out of his head.

"Anybody read ahead?" he asked conversationally. "Anybody finish *Dracula* yet?"

Two hands went in the air, one of them Lennox's.

43

LENNOX

Lennox had only asked that he treat her the same in the classroom as he did everyone else. After that first kiss, when he had blown her off, she had told Booker that she deserved the same respect that every other student in the room deserved and received.

After that blistering night together, the one burned into her memory and her body and her heart, he did. Starting with asking about Eloise and how often she brought her daughter around school and fellow students. He still called on her for class discussions, still seemed impressed with her thoughts and what she shared in discussion. He wished her a good day just like he did everyone else when class was over. And the few times she saw him in the following weeks —whether at Crave, at Caulfield Library, or even Sidecar a time or two—he had been polite.

It was killing her, but Lennox did her best to only die a little at a time. So Eloise didn't see it. She couldn't be sad, hurt, or jealous around her little girl. Eloise came first; she always had. She was careful with the way Booker's courtesies hurt her around Collins, too. It wouldn't do to let her best friend see her mope about a man she should never have given herself to.

But she did her best acting around Booker, himself. As much as she wished there was more to what had happened between them, as much as she wished he would wave her over for conversation at Crave as she had seen him do with damned near everyone else in her film and lit class, she wouldn't let him see it.

She still dreamt about him. About the dirty, sexy things he had done to her body. About the things he showed her he liked, the way he wanted to be touched. She dreamt about sitting next to him at Sidecar, drinking whiskey and sharing long, slow kisses.

Lennox believed him. About the video and the two girls who had blown the whistle on him. After all, if his wife had gone with him to sort the whole sordid thing out, he must not have had anything to do with that video.

But she wasn't sure she believed she was the first student he had ever come onto. As tortured as he had appeared in the beginning of what they did, he had been bold and demanding once he had her in his bedroom. Not cruel, but most definitely not uncertain or hesitant any longer.

Lennox drove herself crazy wondering about it. Remembering him saying she was the only one in the film and lit class that he wanted. And seeing him now so often on campus, always in conversation, often with coed students.

She had seen him laughing with Kara more than once, and even though she liked Kara, she had to wonder if he was fucking her now. Or maybe he wanted to, but Kara was smarter than Lennox, and she had said no.

On the other hand, Lennox had no regrets about the night she spent with Booker. Even if by the time he left Killdare Springs she had died completely and there was nothing left of her but ash and bone, she cherished the night with him.

If asked, especially if Booker could read her thoughts and poked at her for being sensitive or sentimental, she would simply say she was grateful to learn so much about sex and her own body and what she liked. She sure as hell wouldn't admit that she wanted more from him. And by more, she meant not only more sex but more. More smiles. More shared laughter. More conversation.

Leave it to her to fall for someone like Booker Gannon.

A vampire in his own right. Charming and good-looking and sexy as hell, but someone who had slipped in close and sucked the life out of her when she was unprepared. She thought Monty's family was bad. This sort of torture was a completely different level than the fear, the dread, Eve and Joseph McArthur created.

At least March ushered in sunny skies and warmer temperatures. She and Eloise spent time outside. They went for walks and played in the backyard. She started working on her paper for Dr. Gannon's class. As much attention as he gave her now, she thought she could probably write ten pages of gibberish, and either he wouldn't notice and give her an A or wouldn't care and give her an A.

She reminded herself often that she simply had to get through the first week of May, and then she wouldn't have to see him again. She might still hurt, still yearn for him, for his time and attention and kisses, but out of sight would be a step in forgetting about him and letting him go.

But then her mind would wander further down that road and wonder where he would go. What he would do next. Would he still teach? Would he find someone new to seduce? Would he ever settle down and remarry?

Even when she worked herself up enough to hate him, to be angry with him for being true to his word and only taking one night from her, she still wanted him to be happy. If Sofie and Reese had done what he said, if he was innocent and he had lost his reputation and his wife because of that, he deserved to move on and be happy.

"What're you thinkin' about?"

Lennox looked up when Josh nudged her knee. She blinked as she snapped out of her thoughts. Put her legs down and looked at the fireplace, the flames roaring on this particularly chilly March day. Her biology book was open in her lap, even though she'd been lost in thought about Booker. She snapped the book closed and stretched as Josh dropped into the chair across the low coffee table.

"Studying," she mumbled. "Guess I spaced out."

"You started on the final paper in Gannon's class yet?"

Lennox leaned forward to put her book on the coffee table.

"Started thinking about it. Haven't gotten very far, though."

"I hate literature," he groaned.

Lennox snorted. "I wanna know how you keep your GPA up enough to stay on the basketball court."

"By the skin of my teeth." He slouched in the chair and closed his eyes. "Why do I need literature to be an accountant?"

"Why would anyone want to be an accountant?"

Eyes still closed, he smiled and shrugged.

"Because I hate reading."

Lennox picked up her mug, but she only stared at the syrupy remains of the mocha in the bottom. Putting it back down, she sat back and put her feet up again.

"Where was Rupe today?"

"Probably hungover as hell," he answered. "He asked Kara out last night."

"Seriously?"

Josh opened his eyes and nodded. "She turned him down."

"Ouch."

"Gave him the let's-be-friends line."

"It's not a line, Josh," she argued as Josh lifted his gaze over her shoulder and nodded at whoever had joined them. "Sometimes things stay better as friendships."

"Whatever." He watched over her shoulder as the newcomer moved around the end of the loveseat to sit down. Lennox tried not to flinch, to react, when she realized it was Booker. "What're you doing this weekend?"

"I don't know. Why?" She looked back at Josh.

"Let's go out."

Booker paused in the act of taking a drink. Lennox shook her head.

"No."

"Not you and me." Josh rolled his eyes. "I get it. You're too good for any of us. You probably have a guy tucked away somewhere. Maybe someone you know from work."

Lennox laughed out loud. "I'm not hiding anyone, Josh. Just busy."

"Let's get Rupe and go out. He's bummed."

"Mm." She nodded and glanced at Booker. "Maybe."

"What's going on?" He glanced at Josh, trying to pass the question off as a greeting. Lennox wondered what he would have said, if she had said yes, if Josh was really asking her on a date. Would he be jealous?

There was an easy way to find out, but she wasn't interested in playing games. She didn't want to use Banks or Josh or Rupe, and she had no interest in any of them. Not to mention, even if she and Booker could be together, she would rather he just want *to be with her*, not want to keep her *from* anyone else.

"Girl trouble," she announced as she sat forward to grab her book. She felt Booker watching her as she packed her bag and stood. "I'm out."

"Why?" Josh frowned.

"I need to go see Eloise for a bit before I go to work."

"Uh-huh. You dress like a Vegas cocktail waitress when you're slinging drinks?"

"Ass." She tugged the bill of Josh's cap down as she passed him. "You're just mad because I turned you down. Twice."

44

BOOKER

Booker had just come home from a five-mile run and ducked into the kitchen for a bottle of water when someone tapped on his door. Surprised, he took a half second to wonder if it was Lennox. She wouldn't dare come to his house and knock on his door when it was daylight, would she?

Bottle in hand, he made his way to the front door, eyes on the windows in the living room as he passed through. Not so much daylight as dusk, but if Lennox pulled her car anywhere in this neighborhood and walked up to his door at this hour, someone would see her.

He gave the door a yank, irritation and curiosity at war in his gut. Surprised to find his sister on his porch, he could only stare at her. She looked good. Dark hair swept up in a cute ponytail. Her usual makeup routine on her face. Dressed in what he thought were yoga pants and an off-shoulder green sweatshirt, she offered him a big smile.

A little frustrated—whether because Randi had finally come to check on him or because Randi wasn't Lennox and even though it was foolhardy, he had hoped it was Lennox at the door—Booker frowned as he stepped back.

"What're you doing here?"

"Is that any way to greet your favorite sister?"

"Only sister," he reminded her as she stepped inside. She had some sort of slouchy bag over her shoulder, not big enough to hold clothing for an overnight stay. But Booker saw her car at the curb out front, and it was possible she had a bag stowed in it. She started to hug him, but he stepped back and shook his head. "Just got back from a run. I don't think you want to do that."

"You're right." She nodded.

"What's going on?" He pushed the door closed, but he couldn't help looking up and down the street first. As if Lennox might be lurking out there, watching him. He didn't want that; he didn't want any crazy stalker behavior.

But it would be nice if she gave him any indication she had even thought about him since the night they spent together. If anything, Booker felt like Lennox was playing things too cool, like it hadn't mattered much to her one way or the other.

Like it was no-strings-attached sex.

The same as it was for him.

"I finally got my schedule switched up at work," Randi told him. "First weekend I've had off in, like, eighteen months."

"And you decided to give up a free weekend to visit your brother?" He tipped his head and frowned.

"Trust me. I've made my rounds of the bars and the clubs and the—"

Booker held his free hand up and shook his head. "Nope. Stop there."

"Artas is boring these days," she said simply. "And I miss you."

"Killdare Springs is boring, too," he told her. She followed him to the kitchen. "Are you staying for the weekend?"

"If I'm not cramping your style."

Booker snorted. "Yeah. Livin' it up here, Randi."

"So, how's it going?"

Booker tipped the bottle up and drained it one big swallow. Randi watched him toss it in the recycle bin and then lean back on the counter.

"Okay, I guess."

"That's it? Okay?"

"What if I shower and then we grab something to eat? I didn't have lunch today. Last thing I ate was a scone at about eight this morning."

"Okay." She shrugged.

"Where do you wanna go?" he asked as he headed for the stairs.

"Somewhere local," she called in response.

Local. He could take her to Tito's for wings. But he imagined the background of bowling alley noise wasn't conducive to a catch-up session, regardless of the fact that Booker had no plans to share anything personal with her.

Sidecar would be cool, but they didn't serve food. Maybe The Hatch—the restaurant at the front of the building. He'd never eaten there, but now seemed like a good time to try it. He showered quickly and dressed in jeans and a button-down gray shirt. Tried not to think about the fact that it was possible he would run into Lennox if he and Randi went to Sidecar.

Then again, he had heard her tell Josh she had to work tonight. Booker had no idea what time she got off. But odds were if she worked at a tavern, she would work late. He found Randi in his living room, feet on the coffee table, eyes on her phone screen.

"Sexting with someone?" he asked as he snatched his car keys from the table by the door.

She snorted. "Mmm. Yeah. Me and Liza get pretty dirty sometimes."

Booker laughed. He'd met most of Randi's friends, including Liza Roberts. The woman was a tall, pretty blonde who talked too much.

"Don't even wanna go there." He shook his head.

"Wise." Randi put her feet down and stood. "Where ya takin' me for dinner?"

"Place called The Hatch."

"Is it fancy? Do I need to change?"

"Mm." He gave her a once over. "Maybe."

"Okay. Pick again. Too lazy to get my bag right now."

He laughed as he ushered her out the door to the porch. "Good to see some things don't change."

Randi beamed up at him as they skipped down the steps, and Booker directed her to his SUV.

"Do you want bar food? Pizza?"

"Just had pizza last night." She shook her head as she slid into the passenger seat. "So, bar food."

"Either that or go put some jeans on and change your shoes." He pulled his door closed and buckled his seatbelt.

"Bar food it is," she said with a nod.

"How're Mom and Dad?" Booker started the SUV.

"Good." She dropped her phone in the pocket of her door. "Mom said you've been calling her more."

Booker shrugged. He was, but he didn't want to get into the whys of it.

He drove without answering for a few blocks. He was taking her to The Garage. Not sure when he had decided that, not sure parading his sister around the workplace of a student he slept with was a good idea, but now that it was in his head, he couldn't shake it. He wanted to see her. Just to lay eyes on her. To remind himself about the heat of her kiss. Her skin on his. The soft little sounds in her throat that led to the sexy-as-fuck moaning when he was inside her.

He also wanted to see her at work. Just to see how she interacted with people.

Not *people*.

Her *boss*.

Men who frequented taverns like the one where she worked.

Booker hadn't been to The Garage before, but he had looked it up on one of those recent nights when he couldn't sleep because he was thinking about Lennox. Well, to be fair, he had started thinking about the film and lit class, wondering what sort of final papers he would be reading in a month and wondering where he would end up when the semester ended.

Certainly not Artas State. He had loved his time there, but the place wasn't big enough for him now. Even though a year would have passed by the time the next school year started, even though he and Ashley had proved he couldn't have been a part of the video, there was still lingering doubt. With other faculty. Students. Students' families.

"Wow." Randi eyed the building as he pulled into a parking spot across the street. The white aluminum-sided building had seen better days, but he supposed it did resemble a garage. There was a small pedestrian door at the far right and an overhead door he assumed was rolled open in warmer weather. "When you said bar food, you meant it."

He laughed as he locked the SUV.

"One of my students works here."

"Yeah? You've been before?"

"No. But I've heard the food is good."

He had heard that—from several students and from other professors.

"Good. I'm hungry. And I could use a beer."

Booker studied his sister for a moment. "Are you okay? Is something going on?"

"Let's get a beer," she answered with a big smile.

45

LENNOX

"You got plans tonight?"

Lennox looked at her boss with a frown. "Do I ever?"

The old man shrugged. "You can clear out when the dinner crowd goes. Tiffany's good for the night."

"Thanks." She nodded as she reached for the plated chicken sandwich table seven had ordered. "I can always use the study time."

"You study too much," he told her. "Go play with your kid."

She flashed him a big smile as she grabbed the catfish dinner special for table seven and slipped out to the dining area to deliver the food.

"Here we go." She put the plates down with a smile, but she looked up when the door opened on the far side of the tavern. That smile froze on her face when she saw Booker

Gannon lead a cute dark-haired woman inside. What the hell was he doing here? And who was he with?

The two wound through a couple of tables to claim a high-top on the north wall.

"Can I getcha anything else right now?" she asked the couple at her current table.

"We're good."

Assured they were happy, Lennox looked around for Tiffany, the other waitress on tonight. When she didn't see her, she sucked in a deep breath, blew it out slowly, and walked on weak knees to the table where Booker was sitting.

"Dr. Gannon." She hoped her mouth was smiling. That it wasn't small enough to make him think she was jealous. And not big enough to look fake, like she was jealous and trying to prove to him she wasn't.

"Hi." He flashed a smile at her.

She glanced at the woman with him, painfully aware that he hadn't even called her by name. Swallowing down the hurt, she offered the woman a smile.

"What can I get you to drink?"

The woman's face was friendly, almost familiar. She looked at Booker.

"Wanna share a pitcher?" she asked him.

"Damn." He frowned at her over the plastic-coated menu in his hands. "You're making me nervous."

Lennox shifted on her feet.

"How about a pitcher of whatever lager you have on draft."

Lennox glanced at Booker and back at the woman.

"You got it. Do you want me to put in any appetizers for you?"

"Wings," the woman told her. Lennox nodded. She wasn't sure she would eat wings in front of Booker Gannon. At least, not in public. But the idea of eating wings at his kitchen island, him licking her fingers, tasting the hot sauce on his tongue, almost made quiver.

"Be right back."

She stepped away, hoping she wasn't wobbling on her feet. Sure as hell felt like it. Why would he bring a woman here with him? He had never come in here before, but he knew Lennox worked here. It wasn't like she'd been clingy. Lennox hadn't tried to catch him alone. She hadn't left him notes. She wasn't stalking him. Booker Gannon had no idea she was hung up on him. So why did he feel the need to be a dick and parade a woman in here for her to see?

And why did she care?

She put the order in for wings and told Pax she needed a pitcher. And reminded herself to breathe. Her body felt faint, her fingers and toes tingled. She wanted to hate the woman with Booker, but she wasn't a mean person.

Still, the possibility that Booker would take that woman back to his house and undress her and worship her body as he had with Lennox made her want to throw up.

"You okay?" Pax set the full pitcher on the bar and leaned over to look at her closely. "Your face is beet red. You sick?"

Lennox took a deep breath and shook her head. "Fine. Just hot."

She stacked two pint glasses and carried them and the pitcher back to table ten. Maybe she should just think of them that way. The people at table ten.

"Here we go." She set the pitcher down first and then placed the glasses in front of them. "Decide on dinner yet?" She looked at the woman first, because she always took the woman's order first. And because it was easier to look at her, even though half of her considered clawing her face off so Booker wouldn't be quite so into her.

This felt worse than seeing him laughing and talking with Kara on campus. She'd probably have a heart attack if she saw that video of the two coeds rolling around naked together in his bed.

"What's your favorite item on the menu?" the woman asked her, eyebrows arched curiously. Lennox felt Booker's eyes on her. She was glad for the t-shirt and jeans she was wearing, although his stare burned right through the clothing. Good thing the woman clarified menu items, because Lennox's favorite item at the table right now was Booker.

Maybe his hands.

His mouth.

His shoulders.

"The tenderloin is really good," Lennox decided. "But my absolute favorite is the bacon cheeseburger."

"I'll do the tenderloin," the woman told her. Lennox nodded and turned to Booker.

"Don't you need to write it down?" he asked her.

"I have a really good memory, Dr. Gannon," she promised him.

He didn't blush, but he did jerk his gaze away from her and look at the menu again.

"Bacon cheeseburger and fries."

She nodded. "Everything on the burger?"

"No onion or pickle."

Lennox gave them a polite nod and walked away. No onion. Well, of course he wouldn't want onion on his burger. Not if he was going to take this woman home and fuck her senseless.

He liked that phrase. Lennox remembered him saying it to her more than once. She put the order in, delivered their wings when they were up, but only put the plate down with a polite smile. They were deep in conversation. Lennox supposed that was possible for him with a woman like this. She wasn't a student. Booker Gannon could be seen anywhere, doing normal things, with a woman who wasn't a student at Killdare University.

46

BOOKER

"I had a fling. It kind of ended badly," Randi told him. "And I hadn't seen you for a while. So I thought I'd come down here and drink some beer with you."

"Explain ended badly."

Randi took a big drink and looked around the tavern. While it was just a tavern, the interior didn't look as rough as the exterior had advertised. Booker hadn't been in Killdare Springs a year, but he did know this wasn't the greatest neighborhood, and he didn't love the idea of Lennox working here. Waiting on some of the guys he had noticed at the bar. Walking out to her car after a late shift.

"Randi." Booker tipped his head. "What happened? Did he—"

"Found out he was married."

Booker flinched.

"Who was it?"

"An orthopedic surgeon."

"A doctor."

She nodded as she stared morosely at her beer.

"You *know* the doctors at your hospital."

"Yeah. But he was supposedly divorced. Only not really."

"And he let you believe it?"

"He did." She nodded and flicked her eyes up to look at Booker's face. "Dumb mistake, I know. I'm too old to make that mistake."

"Mmm." Booker wasn't judging but commiserating.

"I'm sick of Artas. I'm sick of doctors. I'm sick of nurses. I need a change."

"Like what?"

"I dunno." She took another swallow and shrugged. "Maybe a million bucks and a cottage on the beach. A Cabana boy with a big dick."

Booker squeezed his eyes closed. "Thanks for that."

"You forget that I saw the video. That girl had a rack."

"Randi." He shook his head.

"Seriously. She'll probably have a reduction before she's forty. She'll have back problems. Why do guys find that so..." She trailed off as Lennox approached their table again, this time with their sandwiches.

Booker couldn't keep his eyes off her. Reminded of Sofie and her low-cut shirts, of Reese with her tiny shorts, it amazed him that Lennox Clarke could turn him on with just one look. She was dressed in a black t-shirt with The Garage logo on the back, skinny jeans, and black tennis shoes. One side of her hair was tucked behind her ear, and as always, she wore little to no makeup.

And all Booker could think about was kissing her sweet mouth.

Just one more time.

"Can I get you anything else right now?" she asked them.

"No, thanks." Randi's smile was sincere. Before he could say a word, Lennox nodded and walked away. He couldn't watch her without arousing suspicion, so he reached for the ketchup bottle.

"Why don't you join a dating site?" he suggested.

"I might." Randi nodded. "Maybe when hell freezes over. I don't need to be catfished, Booker."

"Get a cat." He dunked a fry in his ketchup and popped it in his mouth. "Be a cat lady."

"Is she your student?"

Booker snapped his eyes up to look at Randi. "What?"

"Our waitress. She called you Dr. Gannon."

"Mmm." He nodded. "Yeah, she's in my film and lit class."

"She's cute." Randi picked up her sandwich. "You ever think about a dating app?"

"No."

"Have you dated? Since the divorce?"

"You know I haven't, Randi."

"Why not? Killdare Springs is a pretty decent-sized town, right? I'm sure you could meet someone here."

"I'm not sure I want to," he answered with a shrug.

He didn't. Want to. He didn't want to meet someone else. If he wanted anyone, it was Lennox Clarke. But he couldn't have her, so end of story.

"You deserve to move on, Book. To be happy."

"Women suck."

"Some do," she agreed. "Myself included, now that I've had a fling with a married man."

"I'm fine, Randi." He shook his head. "Besides, I don't wanna end up involved with anyone here and then have to pick up and move when the semester's over."

"I get that." She twisted her glass in circles on the table. "Any idea what you're gonna do?"

"Nope."

"Still gonna do that solo vacation?"

"Maybe."

"If they offered you a position here, would you stay?"

"Maybe." He shrugged. "I just. I don't know. I'm up in the air about everything. And I don't know..."

"Know what?" Randi coaxed him.

"How to...how to land. How to go back to normal life. I mean." He picked up his glass and took a drink. "I thought Ashley and I would be together until one of us was dead. Like we said in our vows. I thought we'd have kids together. I thought I'd teach at Artas until maybe she found somewhere she wanted to move to. To raise our kids. And now..."

She watched him patiently.

"Now, I'm paying rent again. I'm working a temporary gig, even though I have my fucking doctorate. I don't know how to settle in anywhere, Randi. Or where home should be."

"Do you like it here?"

He hesitated. Ten, eight—even six weeks ago—he would have immediately said no. Now he wasn't sure he *liked* it here, but he did know he *didn't hate* it here.

He didn't hate all women.

In fact, he hadn't really had time for hatred at all lately.

"Maybe."

"I saw Ashley the other day," she told him.

"Did you talk to her?"

"Just a hello, in passing."

"I made mistakes, Randi," he said quietly. "Enough to make my wife doubt me. The boundaries were definitely blurred, and it was my fault for letting it happen."

They finished their sandwiches, but Booker was still

munching on fries when Lennox came back to check on them.

"Can I get you anything else?" she asked. Her smile seemed a bit forced. Booker wondered if something had upset her. Had one of the men in here said something to her?

"Just the check," he told her.

She nodded.

"Booker said you're in his film and lit class."

Booker glanced at Randi, realizing he hadn't introduced them. At Artas, he would have. Because he'd had nothing to hide there. Now he did. *Now* he had crossed that ethical line, and he had automatically tried to hide it.

"Yeah." Lennox nodded, her smile warmer for Randi than it had been for him. "I'm Lennox. Studying nursing at Killdare."

"Nursing." Randi grinned.

Shit. Randi was a nurse. What if they clicked? What if his illicit one-night fling and his big sister started talking?

"I'm a cardiac nurse," Randi told Lennox. "In Artas."

Lennox nodded. Booker wondered if she remembered that first conversation they'd had in the lecture hall. When she told him she would need to leave Friday classes a bit early, and he had mentioned that his sister was a nurse.

"Nice to meet you." Lennox waved her hand at the plates. "Want me to get this stuff out of the way for you guys?"

"Please." Randi sat back to give Lennox room to work.

"Working late tonight?" Booker asked her, because if he didn't engage her in some conversation, Randi would be suspicious.

"No." Lennox shook her head. "I'm actually out of here in about an hour. Gonna meet Josh and Rupe for a while."

47

LENNOX

She did meet Rupe and Josh later, when she left The Garage. Thankfully, Booker and his—date? Companion?—thankfully, *Booker* was gone when she got off work. The woman with him was pretty, and she had been warm and friendly. Didn't mean Lennox liked her or wanted to talk to her again.

Rupe wasn't heartbroken about Kara turning him down, not the way Josh had made him seem. But Eloise was with Collins, so Lennox stayed out for a couple of drinks with them. She begged off when they decided to go to a frat party. Lennox had no interest in campus parties, not anymore. If she were going to stay out now, she would prefer to go to Sidecar and nurse a drink before going home.

Except what if Booker took that woman there tonight? Before taking her home?

Lennox watched Rupe and Josh shuffle across the parking lot at Tito's before she started her car. She had no idea where she was going as she pulled out of the lot. Home or Sidecar? The only way she could handle Sidecar tonight was if Banks was working. She could hang with him for a while.

She was dead curious if Booker would show up there. With that woman. But if she chatted Banks up for a bit, it wouldn't look stalkerish, right? She wasn't really dressed for a night out, not at a place like Sidecar, but she didn't want to go home and change. For one thing, she couldn't breeze in and out, leaving Eloise behind. And another, Collins would question her. She wasn't in the mood for that. Not after waiting on Booker at The Garage.

If Collins needled too much, Lennox might end up saying something stupid.

She didn't know what the hell they were, but she had feelings for Booker Gannon. Better to bounce them around in her head, by herself, than enlist her friend's help in figuring it out. Collins would have every right to say *I told you so.*

Lennox searched the back lot for Banks' truck, only a little bit relieved when she saw it parked in his usual spot. What she was doing—walking in here to see if Booker showed up, ready to chat Banks up for what reason? To make Booker jealous?—was dangerous.

Never mind Monty's family. Getting tangled up with Booker had been stupid, dangerous to her. To her heart. Yes, Monty's family, Eve especially, might have words for her if she found herself involved in a scandal with a professor. But at this point, she was on her own with her feelings, and the man who had taken her to his bed was becoming her obsession.

She had left her daughter at home so she could stalk the professor she'd had earth-shattering sex with. The same professor accused of assault, sexual misconduct at the least. The same professor Lennox had sworn she wasn't interested in and had slept with and then promised she understood the rules of the game. That she would leave him alone.

Once she parked, she found a sweatshirt she had tossed in the back seat of her car earlier in the week. A Killdare University hoodie. She snatched it and tugged it on over her t-shirt, fluffed her hair, and left the safety of her car. If Banks was busy, she would duck out fast and leave him alone. If Booker showed up, she would not approach him. Nor would she do anything stupid with Banks to provoke Booker.

Satisfied with herself for laying out her rules, she headed into Sidecar, happy to see the end bar stool vacant.

"Hey, Lex." Banks gave her a warm smile. "You alone?"

She nodded. "The guys went to a frat party."

"Not your scene." Banks nodded. "Drink?"

She considered a shot of tequila or five but decided against it since she had to drive home.

"Please," she answered.

"Did you work tonight?"

"Yeah." She pulled in a deep breath as she looked around the dimly lit bar. Soft piano jazz soothed her nerves. Funny how she had grown so used to this place. It felt like home. Maybe she wasn't here to stalk Booker in the

event that he showed up. Maybe she wasn't here to flirt
with Banks, just to rile Booker up. Maybe she was here
because Sidecar had become her sanctuary. She would
touch base with Banks and then go home. If Eloise was
still awake—she would be, because Collins let the kid
stay up and eat sugar, just like an auntie would do—she
would cuddle up with her on the couch for a movie. If
Eloise was sleeping, she would delve into girl talk with
Collins.

About her last date. Or a date on the horizon. Collins often
told her she felt her biological clock ticking away. They
should most definitely be concentrating on finding *her* true
love, not worrying about Lennox imploding with steamy,
sexy thoughts about her professor.

"Have you been busy tonight?" she asked her friend.

He shook his head as he put her drink in front of her. "Just
getting busy now."

She nodded. "Thought I'd bug you for a minute and say hi
before I go home."

"You know I love your face sitting here at my bar."

Lennox laughed and rolled her eyes.

"Monty's parents were here earlier," he told her. His words
turned her backbone to steel. She sat up straight and looked
around. "Relax. They're gone. I saw them leave."

She blew out a quick breath and picked up her drink.

"She can't take her from me. I know that. But she could turn
her against me."

"No." He shook his head. "I mean, the woman is cold, and I

get why she scares you. But no. No one's gonna turn your little girl on you."

"I think she's good to Eloise."

Banks nodded.

"What if I'm holding onto that fear? You know she threatened me about having an abortion."

"Yeah."

"I wouldn't have done it, but she scared the hell out of me. What if I'm holding onto that fear? And really, she just wants to be in my daughter's life?"

"That's a really deep thought for a Friday night, Lex."

She laughed softly but continued, "I mean, seriously, Banks. It just hit me. What if all this time I've hated her because of that fear, and what if she just wants to be Eloise's grandmother? I mean, I don't know that Eloise could feel about her the way she feels about my mom. But—"

Lennox stopped talking when Banks covered her hand with his.

"Breathe."

"Maybe—"

"I think you should just do what you do, Lennox. Be Eloise's mom. And allow Eve McArthur to see her. Just as you have been doing."

"Yeah?"

"It's not like you fill Eloise's head with horrible thoughts and words about Monty's family, right?"

"Of course not."

"Then do what you do. You're a good mom."

She nodded and turned her hand over to squeeze his. "Thanks."

The worry had carted her away there for a moment. And even though Banks didn't know the depth of her worry, her guilt—since she had done something she technically shouldn't have, though not something worthy of losing her daughter—she felt better.

"Gonna make the rounds," he told her. "I'll be back."

She nodded and watched him move away, startled when someone sat down next to her.

"That was cozy."

She hesitated before looking at him. Either he had already been here, somewhere at the bar or at a cocktail table, or she hadn't noticed him come in, but apparently Booker had seen what looked like she and Banks holding hands.

Booker sat next to her, the woman to his right.

So much for the rules she had laid down for herself. She'd broken all but one, and Booker had taken care of that one when he approached her.

48

BOOKER

Randi hadn't wanted to go straight back to the house, so despite her casual attire, he had brought her to Sidecar.

Hoping he would see Lennox. Maybe he had assumed he would see her with Josh and Rupe, although he'd never seen the guys in the speakeasy with or without her. It didn't have the college vibe. Finding her cozied up at the bar with Banks, the guy who had laid that steamy kiss on her a while back, had been a tough pill to swallow. Bad enough to think of her out partying with college guys, especially Josh, if she had a history with him.

But this guy? He was older. Probably not Booker's age, but not a typical beer-guzzling college guy. He was a good-looking guy, and he probably came off as sophisticated to someone like Lennox. And they knew each other well, if Banks was her best friend's brother.

Booker fought a sudden urge to grab Lennox, to haul her up against him, and plant his mouth on hers. To claim her.

Fuck if he didn't want to beat his fists on his chest and roar at every male in this place. Lennox was his.

When had that happened?

When had he gone from one hot-as-fuck night to desperate and possessive?

Lennox sipped her drink and put her glass down.

"Thought you were meeting Josh and Rupe."

Had she done the whole frat thing? Beer pong? Other drinking games? Had she danced topless on tables and spread her legs for some dumbass college kid who didn't know how to pace himself and couldn't get her off before his own race to the finish?

Booker had always assumed that path—the party path— was a given for most college kids. Guys and girls. He'd lived it, hadn't he? All his buddies had. Ashley had told him stories. And as a professor, he had overheard countless stories of the same events.

And yet, the thought of Lennox parading around with a red Solo cup, with skimpy shorts and a low-cut top, slipping into any available bedroom with a random guy for a quick fuck, made him green with envy. And red with rage.

She deserved more, better.

Satin sheets. Rose petals. Champagne.

Lovemaking instead of fast, mediocre sex.

"I did," she answered with a nod. Her face was serene, the complete opposite of the thoughts raging through him. But she wouldn't meet his eyes. "We went to Tito's for a beer. They were going to a frat party."

"Not your thing?"

His heart was going to beat a hole through his chest. What would Lennox think of that mess?

"Nope." She shook her head. "Thought I'd say hi to Banks and then go home. Collins probably gave Eloise pudding for supper with cookies and ice cream for dessert."

He glanced to his right where Randi had her chin ducked, eyes on her phone, as she hammered out a text message.

"Can I buy you a drink?" he asked Lennox. He figured it wouldn't look weird if he bought her something when he got Randi's drink.

Lennox laughed softly. "No. Thanks."

"I didn't introduce you earlier," he said quietly as Randi put her phone down.

"Hey." Banks appeared in front of them, out of nowhere. Booker managed to keep his comment about timing to himself. "What can I get you guys?"

"I need a pour of Lockland. Neat."

"I'll do the same," Randi told him.

"'kay. Lex?"

"I'm good." Lennox shook her head.

Booker watched Banks select the bourbon from the back bar. "Lennox, this is my sister, Randi. She's visiting for the weekend."

Lennox met his eyes with a hard stare. Booker froze, para-lyzed as that serene mask slipped, and something else gripped her features. Hurt. Lennox was hurt.

"Hi, Randi." She leaned around him and offered Randi a warm smile.

"Hey." Randi reached to shake Lennox's hand. "We should talk about nursing school."

"I'd love to." Lennox sounded sincere. "But I need to get home to my daughter."

"Next time."

"Absolutely." She nodded. "Goodnight, Dr. Gannon. See ya Monday."

Booker watched when she slid off the barstool. She had pulled a Killdare sweatshirt on, and again, he wondered if it was hers or if it belonged to one of the guys.

"You leavin' already?" Banks caught her before she walked away.

"I am. See ya." She threw her arms around Banks and planted a kiss on his cheek.

"You okay to get home?"

"I'm fine."

She walked away without a second glance at Booker.

"I'll be right back," he mumbled to Randi. He followed Lennox without waiting for Randi to respond. He was giving himself away, to his sister at least, and yet he couldn't sit here and watch Lennox Clarke leave like this.

He couldn't do it in public, but damned if he wasn't going to march out after her and lay claim to that hot little body.

"You surprised me," he called to her as he stepped outside. Lennox slowed and finally stopped walking, out in the middle of the parking lot. She turned and watched him as he made his way to where she stood.

"What?"

"I've never seen you run."

"I'm not running."

"Yes. You are." He nodded. "This is the first time I've seen fear on your face."

Lennox huffed out a sigh of frustration and tossed her hands up. "You couldn't have told me? At The Garage? That she was your sister?"

"It's not supposed to matter," he reminded her.

"Yeah, I know. But it's one thing to watch you with other girls on campus and something else completely to have you waltz into *my* territory with a pretty woman at your side and not tell me who she is to you."

Booker tensed. "What do you mean? Girls on campus?"

Her laughter dragged over his skin like nails on a chalkboard.

"Look, you told me the rules, remember? You fucked me. It was great. But I wasn't supposed to feel anything the morning I left your bed. It doesn't mean it doesn't rip me apart when I see you talking to other students. Thinking about you giving them the same kind of night you gave me.

I'm not stupid, Booker, but your rules can't keep me from *feeling something*."

Booker moved faster than a snake striking its prey. He wrapped his fingers around her neck and sank his teeth into her bottom lip.

"I told you the only woman I can think about is you. That hasn't changed, Lennox. If anything, it's worse. You are in my every. Fucking. Thought. Every breath I take."

She swallowed hard when he pulled back to look her in the eyes.

"Is that why you came here? To hang on him, hoping I would see it?"

Lennox blinked; her glassy eyes were a knife in his gut.

"It's not supposed to matter," she whispered. "Remember?"

"You. Are. Mine."

He stamped his lips on hers and rubbed his tongue over her mouth until she gave in. The second their tongues touched, he heard that soft little moan in her throat. She wrapped one arm around his waist and drove the fingers of her other hand back through his hair.

"Mine," he repeated.

"I can't be yours," she whispered. "Remember, Dr. Gannon? I can't *be* yours. How many times did you tell me this can't be anything other than sex?"

"Tell me you want someone else." He held her steady so she couldn't look away. "Tell me you want someone else to kiss you, to make love to you like I did."

She sobbed at his words.

"Does it matter?"

"Fuck, yes, it matters, Lennox. *You belong to me.*"

Lennox shook her head. "I don't want to be your dirty little secret, Booker."

He let her go. The gentle push of her fists against his chest hurt more than if she had knocked him back a foot or two. If she had slapped him. He didn't want a dirty little secret. He wasn't sure what he wanted, but he hated the hiding. He hated sneaking around.

It wasn't who he was, and yet, it went hand in hand with who some people thought he was.

She turned away from him, tucked her hands in the front pocket of her hoodie, and walked away. Desperate to go after her, to fix this, he watched her until she approached her car and slid into the driver's seat. Never mind that he didn't know how to fix it. Now wasn't the time for any of it. His sister was inside at the bar piecing two and two together, probably ready to tear his head off.

Lennox was upset, and she needed to get home to her daughter.

Monday at class would be no better for a time to fix whatever was going on. Giving himself all weekend to think about Lennox wouldn't bring him answers. He didn't know *what* he wanted from her, but he wanted more of *it, more of her*.

Obviously, Lennox had some feelings about him, about what they had done together. The problem was that no matter if Booker could get his head on straight, if he could understand what it was about Lennox Clarke that made him breathless and paralyzed with need whenever he saw her or even heard her name, they couldn't be together.

Lennox was terrified of Eloise's grandmother. Booker knew all too well that his reputation for sexual misconduct would reflect badly on Lennox.

And he sure as hell didn't need to lose another teaching position because of misconduct. And this time, he would damn sure be guilty of that and more.

Was Lennox Clarke worth losing his career? And what the hell would he do if he was asked to leave Killdare University?

49

BOOKER

"You wanna tell me what the hell that was about?"

"Not really, no." He settled on the barstool beside Randi and picked up his glass.

"Jesus, Book." Randi groaned. "You're sleeping with her. Aren't you?"

Booker felt Randi's heavy stare, but he refused to look at her. Instead, he fixed his eyes on Banks as he swallowed a mouthful of bourbon. It could be dog-piss for all he cared right now. The guy was closer to Lennox than Booker was, and that pissed him off. What if he knew? What if that guy knew Lennox had slept with Booker?

He didn't care. He didn't care if Banks knew about him and Lennox. But he did care if Lennox had told him. If Lennox had sat here at this bar, nursing a drink, and whispering secrets about the things Booker had done to her body. If Lennox had confessed to Banks that she had feelings for

Booker. If she worried that Booker had used and discarded her.

Booker had no intention of letting this guy step in and mend her broken heart.

That look on Lennox's face earlier—when he had introduced Randi as his sister. Maybe Lennox had been jealous on campus, seeing him talking to other coeds, feeling left out or wishing for his attention again. But she had been hurt tonight. She had believed Booker brought a date to her bar to rub it in her face that he wasn't hung up on her.

He snorted, covered his eyes with one hand, and put his glass on the bar.

"Is she of age?"

"Yes."

"The other ones—?"

"Did not happen," he repeated. "Ever. I never cheated on Ashley."

"And what? Now that your career, your reputation has been dirtied, it doesn't matter anymore? Might as well do the crime if you're gonna do the time?"

He glanced at Randi, aware of Banks hovering near them, a liquor bottle in hand.

"I can't get her out of my head, Randi." He gritted the words out through clenched teeth. "Her laugh. Her smile. Her eyes."

"Do you have feelings for her?" Randi looked at him with wide eyes.

"Maybe." He shrugged. "But it doesn't matter."

"Why?"

"She's in my class."

"So, wait until the end of the semester to go public." Randi swallowed a big drink of her bourbon without a wince. "Does she have feelings for you?"

Booker glanced at Banks. The guy met his eyes.

"You good?"

Booker nodded and waited for him to walk away before continuing.

"I don't know, Randi." He sighed. "What I do know is that she has a little girl, and she's terrified of the father's family."

"What do you mean? Why?"

Booker turned to his sister. "She described them as vampires." He wondered if Randi could read the sarcasm on his face. "The guy as the sexy, irresistible bad boy vampire, and his mom as the evil queen. They have money and status."

"And being with you would look bad," Randi finished. "Because of...what happened at Artas."

"Yeah." He nodded. "Not to mention, I don't really wanna throw another job out the window. My next move might be teaching inmates or someone else I can't hurt."

"You didn't set out to hurt Ashley," Randi argued, "And I'm sure you didn't want to hurt this girl."

"I didn't want to hurt her," he grumbled, fingers wrapped around his glass. He twisted it in circles and avoided Randi's eyes again. "I wanted to consume her. Devour her. And I did. But it wasn't enough. One time wasn't enough."

"Maybe it's not her," Randi suggested softly. "Maybe it's just because you've been alone for—"

"Oh, it's her." He shook his head, his voice quiet but firm. "It's the way she stares at me in class, so boldly. She doesn't back down. Ever. It's the way she walks into the room—any room—and owns it. She's tough, Randi. She's so strong. And yet, she *gave* herself to me. She believed in me, and she gave herself to me."

Randi flinched when he glanced at her.

"She made herself vulnerable to me." His voice came out as a whisper. "Eyes wide open. Knowing I didn't want any ties. That I just wanted sex."

"Except now you want more."

"Now I want more," he agreed, eyes on his glass. "I want so much more. I don't know what the fuck I want, Randi." He swallowed hard and lifted his gaze to find his sister watching him with sad eyes and a deep, concerned frown. "I've only met her kid once. I've never met her friends. She's ten years younger than me. I don't know if I can make her happy. But I sure as fuck wish I could have the chance to try."

"What happened? Outside just now?"

"Well, I made her promise when we slept together that it didn't mean anything. I made her walk out of my bedroom, my house. And when I see her talking to any other male, I wanna rip his fucking head off, so I told her she was mine. Just now. I told her she belonged to me."

"Nice, Book."

"Yeah. Well. She doesn't want to be my dirty little secret, so I guess now she's fucked me. And we're even."

Banks approached slowly, the bottle of Lockland in hand. He tipped his head in askance.

"I don't know what's going on with you and Lex." Banks shrugged. "Not my business."

Booker watched the guy splash more of the amber liquid into his glass and then Randi's.

"Until you hurt her." Banks locked eyes with him. "She and Eloise are everything. Don't. Hurt. Her."

"Well, you might as well take a swing now," Booker announced and held his arms up in surrender. "Because I hurt her."

"Then fix it."

50

LENNOX

"Remember. Formal analysis paper's due by midnight Friday."

The guy who usually sat in front of Lennox was absent today, so she had spent most of the class staring at the back of Rupe's head. He had a cowlick she'd never noticed. She supposed it was because he needed a haircut, and that made it more noticeable.

Collins had been awake on the couch when she got home Friday night; Eloise sound asleep, snuggled up to her. Lennox had managed to keep it together for the drive home, but when she saw her daughter and best friend cozied up together, she couldn't hold the tears any longer.

Thank God, Collins hadn't said those four words she had every right to say. Lennox had picked Eloise up and carried her to bed. When the girl stirred, Lennox had pulled her covers up, kissed her cheek, and then watched and waited for her to get comfortable again. And then she'd cried to Collins.

No big ugly sobs. No buckets of ice cream consumed. Not even a glass of wine.

Just Lennox sharing in broken whispers that of course, she had fallen for Booker Gannon. And while his one-night-only rule no longer stood, he still only wanted sex. Collins hadn't reminded Lennox that she hadn't been ready for the likes of Booker, and Lennox didn't remind Collins that she hadn't gone crazy obsessive and stalked him.

Instead, she had been swallowing the hurt over and over since the night she had spent with Booker. And judging from the way her stomach hurt now, listening to Booker talk about *Nosferatu* and reminding them their papers were due, she was still swallowing the hurt. How long until it burned right through her?

Interesting that her little girl would turn six in just a few weeks, and this year, this winter, was the first time Lennox had given her heart to someone.

"So, spring break next week," Booker continued. She felt him glance at her a time or two, but she couldn't deal with it today. All the other times she had sat in this lecture hall, she wanted him to see her, to want her, to remember what they had done together. Today—after last weekend—she wished she were invisible.

What really hurt, made her angry—at herself—was that her body wanted to betray her. Her body—every inch that Booker had kissed and touched the night they were together—was ready to go back to him. To let him use her for whatever he wanted, as long as he wanted. Watching him roll his sleeves up earlier today, her eyes had locked on the expanse of wiry, forearms, and her belly had fluttered with want. Her panties were probably wet.

If he hooked his finger at her now—if the classroom was empty, and Booker made a move—she would wrap her legs around his waist and hold on for the ride. Knowing that when it was over, he would zip his pants and walk out without looking back.

How had she gotten so lost that she would trade in her self-respect, her heart, for another steamy night with someone who would never love her?

"We have a few articles this week. And *Blacula* when we come back." Booker nodded at Kara when she raised her hand. Lennox noticed the blue in her hair had faded; she wondered if Kara would dye it again. Why hadn't Kara gone out with Rupe? Why wasn't Rupe into her? He couldn't have hurt her like Booker did.

But that said everything, didn't it? If a man couldn't hurt her, she wasn't in love with him. Ergo, love hurt. She almost laughed at her weird, broken logic. She should have listened to Collins.

"Can we read ahead?"

"Ready for the Grady Hendrix book?" Booker asked Kara with a smirk.

"Yes."

"Sure. Just don't skip over the articles, because we will discuss them in class."

Lennox dragged her eyes away from Kara to find Booker looking at her. She held the stare for a moment and then looked away.

"Okay. See you all Wednesday. Read Roberts' article on *Nosferatu*."

When Booker closed his laptop, Lennox shoved hers into her bag, ready to skip out of the room as quickly as possible. She hadn't seen Booker since she had walked away from him in the parking lot at Sidecar. They were just about halfway through the semester; she would just have to buck up and get through the rest of the class. Staying away from him would be wise.

Josh dropped his hand on her head as he walked by her. Lennox flashed him a look of frustration, but he didn't notice. She watched him approach Booker as she stood to leave the room. Booker said something to him, and they shared a laugh.

Booker wouldn't tell Josh they had slept together. At least she could rest easy knowing that he would never share that with anyone. But the very idea of Josh—who had crammed his tongue down her throat once—and Booker—who had rubbed his tongue over every inch of her body—being friends made her shudder with disgust.

At herself.

Because the thought of Booker's tongue on her body made her weak in the knees all over again.

"Lennox."

She jerked her gaze from the door, over her shoulder, to where Booker stood at his desk. Josh slipped by her and headed out. Again, the thought of him and her professor sharing locker room talk made her almost physically ill.

"Can I talk to you for a second?"

"I have somewhere I need—"

"It'll just take a second," he promised her. She stood rooted to her spot by the door as the last of her classmates shuffled by her, until she was alone with Booker.

"Please don't do this," she said quietly.

"Do what?"

She lifted her chin and met his eyes. "Whatever it is you're about to do. Just let it go. I'm following your rules, Booker."

Rather than agree, rather than nod and let her go, Booker tucked his hands in his pockets and moved closer to her.

"I don't know what this is. I don't know where it can go. But I don't think it's fair to either one of us to ignore it."

"What does that mean?" she whispered.

"I told you. You're all I think about. I need you in my life."

"Until when?" She shrugged. "Until the semester's over? Until spring break's over? Until you find the next little lamb to invite home with you—"

"Jesus." He huffed and dropped his head back to stare at the ceiling. "Do you remember that night we had together?"

She laughed softly and ducked her head when her eyes burned with tears.

"I don't mean the sex, Lennox." He stepped closer to her. The touch of his hand on her face, his thumb tilting her chin up forcing her to look him in the eyes, took her breath away. "The way we talked. The intimacy we had that one night together."

Unable to look away, she blinked and nodded.

"Was that special to you?"

"Booker."

"I don't mean the orgasms. I don't mean you telling me it was never like that for you. Did that intimacy mean anything to you?"

She licked her lips when a tear slipped over her face.

"Yes."

"Then why can't you believe it meant something to me, too?"

She sniffled but said nothing.

"I'm here. The same man I was that night with you. I'm here, looking you in the eyes, and telling you that it was more than sex."

"And it still doesn't matter, Booker," she reminded him.

"I think this matters more than anything else." His voice was gruff. He leaned in closer, his breath tickling her lips. "I might be in love with you, and maybe you feel something for me. And it's not fair to walk away from that."

"We can't—"

He silenced her with a kiss. A long, deep kiss.

The door banged open behind Lennox.

"Dr. Gannon—"

She froze when she heard Josh's voice.

"Not now, Josh."

"Oh, man!"

"Get out."

"Well, that's ironic." Lennox rested her head on his shoulder. "The biggest dick in your class just saw us kissing. He's probably already told twenty people."

"I'm not done with you." Booker urged her to look up at him again and sealed his lips over hers for another kiss.

"I can't do this."

She regretted the words the second she said them. Booker dropped his hand and stepped back.

"You don't want this?"

"I do." She nodded and struggled to swallow the knot of emotion in her throat. "But I have to think of Eloise."

"Because being with someone like me will trigger Eve McArthur? This isn't worth losing—"

"Because I won't teach my daughter that it's okay to hide who you are and what you feel. I deserve more than this, Booker. I deserve someone to love me out loud."

"You do." He nodded as he tucked his hands into his pockets again. "I already talked to Richard Isles."

"Who?"

"Dean Isles."

Lennox stared at him silently.

"It's okay. If you really can't do this. If you don't want to try this. But I love you, Lennox. And I don't want to hide that or you. I don't want you to settle for less than everything you deserve. For your sake and for Eloise's sake."

"Booker."

"I told Dean Isles that I have feelings for you. I did not tell him we slept together, but I have removed myself as your professor."

"What does that mean?"

"It means that in case I can't be objective about your work, I have handed all of it over to Chuck Whisman. He's aware, also, that I have developed feelings for you. He will grade your work. You're free to move to his class, but it won't be as interesting. No vampires."

The cute, impish grin on his face twisted her heart.

"Booker."

"If your schedule does not allow for you to move to Whisman's class, you can still come here. And I will continue to have a third party monitor your attendance and evaluate your work. As a man in love with you, I can no longer have a supervisory, advisory, or evaluative role over you."

"What if they would have fired you?"

"What?"

"You went to Dean Isles? What if he would have fired you, Booker? After what happened before, what if he would have fired you?"

Booker shrugged. "What if he would have? I can find another job, Lennox."

She sniffled when he stepped closer to her again.

"But I can't find another you."

She stared at him boldly as tears streaked her face.

"I don't want you to ever look for another me."

"I love you."

Lennox leaned in close enough to brush her lips over his. She let her backpack slide to the floor at her feet and cupped his face in her hands.

"I love you, too."

"Do you forgive me? For telling Dean Isles—"

"Did you tell him we're in this together?"

"No." He shook his head. "But I'd be happy to go do that right now. If you don't have somewhere else to be."

EPILOGUE

Eloise sat primly on the loveseat by the fireplace. The birthday gift Booker had given was in her lap, though she had yet to tear into the pretty paper. She hadn't even touched the purple bow yet. Her mug of hot chocolate sat untouched on the table in front of her. Eloise twisted the little package this way and that, admiring either the wrapping job or the paper itself. Lennox watched her, amused and curious. Normally, presents lasted three seconds in her daughter's grip. Maybe this was Eve McArthur's influence.

Lennox had thrown a party for Eloise's sixth birthday. She had invited Eve and Joseph, and they had attended, even though the party was held at a skating rink. Neither of them had skated, but they had stood together and watched their granddaughter wheel slowly around the rink with either Lennox, Jaxon, or Collins, and her friends. They had gathered around when everyone sang to Eloise, and they both ate a piece of cake.

The dress they gave her for her birthday was frilly and stiff, and though it was adorable, Lennox knew Eloise would hate having to wear it. At least it was yellow, Eloise's favorite color. They had also given her a small acoustic guitar which surprised the hell out of Lennox. Collins had stepped up beside her, most likely to prop her up, when Joseph announced that they would arrange for Eloise to take lessons if she was interested.

The party had gone well, and truthfully, Lennox felt more at peace about the McArthurs than she had since realizing she was pregnant. However, she wasn't ready to vacation with them or even go out for brunch with Eve. And likely, she never would be. But if Eve and Joseph had been overbearing with her in the beginning, maybe it had been their fear that she would keep them from their granddaughter.

She had not invited Booker to Eloise's party. Though torn by the decision, she stood by it. She and Booker had gone together to Dean Isles and talked to him. Apparently, their situation wasn't the norm, but because she was of age and because Booker was single and had come forward about his personal feelings and the desire to protect both her and his career, Isles was going to allow them to date—his word. Thankfully, the details of their relationship had not come up. Lennox had no desire to get into the nitty gritty of what had already transpired between herself and Booker.

Chuck Whisman had already read her assignments and approved of the As Booker had given her. She still worried that Booker would be asked to leave when the semester was over. Where that was once all she had hoped for, now she desperately wanted him to stay. To have a place at Kill-dare University. She had seen the changes in him, aside from everything that had happened between them. He had loosened up in the lecture hall. He smiled more. Talked more.

His passion for literature, for horror, was obvious and contagious. The film and lit class had become her favorite, and she knew most of the students in the class talked about it, about Dr. Gannon, all the time. Even more, Booker's love of teaching, his respect and appreciation for students, was slipping out from behind that shield he had carried into class that first day.

Lennox liked to think she might have been part of that, part of what had brought him happiness and hope.

"I'm sorry."

Booker looked at her when she spoke. He arched his brows curiously.

Across the table, Eloise beamed up at Kara as the girl sat down beside her. The blue had all but grown out of her hair. Now she was thinking about going pink. Josh sat on the hearth of the fireplace watching Eloise, grumbling about how long it was taking her to open her presents. Josh and Rupe had pooled together and given her a set of *Junie B. Jones* books. Lennox knew those books tied the bike she got her for best present.

"For what?" Booker leaned closer to her.

Even though their secret was out, they had assured Dean Isles they would be discreet. No public displays of affection on campus. Lennox's friends knew they were together, although Josh hadn't run off blabbing the day he had found them kissing in the lecture hall. Assuming they all knew,

Lennox had referenced it later that afternoon, after they talked to the dean, at Crave. Kara and Rupe had been floored by the news. Lennox had been shocked that Josh kept his mouth shut.

"That I didn't invite you to her party."

"It's okay," he assured her.

"She likes you." Lennox sighed as Eloise climbed into Kara's lap and finally pulled the bow off the present.

"All the more reason for us to go slowly," Booker reminded her. "Making sure a six-year-old is comfortable with her mom being with someone is a lot bigger than getting the dean's permission to be together."

Lennox laughed softly.

"And we have all the time in the world." He squeezed his fingers into a fist. Lennox nodded. He wanted to touch her, hold her hand. But he wouldn't. Not here at Crave. And not in front of Eloise. Not until Lennox was ready to take that next step. "Maybe when she turns seven, I can teach her to speed skate."

"Maybe not." Lennox narrowed her eyes at him.

"Nope." He shook his head. "Maybe I could teach her to break a tackle."

"She watches football with my dad and brother," Lennox told him. "She could teach you a few things, I'm sure."

They looked back at Eloise as she tore the paper from the gift. Josh cheered her on, but Kara glanced at him with a frown.

"She savors things, Stone," Kara told him. "She's smart."

"She's pokey." Josh pointed at Eloise and grinned when she did.

"Will you read them to me?" she asked Josh. "The *Junie B. Jones* books?"

Before he could answer, she pulled the paper from the hardback book and squealed with delight.

"Mommy, it's *Goldilicious*!"

"Yes, it is." Lennox nodded and smiled. She peeked at Booker. "Yellow's her favorite color. How'd you know?"

"I didn't." Booker shrugged. "But gold is for princesses, and she kind of fits that bill."

"A princess you're gonna teach to break a tackle." Lennox grinned.

Booker shrugged. "Never know when that'll come in handy."

Eloise slithered off Kara's lap and hurried around the corner of the table.

"Will you read it? To me?" She aimed those dark eyes at Booker, and Lennox knew there wasn't a chance he would say no.

"Of course."

Eloise climbed up to sit on his lap and eyed Josh for a moment.

"And then you can read *Junie B.*"

"Nope." Josh shook his head. Lennox held her tongue, before she could snap at him. "How about if you read one to me?"

**

Thank you for reading Lennox & Booker's story! If you enjoyed Naivete, please consider leaving a review on your favorite bookish site!

If you enjoyed Naivete, stay turned for more Killdare University stories!

Sign up for my newsletter to stay up to date!

Broemmer Books

NAIVETE PLAYLIST

To listen to the playlist I created for this story, click here:

https://open.spotify.com/playlist/3LHT3TxUgglQv
G8JZODERF?si=fc6fb8dd032b4a04

I also listened to several Spotify jazz playlists during my prep, writing, and rewriting stages.

SNEAK PEEK AT INTOXICATE ME

Chapter 1

The quirky little blonde wiggled her body against his again. The bar was hopping, and the dance floor was packed, but he'd seen it crazier. She had room to dance; she was coming onto him. Malachi wasn't big on dancing; his buddies had talked him into this. So Roman was getting married. What the hell happened to doing the bachelor party at a strip club? Or throwing a bachelor party at someone's house or a hotel and bringing the strippers in?

What the hell had happened to the *bachelor party*? What the hell happened to his buddy? Pussy-whipped, that's what.

Aria doesn't want to do the traditional bachelor and bachelorette parties. Aria wants to do a couples' night out. Aria wants....

Sure, Mal liked Aria okay, but he wasn't sure he liked the way she was changing his best friend. Hell, they were too young to do this commitment stuff, weren't they? They'd only been out of school for a year or two. Okay, three. And

Roman and Aria had been seeing each other for two of those three years.

Still. Malachi Murphy wasn't about to get caught up in a committed relationship. And he wasn't into nightclubs. Hell, he was a good ole boy. He liked bonfires and Luke Coombs and longnecks. Country girls with long legs.

But maybe this little blonde would do for tonight.

"She's into you, Mal!" Aria leaned close to him and yelled so he would hear her over the music. Some kind of remix of an old Elton John song. Roman arched his eyebrows as if to say why not? Mal turned on the dance floor, barely moving his hips to the beat. The blonde flashed a smile—maybe a bit more manic than sexy—but he had to admit she had some moves. Those little hips gyrated perfectly to the beat of the music.

Hell, why not? Damned near all of his buddies were dancing with someone. Some of them, like Roman, were caught up in relationships. Some of them just feeling the beat, the alcohol mostly, and the hot curves pressing up against them.

The blonde barely came up to his shoulder. Even in the heeled sandals. Mal took advantage of her spin and eyed her from head to toe. Her honey blond curls were piled in a messy knot at the back of her head. The lacey red tank she wore left her tan, toned arms exposed. Mal had a thing for collar bones and long, elegant necks. The tank stopped at the faded skinny jeans painted on her little hips, still swinging to the beat. The denim molded her lean thighs and calves and led him right down to the red fuck-me heels.

His dick jumped to attention. Maybe he wasn't big on clubs and dancing, but that didn't mean he couldn't do it. And damned if her moves weren't sexy as fuck. He could play along. See where it led. The idea of stripping those jeans off her made his mouth dry. He reached for her hand when she faced him again. She flashed another smile. This one was smaller, less certain. Fuck if that didn't turn him on even more.

Thank fuck his sisters had taught them all how to dance. Maybe not the part about grinding middle to middle, but Breena and Sarah had taught him and his brothers how to move on a dance floor. Didn't hurt that they were athletic and well-built. And apparently, they all had rhythm.

Behind him, he heard Roman cut loose with a loud catcall. He knew his buddy was referring to the way he was now moving with the blonde. Fuck it. He didn't care. The rest of the guys were having a good time; he was going to enjoy himself, too.

If the blonde said goodnight when the dance was over, so be it. His daddy had taught them all to respect women.

To read the rest of Mal & Everleigh's story, click here:

Intoxicate Me

ABOUT THE AUTHOR

 Tracy Broemmer is the author of several contemporary romance novels including the 515 Whiskey Series, Shameless Santa, and the Mississippi Queen Trilogy. Tracy also writes women's fiction and is the author of the Williams Legacy series as well as several stand-alone titles.

Tracy's books have been called gripping, emotional, and timely, and readers describe her characters as real and relatable

Tracy lives in Midwestern Illinois with her husband of 31 years. Visit her on the web and sign up for her newsletter at www.broemmerbooks.com

ALSO BY TRACY BROEMMER

The Mississippi Queen Trilogy

Kissing Springs Bourbon Fever Boxset

515 Whiskey Series

The H Books

The Timberton Hounds Novellas